SKY BLUE

OTHER FIVE STAR WESTERNS BY MAX BRAND:

The Fugitive's Mission (1997); *In the Hills of Monterey* (1998); *The Lost Valley* (1998); *Chinook* (1998); *The Gauntlet* (1998); *The Survival of Juan Oro* (1999); *Stolen Gold* (1999); *The Geraldi Trail* (1999); *Timber Line* (1999); *The Gold Trail* (1999); *Gunman's Goal* (2000); *The Overland Kid* (2000); *The Masterman* (2000); *The Outlaw Redeemer* (2000); *The Peril Trek* (2000); *The Bright Face of Danger* (2000); *Don Diablo* (2001); *The Welding Quirt* (2001); *The Tyrant* (2001); *The House of Gold* (2001); *The Lone Rider* (2002); *Crusader* (2002); *Smoking Guns* (2002); *Jokers Extra Wild* (2002); *Flaming Fortune* (2003); *Blue Kingdom* (2003); *The Runaways* (2003); *Peter Blue* (2003); *The Golden Cat* (2004); *The Range Finder* (2004); *Mountain Storms* (2004); *Hawks and Eagles* (2004); *Trouble's Messenger* (2005); *Bad Man's Gulch* (2005); *Twisted Bars* (2005); *The Crystal Game* (2005); *Dogs of the Captain* (2006); *Red Rock's Secret* (2006); *Wheel of Fortune* (2006); *Treasure Well* (2006); *Acres of Unrest* (2007); *Rifle Pass* (2007); *Melody and Cordoba* (2007); *Outlaws From Afar* (2007); *Rancher's Legacy* (2008); *The Good Badman* (2008); *Love of Danger* (2008); *Nine Lives* (2008); *Silver Trail* (2009); *The Quest* (2009); *Mountain Made* (2009); *Black Thunder* (2009); *Iron Dust* (2010); *The Black Muldoon* (2010); *The Lightning Runner* (2010); *Legend of the Golden Coyote* (2010)

SKY BLUE

A WESTERN STORY

MAX BRAND®

COPY 1
FIVE STAR

A part of Gale, Cengage Learning

GALE
CENGAGE Learning™

Detroit • New York • San Francisco • New Haven, Conn • Waterville, Maine • London

GALE
CENGAGE Learning™

LIBRARY OF CONGRESS CATALOGING-IN-PUBLICATION DATA

Brand, Max, 1892–1944.
    Sky blue : a western story / by Max Brand. — 1st ed.
        p. cm.
    ISBN-13: 978-1-59414-945-0 (hardcover)
    ISBN-10: 1-59414-945-3 (hardcover)
    I. Title.
    PS3511.A87S543 2011
    813'.52—dc22   2010048189

First Edition. First Printing: March 2011.
Published in 2011 in conjunction with Golden West Literary Agency.

Printed in the United States of America
1 2 3 4 5 6 7 15 14 13 12 11

ADDITIONAL COPYRIGHT INFORMATION

"Sky Blue" by George Owen Baxter first appeared as a six-part serial in Street & Smith's *Western Story Magazine* (4/2/32–5/7/32). Copyright © 1932 by Street & Smith Publications, Inc. Copyright © renewed 1959 by Dorothy Faust. Copyright © 2011 by Golden West Literary Agency for restored material. Acknowledgment is made to Condé Nast Publications, Inc., for their co-operation.

CHAPTER ONE

Larribee was plain no good. Larribee was low. The Dents did not have to do much thinking. The fact was clear after a single half day of their cousin's company.

His father's letter had pointed out that he sent the young man into the Far West—meaning, in those days, anything west of the Mississippi—in the hope that he might find himself. He said that he had given Alfred every opening and encouragement that he could, but the boy was averse to labor. He hoped that Wilbur Dent would be able to make a man of him. *But,* said the letter, *you'll find Alfred very odd.*

Wilbur Dent had lifted eight hundred pounds of wheat off a scale in a single clean effort. Now he set his jaw and said to his wife: "I'll make a man of him."

She smiled a little, and then forced herself to swallow the smile. "You mustn't be too hard on the poor boy," she said. As a matter of fact, she hoped that her dear husband would flay the youth alive, if by so doing he was able to accomplish the will of the boy's father. For the elder Larribee was rich. He was willfully, almost sinfully rich, and if all went well, if they reformed young Larribee, might not a grateful father then open a door to culture and prosperity for one or more of her own darling sons?

"You mustn't be too hard on the poor boy," she said. But her eye was cold blue-gray, the color of sword-blade steel. And her husband understood perfectly. They never mentioned what the taming of young Larribee might mean to their family fortunes, but they set their teeth hard and were determined.

They expected a high-strung spendthrift, a youth with vices, but also a youth with fire. They were wrong. He had all the vices, but he had none of the fire. He drank to excess, gambled to the value of his last shirt, loved cards and dice and was oddly proficient in their management, never raised his hand to do a stroke of work of any sort, and contributed nothing to the family or to the well-being of his host except a continual flow of lazy, good-natured conversation.

There were two hundred pounds of him, rising to a height of six feet. He looked like a seal. His neck was thick, with the same softly flowing lines over shoulders and chest. He had, above all, the same air of sleekness, and a slightly oily huskiness of voice completed the resemblance.

"We'll soon get his weight down," said the elder Dent.

So he introduced Alfred Larribee to the woodpile. He gave him the introduction in the morning; an hour later the blows of the axe ceased ringing. Larribee had disappeared. He turned up at midnight, singing in a somewhat wavering voice as he came down the front path. Dent was waiting for him, but, when he saw the unsteady figure, clad in torn and ragged clothes, he shrugged his shoulders and let the boy go to sleep unreproved.

He said to Mrs. Dent: "After all, he's only twenty-one. Lots of boys are lazy at that age. Lots of boys drink a bit, also."

Then, the next morning, they got full reports of what had happened to Larribee the night before. Fort Ransome was a thriving little town that had a lot of loose cash generally afloat in it, owing to the sale of outfits to trappers and the shipping of their furs up the river to St. Louis, or down the river to New Orleans. The core of the population of Fort Ransome consisted of the sturdy farmers, like Dent, who kept on clearing land and increasing the acreage of their crops, as well as raising cattle and horses, but the life of Fort Ransome apparently settled around the traders' stores during the day and the gambling houses during the night, with a good deal of activity in the saloons during all of the twenty-four hours.

It was in the Potswood gambling house that young Larribee had been, the day before, inveigled into a game of poker. It lasted until midnight, at which time Larribee had accumulated all the stakes on the table.

Then five angry men glared at one another, swore that so much luck could not be honest, and laid their hands not only on young Larribee, but on the money as well. Larribee managed to escape by diving through a window, but his money remained behind him.

"He ran away," said Fort Ransome. "He's a coward."

But Wilbur Dent led the youth back to the woodpile, patiently, the next morning. In half an hour he was gone again.

Where did he get the money to commence the game, having left his winnings behind the night before?

At any rate, that night he won $1,500 at dice before the following morning dawned. When he left the gaming house, he was stuck up by a pair of footpads and robbed of every penny.

Once more Wilbur Dent was waiting up for him when he returned home; he allowed Larribee to enter his room, and then turned the key in the door. "You stay in there," he said, "until you've decided to settle down to honest work."

How was it managed? They could not tell, but after a day of starvation—not even water being allowed him—the very next night Larribee picked the lock, escaped while the house was quiet, and returned to the gambling halls of Fort Ransome.

He spent an hour helping a busy bartender whose partner was sick. He washed glasses during the hour, and got a generous 50¢ for his labor. At a faro table he turned the 50¢ into $5, swelled this to $100 at dice, and to $1,000 at poker.

Once again, in the dawn of the morning, it seemed to his

gambling mates that luck was more than honestly kind to Larribee. So they went for him in unison, but this time he managed to escape, and fled before them until he came to a barn with a derrick rope hanging out of the well-stuffed upper door of the mow. Up this rope, marvelous to relate, ponderous young Mr. Larribee handed himself. Fear must have made his body light and his arms strong, but, at any rate, he got into the mow in safety, and there he was besieged.

Word came to Wilbur Dent, so he rode over with his three sons and raised that siege, but first he parleyed with the truant from the ground. He demanded a week of honest effort on the part of Larribee, and the latter consented. He consented, also, to turn over his ill-gotten gains, which Wilbur Dent said would be duly taken care of in a proper way.

So Dent put $1,000 in his pocket and took the boy home. He got breakfast and another introduction to the woodpile; this time his host stood by to watch. He showed how an axe should be properly swung, and how its flashing blade should be fleshed to the handle in the wood. So young Larribee took his stance, swung, and at the third stroke broke the axe handle neatly in twain.

A flaw in the wood, declared Dent. And he furnished another axe, with a handle of truest, toughest hickory. Alas, it endured only six strokes, and then that noble hickory stick was ignobly shattered in the hands of the boy.

Wilbur Dent had lifted eight hundred pounds of wheat, but he never had seen such a thing as this happen. Even granting that the boy, from sheer malice and laziness, might have struck a little slantwise with the axe, still, hickory is hickory to every Yankee—a wood, and almost more than a wood, a sort of moral thing, undefeatable except by time.

So Dent laid his hand upon the shoulder of Larribee. It was soft and sleek. He could poke his forefinger, he felt, almost to the shoulder bone, but, when he grasped that handful of flesh hard, he felt that it was filled with ten thousand small fibers. He felt it, and he was thoroughly amazed, for he well knew the difference between fat and muscle.

An axe was too fine an instrument for such horsepower evidently. It was quite easy to understand now how Larribee had trundled his two hundred pounds lightly up the derrick rope that morning. So Dent took him to the field where two of his sons were wielding a great cross-cut saw on several oak trees. He ordered Douglas to the barn; he commanded Larribee to sit down with Derry and take the opposite end of the cross-cut. Dent stood by to watch.

It was a goodly thing to see the bright blade of the saw flashing back and forth, spouting a white gush of wood fibers and dust at every stroke. Wilbur Dent looked with pride on Derry, his oldest son, his favorite of the three, seeing the sway of his strong back and his resolute shoulders. For the oak was tough, the inner grain was hard as iron, and the saw teeth screamed against it.

On the other side of the tree Dent saw Larribee with only one hand upon the saw, and his rage burst out. "Two hands, you lazy loafer!" he shouted. "You'll do your share of this work or I'll have the hide off you!"

Larribee looked at him with a sigh, a melancholy look, and, laying both hands upon the long grip, he thrust forward.

Dent saw the thing that happened, but afterward he could hardly believe that it had not been a dream. It was a new saw, freshly sharpened. Perhaps that was the trouble, for the keen teeth bit too deeply into the metallic hardness of the oak's heart and lodged there. But that saw blade of bright new steel, supple as a sword and mighty, gave with a ripple and a bulge before the thrust of Larribee. There was a clang like a rifle shot, and the blade snapped six inches from the trunk of the tree.

11

"That's a pity," said Larribee, standing up with the mutilated stump of the saw in his hand.

"You blasted vandal!" exclaimed Dent. "The price of this comes out of your own pocket. I'll find work for you." He paused to think. What work, after all? A spade has a wooden handle; he could not set this monster to digging. A pitchfork has slender handle of wood, also, and it would snap at the first mighty heave of those shoulders.

Dent stared at Larribee with actual hatred. *Horses,* he said to himself.

He had a dozen freshly bought plains mustangs of Indian stock, wilder than eagles, wilier than snakes. He took Larribee to the corral where they were now being given a three-day course of starvation before experts attempted to manage them.

"You ride every one of that lot before night," he said. "And if you quit, I'll give you a ticket back to your father and let him handle you. A precious lot you're worth to a ranch." He turned on his heels and marched away, filled with a shuddering wrath. He could understand now why this boy had been held up and mobbed since his arrival in the town. At the gate he turned back and saw Larribee leaning on the fence, his hands folded together, whistling to himself.

CHAPTER TWO

Whatever went on in the mind of this idle, worthless fellow, it was very clear that he did not wish to be returned to his father. He remained out until noon, and then he came back to the house in prompt response to the dinner bell. He carried saddle and bridle, and Wilbur Dent looked him over critically. There was no sweat on his brow, although the day was warm. There was no dust on his torn clothes. There was no limp to his gait.

"How many have you rode?" asked Dent.

"All twelve," said Larribee, and pumped out a basin of water to wash for lunch.

There is no use calling a man a liar until you have the proof of his lie. Dent strode to the outer corral, and there he saw twelve mustangs, and on the back of every one there was the print of a saddle in sweat, and on the heads of the mustangs were the signs of cheek straps. He came back to the house in a muse. There was, of course, some trick about it, but even to have saddled the twelve, to say nothing of backing them, was a feat. He said not a word to Larribee. After lunch they would see.

So they sat down to the table, where the Dents talked to one another and looked sourly as Larribee twice heaped his plate with baked beans, ate six rashers of bacon, and cleaned his plate. Then he poured in a tide of molasses and licked it up with half a dozen of Mrs. Dent's best sour-milk biscuits—golden beauties and her pride. He ate with the mild absorption of a

13

stalled ox, and almost as much. When it came to coffee, his cup had to be filled five times.

West of the Mississippi, hospitality is more than a virtue, it is a religion, but Mrs. Dent could not look on at this havoc. She had to lower her eyes to her own modest portion, and finally she left the table, unable to endure the sight.

Then Wilbur Dent spoke: "Well, boys, Alfred says that he's rode all of the twelve of those mustangs. You, there, Dan, you can take a fling at one of 'em after lunch and see how he's gentled down."

After lunch Larribee extended his large frame under a tree, folded his hands beneath his head, and slept; the rest of the menfolk filed out to the corral gate, looking sourly askance upon the sleeper. His mouth was open; his snoring was deep and vibrant.

"I wish a spider would drop down his throat," said Dan Dent. "I'm gonna get spilled plenty. They're as wild as mosquitoes, those devils. Look at 'em!"

For the mustangs milled as wildly as ever when the four men came to the corral fence.

"He rode 'em, did he?" said Daniel Dent. "He rode a broomstick, is what he rode."

But he went in with his rope and snagged the smallest of the lot. It was not the smallest in spirit, however; it exploded all over the corral, and the others, in sympathy with their brother, exploded, also.

Such a column of dust arose that it looked, from a distance, like the smoke that rises from a burning house. But the head of the beast was finally worked up to the snubbing post, he was blindfolded, saddled, mounted. And all that while he squealed with rage as a pig squeals under the knife—half-human screams. Then Dan Dent gave the signal, and they turned the horse loose.

The mustang, when its eyes were free from the blindfold, hesitated. Then it bucked its way to the corral fence in three jumps, and with the third it skyrocketed Daniel Dent into space. He landed on his head and lay still. He was not dead, but he was badly stunned, and, when they got him up, blood was trickling from ears, nose, and mouth. His eyes were the eyes of a drunkard.

"Go get Larribee," said the father gently.

Derry and Douglas went to the sleeper and stirred him with the toes of their boots.

He opened one eye. His sleek face was flushed with sleep. "Yes?" murmured Larribee in his husky, oily voice.

"Get up and come along," said the two. "The old man, he wants to see you ride one of those hosses out there."

Larribee groaned. He closed his eyes again, but, as a sign that he intended to stir before long, he took a pipe out, then a tobacco pouch, from which he filled the bowl, and lighted the pipe. After a whiff or two he was able to open his eyes again. With the aid of both hands he pushed his reluctant body into a sitting posture.

The two young Dents stood by with contempt in their eyes. But the thought of prospective vengeance kept them quietly waiting. They saw the man roll his hulk to his feet, saw him yawn vastly and stretch, and then they followed him to the little outer corral.

The elder Dent pointed with a rigid arm. "You say you rode them hosses, all of 'em," he said, iron in his voice. "Now you can sashay in there and ride only one of 'em again. You won't have to bother about saddlin' it. They's a saddle already on it. Get in there and do it!"

Larribee seemed in no hurry. He leaned for a moment on the rail of the fence and looked over the little herd. "I left them all quiet and peaceable," he said. "And now you've stirred them

15

up. You know about bees . . . they'll let you alone if you don't bother them."

"Shut up and get in there!" ordered Dent.

Larribee sighed. He opened the gate and walked in slowly. The mustangs faced him in a row, ready to charge. They shook their heads. Their eyes were red with the wild beast's hatred of man and the man smell, the awkward, two-legged, mysteriously horrible enemy of all things.

"Poor boys," said Larribee. "I'm sorry for you. But you've got to have the iron on your teeth and the saddle on your back, because Nature gave you more than you need, and other people will be sure to use it. You, there, pinto, don't roll your eyes. I know exactly what's biting you." He sauntered up, talking in this idle manner.

Daniel Dent, who had regained his wits and his feet, said: "Now watch that hand-made tiger eat him up."

But it was a strange thing to see those mustangs stand as Larribee walked about among them. He took the saddled horse by the bit and led it to the gate. It hardly knew how to lead. It seemed to follow the man by choice rather than by compulsion, and, behold, the whole group walked behind their brother to the gate, and, when he was led out into the open, they hung their ugly heads over the rail and stared after him.

Larribee fitted his foot into the stirrup and then mounted, the saddle twisting a little under his weight. He hunched it straight as he sat upright, fumbling for the other stirrup in the meantime.

"He's not bridle wise yet," he said. "But he's learning."

Before a silent, stupefied audience he steered the mustang slowly around the outer corral. Then he halted it by the gate again.

"Try it now, Derry," said the father as Larribee dismounted in a continued silence.

16

Larribee stood at the mustang's head. It made not a move while he was there, merely lifting its head a little and flattening its ears as Derry Dent mounted. Then the word was given, and Larribee stepped away, and that inspired little fiend deliberately tied himself into half a dozen knots. When he unraveled them, Derry was picking himself up from a dust cloud that filled half the corral.

Larribee caught the panting horse and put it inside the corral again.

"What did you do to it?" asked Wilbur Dent. "Now, you tell me what you did to that hoss?"

"I talked. You heard me," said Larribee. "If there's nothing more on hand, I'll go back and have a sleep."

They let him go because they wanted to be alone for a moment; they craved a conference.

"What good is it, anyway?" said Daniel. "Suppose that he can ride any old hoss, what good is it if nobody else can foller in his tracks?"

"What good is Larribee for anything?" growled the father. "Nothin' except to break handles, and gamble, and drink. A coward, too, that runs away from everybody. The whole town is sneerin' at him. He's makin' a joke out of my household. By thunder, I ain't going to stand it!"

He gave his boys their day's assignment of work and wandered thoughtfully back to the house.

"Anything to do?" asked Larribee as he sat under the shade of the tree.

"Not for you!" growled Dent. He thought for a moment. "Yes, by thunder," said Dent. "You can paint the barn. That's what you can do, and nothin' to break except your neck by fallin' off the platform."

He looked around as he spoke and found that Larribee was not present. The first remark had been enough for him, and he

17

was gone. Wilbur Dent went on to the house, where he found his wife on the back porch, hanging out underwear that she had just washed. She was tired, for the middle of the day was very hot.

"Life ain't nothin' but grease and soap suds, soap suds and grease," she complained.

He looked gloomily at her. She was withered, bent, and time-yellowed. He could not tell whether he was fond of her as a wife or as a cheap and tireless servant.

"Soap and grease is nothing," he said. "There's no Larribees for you to handle."

"Who cooks for the glutton but me?" she demanded sharply. "Who cooks for him and then sets at the table and sees him swaller three portions, like he owned the house, and me, and all of us? A hog is what he is. A fat-faced, sleek, worthless hog. A butcher could make use of him, I tell you."

"A butcher might use him, but I can't," said her husband. "I've got enough of him. I'm going to send him home."

She put her wet hands on her hips, regardless of how the soapy water dripped upon her calico skirt. She stared at Wilbur Dent. "Will, have you gone and got crazy?" she demanded.

"I've give it up," he said. "He's too queer. I will go crazy if I have to be around him long."

"Shut up and be still," said his good wife. "If fire can soften iron, we'll soften him, you can bet."

Chapter Three

Larribee, who had taken what he considered his dismissal for the day, went down the street toward the center of Fort Ransome. He had with him a pocket knife, a pipe, tobacco, and some matches. What he wanted was money. He wanted a drink, and he wanted it badly. Then he wanted to sit down with a cool patch of sea-green felt before him, and either the rattle of the dice or the whisper of cards to make the music that he loved to hear.

There was no pride in Larribee. He wore the same clothes that had almost been dragged from his back on the first night he played cards in Fort Ransome, but he cared not for the rents or the stains on coat and trousers, nor that he looked the part of a loafer.

When handsome young Joe Ransome, son of the major and grandson of the founder of the town, rode up to the Potswood entrance, he tossed the reins to Larribee and called out: "Tie the horse up, my boy!" And he flung a coin into the dust at the feet of Larribee.

Larribee was not proud. He tethered the horse, regardless of the sneers of the bystanders, by-sitters, rather, for they were all lined up in the chairs that backed against the wall of the Potswood verandah. Then he mined in the dust where the coin had fallen and picked up a 25¢ piece. He spun it in the air, watched it glitter at the height of its rise, and was pleased by the comfortable spat of it in the palm of his hand when it fell.

To a poor man, something is an infinity better than nothing, and, besides, to Larribee this was a lever with which he might open important doors after he had finished making it grow.

He leaned against one of the pillars of the verandah. He filled and lighted his pipe, while he looked up and down the row of sneering, hostile faces. He had taken water three times in Fort Ransome, where a man was supposed, first and last, to be a man. But Larribee was not proud. He saw the contempt, but he regarded it not.

"I'll match you," he said to a trapper clad in deerskins from the plains. "I'll match you a quarter against a quarter."

"Oh, you . . . take yourself off," said the trapper. "Your hands ain't clean enough to play with me."

Those who heard the remark laughed loudly. Some of them watched Larribee for a moment with cruelly expectant eyes, but he paid no heed to the rebuff.

He walked down the verandah and leaned against another pillar.

"I'll match you a quarter," he said to a sour-faced man with a long-tailed coat and a wide-brimmed hat. He looked the part of a gambler. The latter stared at Larribee up and down.

"Quarters be blowed," he said. "But still, a principle is a principle. Here you are."

"Heads," said Larribee.

The stranger spun his coin as Larribee spoke. It clinked on the verandah floor. "Heads it is," said the gambler, and kicked the coin toward Larribee, who gathered it up.

"I'll give you revenge," said Larribee, smiling gently.

"Find out some small fry. I don't want to waste my time," said the gambler. "But . . . well, here you are." He spun a 50¢ piece. It went the way of the quarter. He lost $1, $2, $4, $8. Then he stopped in the act of drawing out gold, and squinted at Larribee. "What the deuce does he do?" he asked. He was not angry, only curious.

"He sees 'em as they start up in the air, and knows how they'll fall," said a confident neighbor.

The gambler dropped the gold back into his pocket. "It's a good trick, boy," he said. "It's a good trick for picking up a bit of chicken feed here and there."

Larribee went into the bar. He had a stiff drink of whiskey that was colored juice and raw alcohol. A half-breed, a Negro, a decrepit full-blooded Indian, and a plains trader with a prosperous appearance were all leaning at that bar. Larribee was not proud. He shook dice with the Negro, lost $5, and won $40. He went into the gambling rooms after that.

There were three of them, each turning a corner from the other. For the sake of making more bullets fly wide, said the inhabitants of Fort Ransome, callous but very tolerant.

Larribee found a score of men playing, for it was too early in the day to enlist the interest of the majority. The effect of last night's poisonous liquor had not yet worn off, and they had not built up sufficient enthusiasm on this new day's supply. About sunset the play would grow higher, the players more numerous.

Larribee played red and black at roulette. He lost all but $1 in half an hour's play. He shifted to numbers, playing combinations, and in ten minutes he had an even $100. He put $10 on the nine—the ball clicked home on the nine—and Larribee took $350 from the table.

That was a poker stake. But there was no poker to be played. In fact, no game of any size was going on except in a far corner of the farthest room, where young Josiah Ransome, third of that name, was rolling dice on a blanket, bouncing them off a wall before the call. Larribee joined the group. There were five of them, all well-dressed, all apparently well in funds. They looked coldly aside at him.

"That's my horse boy," said young Ransome, laughing. "Let

him lose his money if he wants to. This is a democracy, gentle-men."

Larribee was not proud. He stood on the extreme edge of the group, at a corner of the table. The house was not represented. It was merely a private game, a gentleman's game. He lost $100 before he got the box, then he won $1,000 in four straight rolls. Young Ransome had lost more than half of it.

He was a well-made youth, straight, tall, with a proud head proudly carried. After the fourth cast he fastened his eyes on Larribee for a long moment, then he left the room and went out into the bar. There he called the barkeeper to one side and said to him: "There's a ragged fellow in the rooms shaking dice, and I think he's crooked. What do you know about him?"

"By name of Larribee, he is," said the barkeep. "He's more crookeder than a dog's hind leg. Dice or poker or matching coins, he's more slippery than a greased pig. You ain't been playing with him, Mister Ransome?"

Ransome stepped back from the bar and surveyed its length. Near the farther end he saw a bulky pair of shoulders, a small head, a jaw made to endure batterings.

"Mullins!" he called. "Leave that whiskey and come here."

Mullins looked about with a scowl, but, when he saw the speaker, he put the glass back on the bar and approached. He even touched the brim of his hat, for the Ransomes were as hereditary princes in the town that had been named after them.

"Yes, sir," said Mullins, at attention.

"There's a fellow named Larribee . . . ," began Ransome.

"I know the yellow dog," said Mullins.

"He's been cheating at dice," said Ransome, "and he's not quite fit for me to handle. Here's a trifle."

"No, sir," said Mullins. "To clean up that little job it'll be a pleasure to me. I wouldn't shame myself by takin' your money for it, Mister Ransome."

He went out onto the verandah and looked about him. He was a known man, this Mullins. He, and no other Mullins, had stood up for forty red, bare-fisted rounds against terrible Jem Richards in the height of that champion's career. Now, older, a little slower, he was still great enough to command a following of his own kind in Fort Ransome. At his nod, three burly fellows came up to him. He said to one: "Go in and find that Larribee. Tell him there's a friend wants him right bad out here. Then you can stand by, you boys, and see a show."

So it was that Larribee was tapped on the shoulder and called forth.

He came unwillingly. The game was good, the stakes were high, and he was more than holding his own after his first fine run of luck. So he came out, frowning a little against the brightness of the outer day.

"You're Larribee," said Mullins. "You called me a son-of-a-bitch a while ago. I'm gonna hear you apologize out here, out loud."

The bystanders grinned, all except young Ransome. He stood rather coldly aloof. He was seeing justice administered, as was his duty. He felt that Fort Ransome should be kept fairly clean.

"All right," said Larribee. "I'm not proud. I didn't call you names. I never call anybody names, Mister Mullins. But I apologize, just the same."

"You sneakin' cur," said Mullins, snapping his teeth like an angry dog to work up his temper. "I dunno that just apologizin' is good enough for me. I'm gonna give you a taste of what's what in the old country. I'm gonna bash in your face for you."

He had talked enough to oil his excitable temper. Now he drew back a fist oddly small and compact compared with the bulk of his arm and the shoulder behind it. He drew it back and hit like a good marksman for the head of Larribee.

Larribee ducked. It seemed as though the wind of the blow

traveled before it and tipped the head of Larribee aside. The massive arm of Mullins went over his shoulder, and Larribee, with a surprised look, appeared to stumble forward and to save himself by hitting at the shirt of Mullins just over the heart.

The great Mullins staggered backward. His face had turned gray in streaks, as though he had been slapped by a many-lashed whip. His body was canted sharply to the left, the heavy fence of his forearms was erected defensively before his face, and he bit at the air with gasps.

"Cheese it, Jerry," muttered one of Mullins's champions. "The rat got in a lucky wallop. You on this side and me on that. . . ."

They charged young Larribee with fists ready like horns, and he swayed down like a man paralyzed with terror, flinging himself face downward upon the verandah floor in token of submission. So it chanced that the swinging punches just grazed the top of his head as Larribee unexpectedly straightened and came erect, as it were, by reaching for the body of one man with his right and for the other with his left.

The two champions sat down. Then one, gasping, with an expression of agony, toppled slowly over on his side.

Chapter Four

It looked accidental. It almost had to be accidental. The trouble was that three accidents do not usually happen in a row, in the course of as many seconds. Even young Mr. Ransome forgot his dignity a little and stared.

As for the famous Mullins, he said to his third companion. "He's a ringer. Take him together. You try his head, me his middle. We'll knock the lights out of him."

Mr. Mullins had not quite recovered his breath, however. For that reason he was a little behind in the charge that ensued, and his gallant friend went nobly on, half a step in the lead, bereft of help by that small but vital margin. When he saw that he was somewhat ahead of his friend, he was not abashed. Neither was he troubled by the sight of the two men twisting and squirming on the ground. Instead, he fairly leaped at the head of Larribee so that the latter, throwing up a hand as to ward off the attack, happened to strike with his closed fist upon the very point of the other's chin.

The impact flung the man backward straight upon Mullins, and the two rolled over and over at the feet of Larribee. Then, for the first time, the spectators found their tongues for a long, wild, whooping shout. They agreed that they had been sold, that yonder sleek-faced youth was some famous character who had chosen to mask his prowess behind a mask of humility. And many a one among them shrugged his collar a little more warmly up about his neck.

Larribee reached into the heap and plucked forth Mullins by the hair of the head. It was a dazed and gaping face that was dragged upward. Not only was there a severe and cramping pain in the body of the ex-pugilist, but he had just fallen on his head, with the weight of his friend's body to push his face into the dust. He panted loudly, and his breath was white with the dust.

"Who was it that wanted to speak to me, Mister Mullins?" asked Larribee.

The eyes of Mullins rolled wildly, and it happened that at this moment he looked toward young Mr. Ransome. He really intended no harm to Josiah Ransome III, but the face was familiar in the general haze that possessed his mind, and he pointed with a vague finger.

"Mister Ransome . . . ," he said.

Larribee dropped him, and, turning about, he sauntered slowly to young Ransome and stood smiling before him.

He was the only one of those present who was smiling at the moment. The onlookers leaned forward in their chairs and gaped, but they did not grin either at one another or at the two who were now facing each other. Young Mr. Ransome looked just a trifle pale, but his head was as high as ever. Larribee was still smiling in his good-natured, rather sleepy way as he stood before the prince of the town.

"Did you send for me, Mister Ransome?" he said.

Ransome looked him over. He tried to think of some cutting retort, but his wits were not particularly active at the moment. So he kept silent and continued to survey the sleekness of Larribee.

"Did you want me so badly," asked Larribee, "that you sent a man in and had three more waiting for me when I came out? You know, Mister Ransome, I'm only a humble fellow. I'm not proud, and I never aspire to a guard of honor. But now that I'm here . . . thank you . . . what is it that you want to say to me?"

Mr. Ransome decided at last what he should do. He turned his back upon the other and said to a loitering boy: "Untie that horse for me, my son, will you?" And he threw a quarter toward the lad.

It was a good enough gesture, and it would have won out, ordinarily, but it happened that the boy toward whom the coin was thrown was so engrossed in the scene before him that he was utterly oblivious of the little streak of light that was extinguished in the dust at his feet. So not a hand was raised to untether the horse of his princeship. He would have to walk down and get the animal himself, and this rather interfered with the dignity of his departure, which was to show that such a ragged fellow as Larribee was entirely beneath the attention of such a man as himself.

Larribee touched his arm. "I beg your pardon, Mister Ransome," he said.

Now, young Josiah Ransome was a fellow of infinite spirit, and, when he felt himself touched by one whom he put down as a worthless vagabond, his blood fairly boiled. He forgot the thin frost of terror that he had felt the moment before, when he saw this sleek mauler of men advance toward him, and, whirling around on one heel violently, he threw off the grasp of Larribee with one hand, and with the other snatched out a good revolver, a shining Colt.

"Keep your hands off, you hoodlum," said young Mr. Ransome, "or I'll teach you. . . ."

He got out this much of his remark in the proper style, but then his gun hand fell into a grasp such as Josiah Ransome never had conceived of. It grated the bones of his fingers against the wood and steel as though there were no intervening padding of flesh whatever. It numbed his hand to the wrist and upward. But what made this all the more unreal and horrible was that the face of Larribee did not alter in the least, but remained as sleekly smiling, as sleepily good-humored as ever, as he said: "I didn't know that guns were manners, Ransome. But if they are. . . ." With this, he literally lifted the young fellow before him and cast him backward.

Mr. Josiah Ransome, as he fell, blindly fired his revolver into the thin blue face of the sky, which was the only basis upon which this encounter could have been described as a gunfight, the usual description in narrating it later on by all those who saw the affair. In falling, young Ransome struck the edge of the verandah, spun over, and fell straight down, a full three feet. His forehead was opened up by the iron edge of the boot scraper beneath, and the blow knocked the wits quite out of his handsome, gay, young head.

No one stirred to pick him up except Larribee himself. He gathered Josiah Ransome in his arms, carried him into the saloon end of the Potswood place, and with his own hand poured a dram of whiskey down the unconscious throat.

Ransome wakened with a coughing and spluttering. A doctor was called to sew up the spouting, gaping wound, and, in the midst of the confusion, Larribee quietly got out of the mix-up and went home.

The first person he saw was Mrs. Dent, who cried out: "Have you been stealin' chickens, you great big thing? What's that blood on your coat?"

"Just a little accident," said Larribee.

"Get out to the barn," she said. "Mister Dent, he wants you."

So Larribee went out to the barn and received hard words, and that was why he happened to be mounted on a scaffolding, slowly, slowly drawing a paintbrush back and forth over the rough boards, whistling gently to himself, squinting at his work as though he were a landscape artist, when Marshal Steve Hannahan came galloping out on his foaming horse.

Marshal Hannahan's horse was always foaming. That gallant rider could chafe it into a lather in no time at all. It was said that Fort Ransome had to keep quite a string for the marshal. He must have his ration of four horses a day, or else he would have had to walk on some of his commissions. He always looked as though he had just dismounted. If he went into the saloon for a drink, it always appeared that the wind of his gallop was still blowing and parting his fine, blond mustache. He had a shining eye, nervously compressed lips, and, having been marshal for six months, people admiringly laid bets and gave liberal odds that he would not last out the year. For he loved battle as a good horse is said to love it, and entered fights uninvited as though there were not enough to occupy him in the regular routine of his business.

There was a five-foot gate leading into the Dent corrals, but the marshal did not stop to unbar it. He simply leaped his mustang across it, and though the rear legs of the mustang knocked off the top bar of the gate and left their skins behind, though the blow nearly tumbled the poor brute on its head, the marshal gave the thing not a thought as he dashed on and pulled up under the scaffolding of the painter.

Wilbur Dent had heard the crash of the broken gate and came hurrying out from the barn prepared to swear, but, when he saw the marshal, he thought better of it. He was the silent witness to what followed. The marshal was in a rage.

He called out: "Are you the blackguard by name of Larribee who's been rioting at the Potswood?"

Larribee stopped painting, restored his brush carefully to the bucket of paint, turned a little on the scaffolding plank that supported him, looked down with attention at the marshal, and then, as a puff of wind blew Hannahan's coat open and showed the flaring steel medal inside, Larribee raised his hat in salute. "I've been at the Potswood, sir," he said.

The marshal was hot. "Don't you 'sir' me," he said. "I'll have you know who runs Potswood, and I'm the man. You dice-throwing, card-marking vagabonds I'm going to put down and give the decent people a show in this town. Climb down off that scaffold and I'll give you a lesson."

"Well, sir," said Larribee, "if you'll just hand that ladder over here, I'll come right down."

"Hand you the . . . hand yourself the ladder, confound you," said the marshal. "Get off that scaffold and get quick, or I'll have you down, ladder or no ladder. I'll have you down in such shape that you won't be getting up again in a hurry. I'll teach you to blackguard and riot. I'll teach you to slug the first citizens of Fort Ransome. I'm going to make an example of you."

He made his quirt sing through the air as he spoke, as though he intended to scorch his lesson into the hide of Larribee with those lashes. The swinging of the quirt made the mustang swerve and rear right under the scaffolding. It was so very close that one of the marshal's legs scraped against the wall of the barn, and Larribee was so alarmed that he started violently and uttered a faint exclamation that Daniel Dent said was: "Well, well, sir!" At the same time, his careless right hand tipped over the bucket of white paint, so that the entire contents spilled straight downward and exactly hit the center of the marshal's upturned face!

The mustang, at the same moment, alarmed by that downward flashing stream of white, bucked with all its might, and the marshal came out of the saddle and landed in a violent sitting posture in the dust. Even then he upheld his high reputation. He was blinded with pain, but he got his two guns into his hands and fired two shots at the exact moment when he landed in the dust.

Chapter Five

Dent was in agony lest his laughter should be heard. He almost choked on the way to the house, toward which he hurried the marshal, but he managed to get out a word of condolence. When the marshal swore that he would cut Larribee joint from joint and feed the separate members to the buzzards or the crows, Wilbur agreed that it was a very good thing, and that the boy was as near a zero in worth as any human he ever had seen.

Mrs. Dent, as rapidly as she could, despite frequent liftings of both hands toward the low ceiling of the room, washed the paint from the marshal's face, washed and combed it from his silken, blond mustache, but, do what she would, the mustache persisted in clinging hair to hair, giving the dashing marshal somewhat the air of an adolescent mandarin. As for his magnificent, sweeping coat and trousers, they were ruined beyond repair.

When the marshal could see again out of his bloodshot eyes, he turned a dreadful purple, and his face swelled until it seemed that his neck scarf would burst asunder. He was forced to ask for a fresh outfit, and got one of Derry Dent's, which fitted him only in random places. Wilbur Dent was handing him the articles desired and, in the meantime, learning about the atrocities that Larribee had perpetrated at the Potswood. The more he learned, the more strangely his eyes were lighted, but he continued to nod approval of the threats of the marshal, now in a dangerous mood.

31

The marshal was in the act of carefully winding a scarf about his throat when they heard a quiet voice just outside the door, the husky, rather oily voice of Larribee, saying: "When the marshal's dressed, will you tell him that I'm waiting for him on the back porch . . . to apologize?"

Hannahan paused. His thoughtful glance met Dent's, and then, still more slowly, the marshal finished tying his scarf. Now that he was dressed, he stalked from the room, and, turning just outside of it, he glared down the narrow hall toward the rear of the house.

Wilbur Dent waited the whole half of a second before he said: "If I was you, Marshal, I'd not bother Larribee about his . . . apology. I'd get right into town and have the doctor give me a lotion for them eyes. They look mighty inflamed, sort of. You take a man in your sort of a job, Marshal, he's gotta have good eyes with him."

The marshal made one long stride toward the rear of the house after hearing this speech. Then he checked himself, as though with an effort.

"You've got sense, Dent," he said. "I'd better see a doctor at once."

He left the house by the front door and went to get his mustang, which Derry Dent was holding for him. Once in the saddle, the dashing marshal turned.

"Mind you, it's not the last of this!" he exclaimed.

"I reckon it's not," said Mr. Dent, nodding his head.

It was not until the marshal had dashed away at his usual frantic gallop that Wilbur Dent raised his head. A fit seemed to have seized him. Turning toward the house, he staggered violently. His feet moved drunkenly forward, then back. He reeled. Odd choking noises came from his throat, and he clasped his ribs roundabout as though an explosive force were threatening them. When he got to the big tree, he leaned weakly against the trunk of it. No shame seemed to dwell in the strong heart of Wilbur Dent. He actually drew out a bandanna and applied it to his streaming eyes as, with one hand stretched before him, he went uncertainly forward, feeling his way blindly to the house. Finally, when he had gained the safety of the dining room, he flung himself down in his big chair and shook from head to foot.

His good wife came in from the kitchen, bursting with emotion. "A fine piece of baggage we've got on the place!" she shouted. "Disgracin' us . . . disgracin' us in the eye of the law, what's more. Wilbur Dent, what's the matter with you? Have you got a fit?"

"Cousin Wilbur," said the voice of Larribee from the back porch, "did you see any of the marshal when he left? I've been waiting here to . . . apologize."

"Larribee . . . Alfred," groaned Wilbur Dent. "Come in here to me, at once."

Larribee entered, saying: "I'm mighty sorry about spilling that paint, too, Cousin Wilbur."

"You witless, graceless thing, you!" screeched Mrs. Dent.

Wilbur Dent kicked back another chair. He leaned heavily across the table and peered at Larribee as though he saw the latter at a great distance.

"Set yourself down, Alfred," he said. "Set yourself down and look me in the face, you scamp, if you can. Tell me that you knocked young Ransome galley west . . . if you dare."

"Mister Josiah Ransome?" screamed Mrs. Dent. "Oh, heavens above!"

"Oh, get along with you," said her husband, beginning to choke. "Get along with you and fetch me some coffee. And bring two cups. Oh, my achin' sides. Alfred, I'm a dyin' man. Did you see the marshal's whiskers?"

"Why," said Larribee thoughtfully, "as nearly as I remember, the marshal's whiskers were rather lost, when I last saw him. They seemed to be . . . behind a cloud, so to speak, and. . . ."

A stifled cry came from Wilbur Dent as he buried his face in his bandanna and rocked slowly back and forth. With one arm he vainly strove to embrace his tormented body and give it rest. At last he lay helplessly back in his chair and allowed the tears to course uninterruptedly, shamelessly down his face.

His wife, coming back to the door of the room from the kitchen, almost dropped both the coffee pot and the cups. "Wilbur Dent, you're laughin'!" she exclaimed. "Upon my honest soul alive, you're laughin'!"

"I ain't laughin'. I'm dyin'," he said.

But the first mouthful of coffee seemed to revive him. He rested his forehead upon one hand and groaned for some moments with every breath he drew. "They said that Hannahan would never finish out a year of office. And he won't, for he's finished now," said Dent. "He's gonna go out, not foot first to a grave, but headfirst, blowed out by the laughin' of all of Fort Ransome. Cousin Alfred, dog-gone my spots, if I ain't been mistaken in you. I didn't know you at all. Take my hand, and mind you take it careful, because it's the only right hand that I've got in stock. Alfred, I'm a proud and happy man to have you for kinfolk. Alfred, you can set right here on my front verandah and rest your spurs on the rail and sleep all day and gamble all night, and Wilbur Dent is a liar if he won't be proud to have you."

"Hold on, Cousin Wilbur," said Larribee.

"I mean it. This here is your home. This table is what you're going to eat off free as long as you'll stay with me. Mister Josiah Ransome! Ha! Ha! Ha! If only I could've seen him land on his lily-white brow. But I seen the marshal, and that was a chapter out of Revelation. Why, Alfred, you've gone and made a fool out of me. I thought you were just a bad boy. I didn't know that you were a regular larrupin' Larribee. But this here is your home, lad. Mind you that."

Larribee smiled on his host, and then a far-off look came in his eyes, and he sighed. "It would have been very pleasant, Cousin Wilbur," he said, "if things could have gone along as they were going before. But now that you make me so welcome, I'm ashamed of myself. I wouldn't mind loafing in spite of you, but I couldn't take any pleasure in doing nothing with your permission. I hope I don't sound like a fool, Cousin Wilbur?"

Dent actually stroked the hand of the boy, and then he patted it. "You do what you want to do," he said. "Whatever you do will be all right. Only, I want you to know that I'm proud of you. Reach me that jug from back of the door, boy. There's close onto twenty gallon of honest liquor in there, not the rotten stuff that they sell over the bar in this town."

Larribee brought out the great earthen jar and fetched a glass from the cupboard at the end of the room.

"Two glasses, two glasses!" cried his cousin. "Great immortal Walter Scott! D'you think that I'd drink by myself with you in the room, my boy?"

"Thank you," said Larribee as he filled the glass of his cousin, "but here's a glass that's more to my liking." And he swayed the massive bulk of that jug aloft while Dent watched him, amazed, half rising from his chair in sympathy with that tremendous effort. Mrs. Dent herself, who many a time had pulled and hauled, tugged and rocked at that jug to move it from its corner on cleaning Mondays, paused in the kitchen door and pressed her wrinkled hands together as she saw the gray jug tilt over the raised elbow of Larribee, while, with one hand on his hip and the other on the neck of the monstrous flask, he placed it against his mouth. Then for a moment the Dents stared, and heard the gurgling of the liquid.

Larribee lowered the jug and swung it lightly back to its place, slapping the big cork back into its neck. "That, sir," he said, "was a drink fit for a man to last him a week, and out of a man's cup, I'd say. To your honor and your luck, Cousin Wilbur, and may your jug always be full, I say. I didn't know that I had such cousins in the world, or I should have been here long before."

Wilbur Dent tossed off his glass with a grin. "Seems like I'm drinkin' out of a thimble," he said, "after watchin' you handle that wee jug so. Seems like the three fingers I've had hardly had a taste in 'em, and hardly a bit of smoke or burn. Havin' you around for a year or two might make a man out of me, Cousin Alfred."

The small voice of Mrs. Dent spoke from the kitchen door. "And, Cousin Alfred," she said, "I wouldn't be minding a wee drop myself."

CHAPTER SIX

Hannahan did not leave Fort Ransome; he was not laughed out of office. Neither did Mullins withdraw from the town where he had been so badly beaten, nor did young Josiah Ransome III take a vacation. The reason was that there was a new object of interest in Fort Ransome the very day after the affair at the Potswood.

This was not the arrival of a new regiment, or some foreign duke or prince. It was the arrival of something in which Fort Ransome could take a far more intelligent interest.

It was a horse, a stallion, pale-blue, whose mane and tail matched his body color, so that on the whole he was the tint of the horizon when seen at a little distance, and this was the reason for his name, Sky Blue.

With the stallion came his owner. He was named Dan Gurry. He was a short, stocky fellow with a bright and steady eye and the air of one who has persistence. That air was not an illusion. Fort Ransome learned that four years ago he had bought this thoroughbred colt when he was less than a yearling, and had got him comparatively cheap for two reasons: the stallion was both an unusual and a washy color, and was so scrawny of body and vast of limb that no one could believe he would amount to very much. Nevertheless, his bloodlines were excellent, and Dan Gurry had to pay a cool $1,000 for the colt.

Then he spent four years raising him. He saw that he had the best grass in Kentucky, the cleanest oats, the purest water. He spent his savings freely and saw him grow to the prodigious size of seventeen hands, to a fraction of an inch—not seventeen hands of sprawling malproportions, but seventeen hands of smoothly muscled strength and symmetry. When one looked at his quarters, wide and square enough to fill a door, one could swear that this horse would never gallop. But when one saw him in profile, the shortness of the back, the daylight under him, the amount of ground he stood over, one vowed that here was a speedster of the first rank. From the front he had the head of a king and the shoulders of an Arab. To make the picture perfect, one had only to stand at the pasture fence and watch the monster gallop across the field. It did not gallop. It simply bounded across.

There was one fly in the ointment.

The reason that Sky Blue had come to the age of five years without a track engagement was that no jockey could sit his back. The best that the Eastern and Southern stables could offer had been tried, and they had failed.

In speaking of this, Dan Gurry had said: "I've heard about your boys out here. I've heard that they can ride anything that wears a hide. Now I want to see. I paid a thousand for this colt. I'll pay another thousand to anybody who can ride him three times running. That offer stands. You fellows tell about it in the saloons, will you?"

Tell about it? They could talk of nothing else.

On the very first morning, Fort Ransome gathered to see three riders of celebrity mount that running machine. One was a frontiersman, one was a full-blooded Comanche, those kings of plains riders, and one was a half-breed from the Sioux nation. They did their best. They were not content with one fall, but tried several times apiece, and their average endurance on the back of the stallion amounted to something like a minute and a half. When Sky Blue bucked, he bucked with three years of experience behind him.

Fort Ransome gathered to watch the show continue that afternoon.

It began with Joe Creary, who had been riding broncos down by the Río Grande, broncos with educated dispositions and a full command of the whole vocabulary of pitching. Joe was well-known. In addition he was miraculously sober. When he appeared, the odds on him were quoted at two to one. Some people pitied Sky Blue once Creary's legs were forked over his back.

But the second time the stallion bounded into the air and landed on one forehoof, the face of Creary wore an abstracted look. During the next maneuver, when Sky Blue executed a snap in the middle of the sky, Creary came off and fell all the dizzy way to the earth below. He landed flat on his back, and, although he was unconscious when they picked him up, he bent backward in the middle and suddenly screamed with agony.

The sound of that yell brought the sweat out on the upper lips of the hardiest in Fort Ransome. When Creary was carried off the field, the line of other ambitious applicants dwindled suddenly away to nothing.

Then Wilbur Dent said to his cousin: "Look here, Alfred. I ain't askin' you to hunt for trouble. But a thousand dollars is a thousand dollars. If you can hypnotize twelve man-eatin' mustangs in a morning, maybe you can hypnotize Sky Blue in an afternoon. What do you say?"

Larribee looked across the corner of the corral toward a section of the crowd that contained the bluest blood in Fort Ransome. The Rigby Petersons were there, and the Walters family, and so were the Ransomes themselves, headed by the dignified major with his mustache shining like marble. Even young Josiah Ransome III, with a broad bandage around his head, had braved the public eye and the tongue of ridicule to stand there and see the horse show. With the Western Ransomes stood their Eastern cousin, Arabelle Ransome.

She was not looking into the corral at the prancing stallion and the dangling, flopping stirrup irons as he cantered around the enclosure and then took his lordly stand in the center of the arena. She was looking straight over at the Dent delegation, and among them she had singled out big Larribee. She was one of those girls people look at twice. Her eyes were underlined in royal purple that was not the shadow of fatigue—the rose of her cheeks denied that. And something about her took the eye and kept it. If she turned her head, one looked at the brown and golden roundness of her throat. If she parted her lips to speak, one strove to catch the sound of her voice even a hundred yards away. She was looking at Larribee as though he were a new sort of animal, and he was looking back at her.

"Look over there," he said to Wilbur Dent.

"You mean the Ransome girl?" said Wilbur Dent. "They say it's gonna be a match betwixt her and young Josiah, blast him."

"No," said Larribee, "I don't think that she'll ever marry a loser."

That was the only answer he made to the remark of Dent about riding the horse. The next Dent knew, there was Larribee, actually striding in among the Ransomes on his way somewhere else, as it seemed.

"The fool," Dent under his breath. "He'll get himself tapped over the head one of these days. And even a Larribee's head is not as tough as iron, quite."

But Larribee, sleek and sleepy of eye, moved onward as though he hardly realized what people were about him.

He heard the girl's voice saying: "I hear the fellow is a horse tamer, too. But I suppose that he does his horse taming at home."

"Hush, Arabelle," said Mrs. Ransome. "Hush, child, or the

creature will hear you."

"He's heard me already," said Arabelle clearly.

Larribee turned his head and raised his hat. It was a battered hat. In his first fracas in Fort Ransome it had received something more than its due share of attention. "Of course I've heard you," said Larribee. "But I like my neck more than I like a thousand dollars. Don't you?"

The Ransomes looked coldly upon him. Young Josiah, equal to the occasion, proved himself a true scion of the blood by not turning his head, but keeping his frosty glance steadily upon that huge horse.

"There's your chance at glory," said the girl. "And a lot more newspaper talk, too." She pointed toward the stallion in the center of the corral.

But Larribee looked back at her, and at her only. "I think Creary's back is broken," he said.

"You have a spine of your own," she said.

"It's made of stuff like Creary's," he answered.

"I'll bet that you'll try to ride that horse, though," she persisted.

The Ransomes tried to stop her, but she waved them away.

"What makes you think that I shall?" he asked.

"Because someone dares you to," she replied. "Isn't that reason enough for you?"

"Would you bet against me?" said Larribee.

"I'd bet that fiend of a horse against the world," she said.

"What would you bet?" asked Larribee.

"Why, anything you want."

He pointed. "There's an emerald on your finger," he said. "Will you bet that?"

She looked down at the ring. She looked back again curiously at Larribee. "I'll bet you the value of the ring . . . it's about a thousand," she said. "But the ring has a sentimental value. I don't want to part with it."

"But this is a sentimental bet," said Larribee. "I'll bet you a thousand against the ring that I can ride that horse around the corral."

She stared at him. And he stared back.

"I told you that the ring was not up for betting," she said.

"Oh, it will be," said Larribee.

"What makes you think so?" asked the girl.

"Because you'll do almost anything to see me piled in the dust," replied Larribee.

"What's your reason for thinking that?" she asked.

He shrugged his shoulders and nodded his head toward Josiah Ransome III. "Because of the crack in that head," he said. "You want to put the Ransomes up again, even if it takes a horse to do it."

"Arabelle," said Mrs. Ransome, "I forbid you to speak to this fellow again."

"Arabelle," said Larribee, "you'd really better not. For if you lost that ring, what would somebody say to you?"

Her face flushed hotly. "I won't let him brag and talk me down," she declared.

Larribee took out his wallet and counted out the money slowly. "Here's a thousand that grew out of dice and cards," he said, "with a little whiskey flavoring. Your cousin might hold the stakes."

"Arabelle!" exclaimed Mrs. Ransome.

But Arabelle, looking steadily at Larribee, twisted the emerald ring from her hand.

Larribee walked straight up to Mrs. Ransome and held out the money. "You don't need to be ashamed," he said. "My backbone is worth an emerald ring, I think."

She gestured as though to ask the stiff-backed major to her assistance, but, before he could stir, she suddenly reached out her hand and took the sheaf of money.

Larribee turned away.

"My dear," said the major, "what are you thinking about?"

She was the gentlest woman in the world, but her answer staggered him. "Today," she said, "I'm thinking my own thoughts for a change. Arabelle, I'll trouble you for the ring, if you please."

And Arabelle handed it over.

CHAPTER SEVEN

Dan Gurry was walking up and down in the corral. He was greatly troubled, but he did not speak loudly. His emotion was too great for that.

"Gentlemen," he said, "I'm mighty sorry about poor Creary. I don't mind saying that I'm going to look after him, and the doctor says that he's got two chances in three of walking again . . . someday. For my part, I'm making my last stand and my last try. There is the finest piece of hossflesh in the world, bar none. That's my opinion, and I ain't alone. If I could get that hoss onto a racetrack, I'd make history with him. I've got reasons. I've seen him in the pasture along with Bright Hour, that mare that's burned up the tracks south and north. And I've seen him run past Bright Hour as though she were hitched onto a dray.

"I ain't lyin'. I've invested four years in Sky Blue. I've invested more than time and money, too. Now, gentlemen, I've got an idea that riders as good as any in the world are right here in Fort Ransome. I ain't going to go to Russia to try Cossacks. If Sky Blue can't be ridden here, he can't be ridden anywhere. I ask you, gentlemen, if there's one among you that'll try to back this colt. I offered you a thousand. That's nothing. The man that can break this colt . . . and three ridings I'll call breaking . . . I'll give him a quarter interest in the stallion."

He paused. The Ransomes looked toward the big form of Larribee, but he lounged easily, resting one arm against the corner post of the corral, and regarded the situation with no apparent interest. And no one volunteered to ride the stallion, even for the sake of the one-quarter interest in him. Tough as they were, those men had seen Creary smashed like rotten wood, and they held back. It looked like the stallion's day.

Gurry was in despair. He stood stockstill at last, and, dropping his fists upon his hips, he said: "Gentlemen, I'll give a half interest in Sky Blue to the fellow who can ride him three times. It's not so much, if anybody can climb into the saddle and stick there for a time. There's somebody in the world who can turn the trick, I know, and the minute that he rides this horse, that's when Sky Blue will make both of us rich, and rich quick. I'm offering you a half interest in Sky Blue, any man of you who can stick in the saddle."

The Ransomes looked toward big Larribee, but still Larribee did not stir.

"Mind you," went on Gurry, "though Sky Blue certainly pitches a bit now, he wasn't always that way. He never showed an ugly streak. He's the wisest and the gentlest horse that ever went through my hands. But he's not the same when a man climbs into the saddle. The minute that the weight of a rider comes over his loins, then he starts to raise Old Ned, as you seen. I don't know what the explanation is. He acts like a fiend. But I guess there's something that even his wise old head is afraid of. That's all. If any one of you can get that wrong idea out his head, he'll have an easy ride of it." He paused again. "Well, then," said Gurry, "there's an end of it. And Sky Blue will have to run in the pasture the rest of his days and be broken up for dog meat in a few years."

A stir and a muttering went through that crowd. As brave horsemen as ever rubbed saddle leather with their knees stood about the big corral, the appeal that Gurry made was reinforced by the picture of Sky Blue in the center of the arena, with the wind ruffling his mane and his tail, and his fearless eyes turning from side to side.

"Gentlemen," said Gurry, "he can beat the wind and carry a mountain."

Looking at the stallion, Gurry's statement seemed almost credible.

However, though the crowd muttered and stirred, every man was looking around for some other to be the hero.

Potswood, the gambler, had only one leg. The other had been almost deliberately shot off him in a brawl during his early days. Now he had two of his followers lift him up on their shoulders. He was a little man who wore a forelock hanging, like that with which Napoleon is so often pictured. His face was round and red as a beet. He always looked as if about to explode with anger, and as a rule he was. Now he was in a plain fury.

"Ladies and gents!" he shouted. "If it wasn't for the ladies, I'd say what I thought of the two-legged things I see around here wearin' pants. They ain't men. I come from a part of the country where the women would tuck up their skirts and hop into the saddle sooner than see a hoss go without a challenge. I'll give something extra. I'll tack another thousand onto what Dan Gurry offers to the boy that can ride the stallion three separate times. Step up here, you boys that pretend you got blood in your bodies. A thousand for yourselves, and Fort Ransome saved from a pile of shame. Every town west of the river will laugh at us when they hear how we let a horse stamp in our faces."

A number of people set up a hearty clapping of hands as Potswood was lowered to the ground again. And the loudest applauders were the very men who, under different circumstances, would have tried their luck at once on the back of the big horse. But now they were still looking around, as though they felt no burden of responsibility and were expecting some more worthy champion to appear. The fact was that their last picture of the stallion in mid-air, snapping Creary loose, still overawed them. Such an incarnation of power and cruel intelligence they never had seen before in horseflesh, and not a man there moved to enter the corral for a long moment.

Then Larribee leaned over to the side, slipped between the bars, and walked quietly toward Gurry.

The applause instantly ended. There was one breathless whisper of—"Larribee."—some adding—"The tramp."—and others—"The Dents' fighting man." But he looked more like a tramp, in his ragged, torn clothes, as he approached Gurry.

The latter was new to the town and had heard nothing of the recent exploits of Larribee. He merely said, as he looked over the sleek face and shoulders of the man: "You want to try Sky Blue?"

"Yes," said Larribee.

"You ain't drunk, friend?" asked Gurry.

"I'm to ride him three times. Is that the idea?" asked Larribee, ignoring the question.

"You ride him three times," said Gurry. "You can lump the three times together, if you want. If you take the kinks out of him the first ride, you can try him again the second a few minutes after you've got off him. But three times he's got to be backed and rode. I've seen too many hosses backed once, and then pile their rider the second try."

"Well," said Larribee, "I'll make my try with him."

And with a nod to Gurry, he sauntered on toward the stallion.

"Look," said Arabelle Ransome. "He hasn't even spurs on his heels, nor a whip. And yet he's going to try to ride that demon of a horse. What sort of man is he?"

"Arabelle," said Mrs. Ransome, "I don't want to be too short with you, but the manner in which you've carried on. . . ."

47

"Oh, hush up," said Arabelle. "You're so excited your ownself that you're ready to run away, and you know it."

Mrs. Ransome did not even answer; her eyes were fixed straight before her on the stallion and the man who approached it.

Young Josiah Ransome, looking gloomily down, saw a thorny bur rolling at his feet. He picked it up idly, because he had to have something to do with his hands in order to keep his tongue quiet. There were many things that he wanted to say to his cousin, Arabelle. And he knew that to utter them would be his ruin, so far as she was concerned. So he gripped the thorny bur gently and felt the stickers, hard and pointed as needles, pass through the callous skin as though it had been tissue paper. The pain relieved him and half occupied his attention.

In the meantime, as all the onlookers pressed gradually closer and closer to the fence, Larribee walked up to the stallion, not from the side, but straight on toward his head. Sky Blue endured that approach until the extended hand was a foot from his nose. Then he bounded a rod to the side and waited again, snorting, his head raised and his neck arched so that the mane seemed like the decoration on an ancient helmet.

Larribee paused and laughed, and then he went slowly on toward the horse again.

Sky Blue canted his great head a little to the side as he listened. It seemed to him that he had heard this voice before, somewhere in the beginning of his life. It called up to him, very vividly, the smell of corn, yellow as gold and still ripening on the cob, the sweet scent of the feed box, and the whistle of the wind through the grass on a bright spring day when the clouds go over the heavens in little companies of twos and threes.

Then he thought of a winter day when the sun was shining through for an hour, and he could stand on the lee side of the barn and soak up the warmth like a sponge, and let it seep through his blood and penetrate his bones with comfort.

He shook his head to get these fancies out of it. He shook his head, and found that the hand of the man was close to his nose. He sniffed at that hand. There was a good smell about it. It came out to meet his sniff, and the strong tips of the fingers rubbed him between the eyes, never against the curl of the hair or the grain of it there, but downward, with the touch of one who understands how a horse should be caressed.

At this moment something happened to Sky Blue very much like what happens when an electric wire bearing a strong current is grounded. In a trice a current was flowing through the stallion, and the touch and the voice of the man were as one, soothing him. He allowed that hand to take the reins of his bridle and draw them over his head, lingering an instant to rub the ears. Then the stranger stood beside him.

"What's the matter back here?" asked Larribee. "What's the matter with you under the saddle, old son?" He loosened the girths. He passed his hand under the blanket and over the back and the loins, smooth and damp, like steamed silk. On either side of the backbone there was a deep sheeting of muscles, as hard and elastic as rubber. From that point, arching back across the hips, over the mighty quarters, there was one long succession of interweaving, interchained muscles hooked at last to the hocks and tapering down, through iron-hard sinews, to the fetlock joint and the pastern.

"By Jove," said Larribee as something broke loose in him like a freed river from a dam, "there never was a horse before. This is the only one."

CHAPTER EIGHT

Big Sky Blue, turning his head, took the stranger by the shoulder. He had the power of a lion in his jaws, and Larribee half expected to hear the sound of his own bones crunching. The agony was exquisite. But he merely said, playfully: "That shoulder is a joint, and not an apple, Sky Blue, old fellow."

The stallion loosed his hold. He reached higher. With a flick of his upper lip, he knocked the hat from the head of the man and nibbled at his forelock.

Suddenly Larribee laughed aloud. There was a ring of joy in his laughter that ran like quicksilver, flashing through the crowd in that corral. They knew that Larribee was not afraid.

Poor Dan Gurry, overcome with excitement and hope, bowed his head in both hands and would not look again for a moment, lest he should be disappointed.

In the meantime, Larribee rubbed the nose of Sky Blue with his fingertips. The stallion nipped at the fingers, and Larribee slapped him soundly across the muzzle.

It brought a squeal from Sky Blue. He reared, towering above Larribee. But Larribee did not move from under the impending blow. He simply laughed at the monster and called out to him: "You old idiot, you!"

The stallion rocked lightly back to the ground and a gasp of relief came from the spectators. They would not have been surprised to see the daring fellow crushed to the ground, his life smashed out by the stroke of two massive sledge-hammers.

Instead, Larribee tightened the cinches again. He laid a hand on the pommel of the saddle, he put his foot into the left stirrup, but, miracle of miracles, he did not pay the slightest attention to the reins. He merely allowed them to dangle loosely over the horn of the saddle.

The stallion was ready for trouble, now. Whatever men were to him when they walked the ground, they were another matter once in the saddle. Never a man put foot in the stirrup without reminding him of his colt days, a bright May day, when the turf was soft and fit for galloping, when the very sinews of a young horse yearned to be stretched by a mighty run. He had taken the bit readily. He had permitted the saddle, in spite of its jangling stirrups and squeaking leather, and its flexible arm that ran around his body, thin as a web and strong as iron. But when man sat in the saddle, a red-hot pain seared his very soul. That he could not forget. The fear of it turned him mad, reddened his eyes as they were reddened now.

Someone screamed from the fence line of the corral: "Larribee, Larribee! Mind the reins, you fool!"

It was Wilbur Dent. Dan Gurry whirled about. His face was swelling and livid with passion, patched blue and gray. He spoke softly, through his teeth, and yet every soul present heard him: "I'll shoot down the first man that yips again. It's brains and not reins that'll ride old Blue."

With his foot in the stirrup, Larribee paused for a moment, and then his right hand fumbled under the saddle, under the blanket, just at that point where there is most spring in the back of a horse, where the muscles are most supple, that long half loop of power that hurls the horse forward. At that point he brought his hand to rest, and he felt the stallion's flesh quiver beneath his touch. He felt the power crawl beneath the skin, stiffening to iron, and then the whole body of the great brute shuddered.

51

"Old Blue," said Larribee gently.

The horse turned his head. He looked back curiously and some of the fire left his eye, for the hand of the man lay on the very nerve center of that old pain, that old agony of terror that he never could forget. Gradually he relaxed. He listened to the voice of the man, and that voice rippled and ran through his soul as the sound of spring waters that bubbled out of the side of the hill and all summer long ran down the thirsty slope.

"I understand," that voice seemed to say. "I know all about everything. We've been a long time apart, you and I, but now we're together."

Sky Blue sighed; every cell of his great lungs distended, and, when that mighty breath had been taken, he felt the pressure of the man as he lifted himself up.

There was no start, no sudden upward thrusting, no wrenching of the tender corners of his mouth. There was only a big weight just behind his withers, where a horse can stand weight the best, and always the good right hand upon that nerve center, that center of memory, under the rear of the saddle.

Sky Blue prepared to tremble. But the shudder was only a partial one. He flexed his knees a trifle and sank lower behind, ready for the first mighty bound into the air. The thousand tricks of the fighting game flashed through his cunning mind, that mind so trained and sharpened by his countless duels with clever riders. He had won them all, from the first pain-inspired combat. He would win this, also, or die fighting. He would break this new tyrant.

Yet it did not seem the same as the other battles. The voice of the man went on, soothingly, and always the head of the stallion was free. This amazed him more than any other thing. For he knew that man ruled by the reins and the grip of the bit across the under jaw. He knew, when his head was drawn back close to his breast, as had happened now and again, he was powerless to buck until he had managed to stretch out his head once more. But here there was no effort to hold him in such a fashion. Here his head was as free as though he stood unbridled in the pasture.

Above all, the magic of the man's hand was on the tender place beneath the saddle blanket. Gradually that hand was withdrawn, and the full weight of the rider slipped softly into the saddle. Sky Blue thrust out his head, and trembled like a racer ready for the start. But once more the hand of the rider reached under the blanket and reassured him.

It was very odd. There was no mighty gripping of his sides and yet he felt surpassing strength in this fellow who had mounted him. There was not the usual quick, frantic fumbling for the stirrups. There was no stab from sharp spurs that cut into his flesh.

Instead, Larribee sat sidewise and slapped Sky Blue on the shoulder, and, as he fumbled for the right stirrup, his heel fearlessly, carelessly, rubbed and tapped against the sensitive side of the horse.

Sky Blue shook his head again, so that the bit and the bridle rattled, and again a faint gasp, like a sound of approaching storm, came from the crowd that watched.

Dan Gurry, his face now utterly gray, leaned back against a corner post of the corral. His lips moved. Those who stood near said that he was praying. Those who stood nearer declared afterward that he had simply been cursing softly, but, in fact, cursing was the only kind of prayer he knew about.

Arabelle Ransome murmured to herself: "He's not afraid. Look at him. He's not afraid. He's going to make that horse believe in him. I never knew a man could be like that."

She had gripped, as she spoke, the arm of Mrs. Ransome, and that dignified lady was heard to remark: "Be still, you silly little thing."

But out there in the center of the corral, big Sky Blue stretched out his long, glorious neck and with his ears flattened he said as plainly as words: *Now, try me, you. Try to hold me. Try to crush my chin back against my breast. Try to master me, if you dare. Here I stand, for all to see. It's a fair fight.*

He waited for the bite of the spurs and the rasp of a harsh voice, the grip of constricting legs, and, above all, for the iron of the bit in his mouth and the electric currents of hatred and fear flowing in fast tremors down the leather reins.

Instead, Larribee slapped him on the shoulder, and then on the neck. "Are we going to wait here a while, old Blue," he asked, "or are we going to move along presently?"

The stallion swung his head around and sniffed at the knee of his rider.

And the hand of the man reached down and slapped him gently across the muzzle. "We're friends, Blue," he said. "That's what we are."

The stallion was on the verge of plunging into the air, but the tap upon the nose had set it tingling. He paused to lower his head almost to the ground. He sneezed, and then he broke into a gentle trot. The reins flipped and flapped upon his neck, the man sat with perfect poise in the saddle, and from the watching crowd a shout that was like a roar of anger went up. Sky Blue heard it and leaped a dozen yards to the side. He expected, as he plunged, the control of the spurs and the bridle, but it did not come. Larribee shamelessly took hold by a handful of the mane and steadied himself against the movement. And that was all.

Then the reins began to be gathered, gently, slowly.

But Sky Blue was not to be deceived. He felt that man was stalking him, attempting to surprise him, and the moment the reins were straight, he thrust out his head suddenly, his neck stretched to its full length, and bolted straight ahead.

Behold, he had whipped the reins right through the hands of Larribee. There was no pull, either backward or to the side. He was allowed to gallop at his own sweet pleasure. From the very ends of the reins down to the iron bit between his teeth and thence upward to his wise brain, there came to the stallion from the hands of the rider a rhythmical assurance that as the horse would have it, so would the man be pleased, and all was well with the wind of the gallop blowing upon them both.

They moved as one. The sway of the man in the saddle was as the sway of the horse in a long and easy rhythm. He heard Larribee laughing; his neck was slapped by the strong hand of the man.

Instead of bucking, instead of striving to knock holes in the pale sky above him, the stallion began to frolic as he had frolicked of old in the pasture fields. He threw up his heels, but only in joy; he swept around and around the big corral at a speed that not a man of all those who watched ever had seen before.

At last he dropped to a trot. A slight pressure on the bit told him to stop, and Sky Blue came to a full halt in the center of the open space.

CHAPTER NINE

When the West opens its throat to shout, it remembers the Indians that once filled its plains, and the sound splits the sky. So it was now that big Larribee had got the stallion under control.

For under control he plainly was. He had not bucked a single jump of the way. Although he had seemed to bolt, at first, he had given up even that means of protest and now jogged peaceably forward—Larribee actually giving the blue horse a round thump in the ribs with his heel.

He rode to the barred gate of the corral and just paused there to speak to Gurry.

"He'll do," he told Gurry. "He'll win some stakes that will choke you to swallow 'em."

"You can get choked by 'em, too," said Gurry. "I'm for you, Larribee." Those words came out of the trainer's heart.

Potswood could be heard shouting in the distance, parting the crowd before him with loud words accompanied by blows freely delivered with his walking stick, with the aid of which he hobbled forward. Some of those blows might well have been resented, were it not that on either side of the gambler walked a brace of his ruffian bouncers who did duty of a night in his gambling house.

Potswood came up through the crowd brandishing a purse or, rather, a double-ended bag-shaped wallet of chamois skin. He was striking right and left with this, and the gold within jingled loudly. As he came close to young Larribee, he shouted: "Here, Larribee! Here you are, boy! You can have double this, the first time that you lack a stake in my house."

Larribee turned to the gambler, nodded, and waved his hand cheerfully. "You save that money, Potswood," he said. "Split it into ten sections, and give it to the next ten poor fellows . . . not the ones who want to gamble, but the ones who have had their fill of cards and dice and are leaving."

Potswood hesitated and seemed of two minds as to how he should take this suggestion, but the hearty clapping of hands that greeted this most unexpected act of generosity caused Potswood to side with the apparent majority. He waved his hand to Larribee and called back loudly that he would do exactly as he was bidden, and that he would take a pleasure in doling out the money in this manner.

This last act of Larribee's was of great importance in the mind of one of his observers, for Arabelle Ransome exclaimed to her hostess: "You see? You see? It's not the money that he's interested in."

"Money? Stuff," said Mrs. Ransome. "Whatever put such an idea into your head in the first place? The boy's a hero! A downright hero!"

When her son heard this remark and saw Arabelle nod with the utmost gravity, he squeezed his hand together so hard that the spines of the bur almost pierced his palm.

Then Larribee came through the crowd. He was big enough at all times. He looked like a giant on the back of Sky Blue, and the people gave way before him, opening a long lane of considerable width, for the stallion was dancing and prancing now that he had such a mob of strangers around him. No stiff rein checked him; it was only the gentle voice of Larribee that kept him in control.

So he came straight up to Mrs. Ransome and dismounted,

thereby definitely putting an end to his first ride on Sky Blue.

"I hear that you have something for me," he said to Mrs. Ransome.

"Yes, indeed, I have your money," she said. Then she placed the ring in Arabelle's hand. "You can talk to her about the other thing," said Mrs. Ransome.

Her husband came up with a stern and forbidding air and stood by, but Arabelle stepped straight up to Larribee.

"This ring," she said slowly, "belongs to you, I suppose. But it's only mine to keep on a sort of trust, I suppose I may say. I've no right to give it away to a man whom I've met today for the first time. I'm going to ask you not to wear it."

He took the ring and looked down at it. It was a broad golden band with a plain setting, such as a man would be likely to prefer. The emerald itself was big, with a broad-faced table cut, and it was by no means free from flaws. Looking down into it, he saw the dull blue-white of several small fissures. Nevertheless, it was a handsome stone, and the face of it bore an incised design of a coat of arms, supported by a unicorn and a lion rampant on opposite sides. He tried the ring on the fourth finger of his left hand. It would not pass over even the first joint, but with some pressure it was got onto his small finger on the same hand.

He said: "If it were a looser fit, I'd take it off and wear it in my pocket, but it's so snug that I'm going to leave it where is."

"Young man," said Mrs. Ransome, "don't be rash. If you wear that ring, it will cost you a pretty package of trouble one of these days."

"I suppose it will," said Larribee, "but I've an idea that it likes the open air and the sun, and I like to see it. Arabelle, this is a better day than even a blue sky could make it."

Arabelle looked him straight in the eye. "I ought to tell you what that ring means," she said, "but you're so proud, my friend, that I won't. Only, if you can keep it safely on your hand for a year, I wish that you'd let me know about it."

"At the end of a year," said Larribee, looking back into her eyes with a glance as straight as hers, "the ring will be on my hand if the hand is still mine."

If there were a little bravado about this, he covered it with a chuckle, and, remarking that it was time for him to give the stallion its second trial, he got into the saddle, this time with a bound, and rode off through the shouting crowd.

Major Ransome was almost exploding with rage. He had not spoken while Larribee was present, partly because he would not demean himself by speaking, as he put it, to a common adventurer, and, secondly, because he hardly knew what words to address to his wife and his young cousin. For he felt that no language could be quite strong enough.

As soon as Larribee had gone off on the stallion, Major Ransome said in a low, almost a choked voice: "My dear, I don't know what's in your mind."

Mrs. Ransome was a small and rather a thin woman. She had been a pretty thing in her day, but her day was a short one and left her to an early, scrawny middle age. She was usually sweet-natured, and her husband was amazed when she turned about to him with a sparkling eye and exclaimed: "Josiah Ransome, what in the world are you talking about?"

He was justly indignant. "I'm talking about the vagabond you've seen fit to pay attention to here with everybody looking on . . . the same ruffian who attacked your own son."

"My own son has been hungry for a dressing down for years," said Mrs. Ransome, "and I'm mighty glad that he got one at last. It may do him some good and get a little of the precious starch out of his backbone. As for speaking to young Larribee, I give you my word that I've never before seen a man that I'd rather know. Arabelle, here, agrees with me."

"I do," said Arabelle, and she put her arm through that of her hostess, and smiled back over her shoulder toward the retreating form of big Larribee.

The major could have swooned with mortification had he been a shade less of a man than he was. However, he had both pride and courage and he said, lowering his voice so that, as he thought, the bystanders could not hear him: "It's an outrageous thing and a mysterious thing. Burly bullies and bruisers, it seems, are your fancy just now, my dear. What on earth," he added, in a still lower voice, "do you mean by speaking out so that everyone present can hear you? Are you quite mad?"

"No, Josiah," she said. "I'm not mad. But I'm tired. I'm tired of a lot of things. And just now I'm chiefly tired of the Ransomes . . . all except one." With that, she actually turned her back upon the major, and took the arm of Arabelle more closely inside her own.

The girl returned that pressure. They went off a few steps together, and there were more than a few covert smiles turned toward the major.

He sought comfort with his son. "Women, by heaven," said the major, "need discipline more than soldiers and, by the eternal, they're going to have it." He fanned his mustaches out to either side with his thumb and forefinger.

"Arabelle has mother all excited," said Josiah III. "That's the only trouble. Poor Mother, she can be influenced, you know. And Arabelle's a rebel, it looks to me." He smiled as he said it, a sick, wan smile, for his whole heart yearned after her in bitter longing that was almost like hatred.

"Arabelle is young," said the major heavily, "but youth is a fault that corrects itself. A little patience with Arabelle, my boy. A little more patience and you'll see everything turn out well. One mustn't forget that she's been badly spoiled. Wealth like hers is able to corrupt even saints." He licked his lips and added again: "Even saints."

As for young Josiah, he had not the girl's wealth in mind. He would have had her willingly, if she had brought with her nothing but beggary and her loveliness.

In the meantime, Arabelle was saying to Mrs. Ransome: "I've got to tell him what the ring means. Of course, I can't let him go off without knowing all about it."

"Of course, you can't," said Mrs. Ransome. "But I'll tell you one thing, my child."

"What's that?" said Arabelle.

"Whatever you say, he'll never hide the ring."

"Why do you say that?" asked Arabelle.

"I say it because it's true," said Mrs. Ransome. "He's filing his claim. He's warning you that someday he's going to marry you, and well you know it."

"Oh, stuff," said Arabelle, "I never heard of such a thing." She looked straight before her, not at the people, but at the brilliant white clouds that were sailing out of the east, each shining as though a separate sun, or a moon, at least, were hidden in its depths.

CHAPTER TEN

Now, when young Larribee rode the stallion through the crowd once more, he was reining it right and left, and he seemed, indeed, to be using the strength of his hands freely. As a matter of fact, his touch was softer than the fall of feathers. He was simply suggesting to the great horse, as it were, how it could pick and choose its way through the human mass.

When Sky Blue felt the twitch upon the bit and turned his head a trifle, he could not help seeing the gap that always appeared in the throng. So he responded readily, and, after a few times, he was able to understand that the man was not fighting against him, but was simply helping him, from a superior angle, to solve the difficult problem of working a way through that mass.

The stallion was happy as a man is happy in finding a true companion, a sympathetic spirit. He had had stable friends and pasture mates, of course, but this man was different, in that he could give more than the beasts could ever give. The man was neither more nor less; he was different; he seemed to understand, and there was always that mysterious electric current flowing down through the reins as if through charged wires, and there was always the genial flow of that voice, awakening an answering harmony in the mind of the stallion.

Dan Gurry had broken through the crowd. He was quite pale, and his eyes burned under the deep shadow of his brows. His voice was low, and carried through sheer vibrancy. "Larribee. Larribee?"

"Yes, sir?" called Larribee.

"Try him in the open. Try him across the fields. Let him have his head on the straightaway. Wait a moment. Where's Colonel Pratt and his thoroughbred? He's surely here."

The colonel was there. He was found, and he came forward, a straight, lean, iron-gray man of sixty, with a stern face. He was riding a mare. She was ten years old. She was a little over at the knees and she hobbled a little in her walk. But her gallop was still the true swallow's flight, across country or over the level. The colonel loved her as the apple of his eye.

"Well, Mister Gurry," said the colonel. "What will you have of me?"

"You've got a fine mare, Colonel Pratt," said Gurry. "I just saw her this morning, and I didn't need to have her pointed out to me. I could see her points. She can move, sir, I'll put my bet."

"Yes," said the colonel with considerable pride. "She can move a little."

"Now, then, sir," said Gurry, "not that I want to offend you, sir, or to bother you too much, but I would lay a little wager, just in friendly rivalry, sir, that if you'll try her against the stallion, he'll beat her . . . and he has a two-hundred-pound man on his back, too."

The colonel weighed a hundred and thirty, dressed for the field. His mare was in perfect fettle, iron-hard, her ribs showing when she stretched out in a gallop, whereas it was plain that the stallion lacked exercise, and there were ripples along his flanks that were not muscle, but sheer fat. The colonel was a fair man.

"I gather that you've never trained that stallion across country, Mister Gurry?" he said.

"He's jumped pasture fences for his own pleasure," said Gurry, "and that's the only training he's ever had."

"The very best training in the world, in some ways," said the colonel. "That's why the Irish horses jump so well. Still, a man in the saddle makes a difference. And two hundred pounds of man on a horse that he's not familiar with is. . . ."

"I understand you," said Gurry. "Still, I'm fair mad to see the foot of Sky Blue tried out, sir. Now, you take a spin across to that bunch of trees and around them . . . I'd call that about half a mile out, sir, wouldn't you?"

"I'd shoot it for a thousand yards," said the colonel, turning a critical eye in that direction.

"Now, then," said Gurry, fairly panting with eagerness, "just in the purest friendship, sir, would it interest you to try the mare against the stallion for five hundred, sir?"

"I only bet . . . ," began the colonel. Then he changed what he was about to say, for he was scrupulously polite to everyone, even those who he considered whole worlds beneath him in social stature.

"You don't need to tempt me with a bet, Mister Gurry," he said. "I'll try the mare against the stallion, if you wish. And we'll both keep our five hundred dollars safe, if you please."

"Thank you, Colonel Pratt," said Gurry. "That's a gentleman's offer, and it's a mighty great pleasure to me, sir." He hurried to the side of the stallion and Larribee. "D'you think that you can jump him?" he said.

"I can ride him over a mountain of glass," said Larribee through his teeth, for the joy of a new power was making all his nerves jump with joy. In the saddle on that horse, he felt complete for the first time in his life. He had a sense of pride as high-headed as the pride of the stallion he rode upon.

"Then take him across those fences," said Gurry. "He can jump them in his stride, I think. I've had him hop over seven feet, with nothing on his back, if he wanted to get to the other side. Let him go his own way . . . but I won't give you advice,

Larribee. Only, if you find him getting away from the mare across country, try to hold him in a little as you reach the stretch of road, there. It's only a quarter of a mile or so to finish off, I should say, but I'd give a leg to see him tried against some good blood, like that. I know that she's not the finest racer in the world. But a racer she has been, and a prime one, and she is in the fittest kind of shape. It'll be natural talents against training and blood and all. Now, then, Larribee, bless you, and try to give us a fair show of what he can do."

Larribee simply nodded his head. The colonel was leading the way out from the borders of the crowd, which had heard the news in the wake of one swift whisper. So Larribee rode the stallion out behind the mare.

Behind them the murmuring of the crowd was like the humming of a great hive of bees in the ear of Larribee. And he could hardly keep from laughing, there was such joy in him.

The colonel turned in his saddle. "Mister Larribee," he said, "you've done a brave and brilliant thing today. In the matter of this little trial, if it is your wish, I'll ride the mare just hard enough to make an even show of it."

"Colonel Pratt," said Larribee, "that's mighty kind of you, but, if you please, take everything you can out of the mare. I think you'll need to if you're to make a good showing with her." He smiled a little, in spite of himself.

His words had been quite enough. There was no need for the smile. The colonel turned a bright pink.

"Very well," he said. "Are you ready?"

"Ready," said Larribee, straightening the stallion toward the mark.

"Then here we go," said the colonel, and he sent the mare away like a shot.

Larribee spanked the side of Sky Blue with his hand. And the stallion merely turned his head, curiously. A shout of disappointment and amusement came from the crowd. Larribee could hear, he thought, the groan of Gurry. So he called softly to the stallion, and the big fellow broke into a trot, than a canter. As Larribee called a second time and struck his heel against the side of the roan, Sky Blue caught sight of the mare winging her lovely way across the first fence. In that instant he knew, and, half a count later, Larribee was almost torn from his seat by the lurch of the horse gathering way. In two bounds he seemed to be at full speed.

He did not jump the fence—that is, there seemed to be no extra lifting of legs, no gathering to clear it—but one instant it was before Larribee, and the next instant he was over it, and the fence was well behind. He gasped. Before the gasp was well finished, a ditch opened before them, and he almost fell out of the saddle as the stallion jumped thirty feet to clear it!

So rapidly were they going, the landscape near at hand dissolved softly, in a blur, and the distant hills went walking smoothly and steadily past them. The blast of that galloping tore at the mouth of Larribee, and fluttered his eyelids. He bowed forward to butt it, and out of his lips came a thin, small, sharp, straining cry.

Sky Blue lifted his head and pricked his ears. He thought that he had heard that sound before, the scream of a hawk, half lost in a windy sky, or was it the far-distant neigh of a neighboring stallion from another hilltop? But, with pricked ears and head lifted for a moment, he listened to the cry of joy that had rushed from the throat of the man, and in that instant they were welded together, made of one flesh, of one brain, of one mighty spirit.

Strength was in the grip of the man's knees, but only enough to keep him in true rhythm with the stallion's gallop; strength was in his pull upon the reins, but only enough to balance the striding of Sky Blue.

They caught the good mare at the clump of the trees, and the colonel looked around at them as though the earth had been split and the steeds of Poseidon had risen out of the gap.

All the way back from the trees to the head of the straight road, the mare led, but Larribee was holding the stallion in, not by might of hand, but by talking quietly and using the reins for suggestion rather than control, so that Sky Blue ran with one ear forward, and one ear canted back to listen.

In this manner they reached the straight road with the mare a good two or three lengths in the lead. And then Larribee called on the big horse. He called on him in spirit, and he called on him in fact, with a great ringing voice, and Sky Blue reached the mare in half a dozen bounds.

Larribee would never forget the startled, bewildered face of Colonel Pratt as he and his mare were jerked away to the rear. After that, he forgot the colonel, forgot the mare, forgot the race. He was only intent upon the dazzling speed of the blue horse.

CHAPTER ELEVEN

Sky Blue was dark with sweat, and the big horse was dancing and prancing when at last it drew up before the crowd. They did not shout. But men and women went about looking at one another with foolish smiles, as people do when something a little past the expression of words has been observed. So they looked at one another, and they shook their heads and grinned.

Dan Gurry came with his face as red, now, as it had been pale before. As Larribee dismounted, Gurry took one of his big hands in both of his.

"They say that there's nothing in luck," he remarked, "but I felt my luck stirring in my blood when I seen Fort Ransome. I felt my luck even when Creary went down. They can say what they want, but I smelled my million when I seen the old town. I smelled it from the far side of the river."

Other people said nothing at all to Larribee. They were too busy looking at this superhorse, this long-striding miracle. Sky Blue was safe enough to examine. For a mere moment after the race had ended, the stallion was cropping the grass, keeping his head close to the boots of his rider.

So Colonel Pratt found the blue horse when he came in on his badly blown mare. She had had every advantage of weight, of the start, and of professional training, as the colonel himself had pointed out, and yet she had been left hopelessly behind.

"I was dancing in the air," said Colonel Pratt frankly, "like the tail behind a kite in a high wind. And Sky Blue went past

68

me with a rush and a roar, like a fast train on a downgrade. That's the way he went. By the way, Mister Gurry, what sort of price do you put on your horse? He's a good one."

"Did you ever see a thoroughbred that color?" asked Gurry.

"No," said the colonel. "I dare say that he could hardly be a thoroughbred."

"I dare say he is, though," answered Gurry grimly. "And I dare say that I got his papers in my pockets. His blood's as thorough as ever was seen, color or no color."

The colonel blinked. "Well," he said, "granting that he's a thoroughbred, a good stayer, and plenty of foot, what might his price be?"

Gurry looked at Larribee with a faint grin and an unearthly light in his eye. "Larribee has a half interest in him now," he said. "And Larribee is the only man that has rode him. Ask Larribee what his price would be?"

Larribee looked at Pratt with a smile. "The pound of flesh nearest to my heart, Colonel Pratt," he said.

The colonel nodded. "I understand, Mister Larribee," he said. "I understand perfectly. And I value you all the more for your magnificent horsemanship and for your understanding that the value of horseflesh is something more than dollars. Keep the blue stallion, and may he bring you much good, you and Mister Gurry. I've been badly beaten. But I value my mare as much as ever. The finest horse may be passed by a thunderbolt."

In after days, this speech of the colonel's was much quoted. Even at the time, it quickly went the rounds of the crowd, for Pratt was, of course, a noted horseman.

Men pressed in from every side to pat and stroke the stallion, admiring him and shaking their heads over him, while Gurry and Larribee stood together, talking earnestly.

Gurry wanted to get the stallion in training at once. It might be difficult enough, he said, even though Sky Blue had been ridden by one man, to make him submit to the riding of another. It would be best to go about the thing immediately, and to expect many upsets, before they found some tough jockey, with wit enough to manage Sky Blue.

They were talking in this manner together, calmly aware of the crowd about the stallion as parents are aware when strangers admire their children, and neither of them realized that the stallion was that moment being stolen from them.

It was tall and handsome young Josiah Ransome who came near to the stallion, and, as he came, he saw the face of lovely Arabelle Ransome, bright, and enthralled with admiration. As he saw this, he flexed his fingers a little, and the thorns of the bur thrust deep into the bleeding palm of his hand. This was what gave him his thought.

He put his right hand upon the back of the horse, and under the cantle of the saddle, under the blanket, where it was raised a little by the saddle's forward pressure, he passed the bur. The big thorns instantly thrust into the woolen blanket and young Ransome stepped back, content.

"If they find it," he said, "then my luck's out. If they don't find it, then that bully, Larribee, that slugger, will show Arabelle how hard a man can fall."

Almost immediately afterward, Gurry asked Larribee to take the stallion back to the stable. And, he said, the next day following they would start for Kentucky. They would go to a little private track he knew of, half hidden in the woods, where they could train the big fellow, take their time and groom him for big matches.

So Larribee, nodding and smiling, gathered the reins back on the pommel, and sprang into the saddle. He gathered the reins. He thrust his right foot into the stirrup, unhampered, for the stallion stood as still as a stone. Into the soft of his back, into the remembered place where a fool of a stable boy once had placed a bur, just there he felt again the downthrust of the pain and the fire of the torment worked through his very brain. So he stood for an instant, incredulous, for this was a thing not to be believed. He had trusted the man, and the man had trusted him with a loose rein. And now?

Larribee spoke to him cheerfully and bumped his ribs with his heel.

And Sky Blue responded. He responded as gunpowder responds when a spark is dropped into it. He bounded toward the sky, and, dropping out of it, he smote the ground, and the descending weight of the man on the saddle crushed the thorns to their full length into the flesh of the horse. It was not the present torment alone. It was the remembered pain as well that tore at the spirit of Sky Blue. He screamed with fear and rage and horror, and then he began to fight.

Fort Ransome is no more. The walls of its blockhouse have burned, and an irregular square earthwork marks the site of the little stronghold. The town, also, has gone. Its houses are down, and the plow travels once a year over the former location of post office and courthouse. But still there are oldsters, here and there at campfires and in bunkhouses, who will listen when cowpunchers tell of great and epic battles between men and horses. They listen, and then they smile, and at last they may describe the fight between Sky Blue and Larribee.

The stallion fought with cunning and with the skill of a trained warrior. He was far readier to die than to submit. He had to fulfill not only his hatred of all men, but especially of his deceiver who had, as it were, promised him love from the first word, and who now turned against him. And the man fought with the desperation of one who has entered the Golden Gate and struggles to keep from being thrust out again. He had had beneath him such a horse, he felt, as no other man ever had ridden. The wind of the gallop still seared his eyeballs. The joy and the glory of flight were in him as though he had ridden an eagle through the heart of the sky. He had been transformed. And was he to be dragged back to the earth again?

He fought with the wisdom of a perfect rider. He fought with the strength of four men. His balance was perfect. The grip of his knees would have broken the ribs of a smaller beast. And the weight of his hand on the reins was leaden. It was too heavy, in fact.

Fairly and squarely, before all of those watching eyes, Larribee was beating the stallion. When the horse hurled himself backward, as though anxious to break his own spine or the body of the man in the saddle, Larribee was out of the saddle, and, as the monster horse lurched upward, Larribee, like foam, was riding the wave again.

When Sky Blue did his sidewinding, Larribee clung with his mighty leg grip, and when Sky Blue tried that last and deadliest of all tricks, spinning in a short circle, Larribee maintained his balance. When the great horse bolted, trying to scrape off his rider against the nearest fence, Larribee pulled on the reins until the head of the stallion came slowly and surely back, close to his breast, and he was half blinded and all his movements constricted.

So hard did Larribee pull, in the excess of his power and in the confidence of an ultimate victory, that he drew with all his might, at the last, and the big double reins, almost strong enough to serve as traces for a team of horses, burst apart in his hands.

The ends dangled wildly. In the recoil, his body bent far back over the pommel of the saddle, and Sky Blue did not miss the opportunity. There was a low-growing tree in that field, with branches that thrust out on either side, and Sky Blue had tried for it more than once in the course of that battle.

Now, as the rider suddenly reeled far back, the horse found himself near that chosen goal, and, half wheeling, he made for it like a bolt from the sky.

They saw it. Every pair of eyes saw the move and understood, and a single, short, wild cry of horror broke from the crowd as if out of a single throat.

Young Ransome, his face gray-green, narrowed his eyes and looked. Then he glanced aside for one instant to see his cousin, Arabelle, with expressionless eyes, like the eyes of a statue, her face marble-white.

Then Sky Blue struck the branch of the tree. He should have crumpled and killed his rider. But the man was still sloped far back in the saddle, and the weight of the blow was received on the pommel, reënforced for taking the shocks of fifteen-hundred-pound steers on a forty-foot rope. That pommel and its supports were shattered to bits. The saddle itself was a battered pulp. The force snapped the girths, and saddle and man fell limply to the ground.

But while the stallion galloped away, free except for his bridle, the rider lay, senseless on the field, without a broken bone, without a scratch upon his body. Some men said that that was the greatest miracle of all.

CHAPTER TWELVE

Of the crowd that watched the breaking of Sky Blue, that attempted breaking that so nearly succeeded, perhaps a hundred and fifty had horses, and, when the stallion shot across the fields, ears flattened, neck extended, tail blown straight out by the speed of his going, every man and boy who had a horse was on its back in instant pursuit.

Except for that, perhaps, none of the remainder of this chronicle would be narrated, or all would have been so changed it would have made a much shorter history. But those honest riders, nearly all on tough, plains mustangs that can run all day before they drop, spurred and whipped forward as if for an incalculable prize. And the harder that cloud of pursuit labored to the rear of him, the greater distance the stallion put between him and the man-ridden beasts behind.

Of all the riders present, the only exception to the general pursuit was Colonel Pratt. His mare already had been badly winded. He was not such a fanatic as to try her paces against the horse when he carried not even the weight of a saddle.

Instead, he joined the other half of the throng, which surged forward to gather about the spot where Larribee lay unconscious.

Dan Gurry was there, also, but Gurry was practically useless. His eye was glazed. His look was staring and vacant. He could not find an answer for those who addressed him. For he had seen a star plucked out of the sky and lying, as it were, in the palm of his hand, then snatched away and cast far off.

He did not think of immediate pursuit on horseback. He would about as soon have mounted a mustang to catch a comet in the heavens. So he ran, instead, toward Larribee.

A dozen men picked him up and then they put him down, for the calm, cold voice of Colonel Pratt spoke to them, called them fools, and bade them to put the man down at once.

They laid Larribee on the ground, and Colonel Pratt kneeled on one side of him. On the other side was Arabelle Ransome. She had got there among the first, somehow, running like a deer and picking her way through the swerving crowd, just like a hunter through a pack of buffalo.

The colonel, without undue haste, took out a knife and cut away the coat and shirt of the fallen man. And Larribee lay still, without a sign of internal damage, except for a thin trickle of blood that ran down from his nostrils and two thin streams that ebbed from his ears.

The colonel saw them and quietly said: "At least, he's alive. His heart is beating, or the blood wouldn't flow. You hear the heart beat, Miss Ransome?" For her ear was pressed to the broad breast of Larribee.

She straightened suddenly. "His heart is beating, well enough," she said, "and it has a good, strong thump to it. I think he'll be sitting up in a moment."

She was right. Larribee sat up suddenly and looked around him in bewilderment, grasping at the group on either side, and seeming as one who expects to find a mortal enemy nearby.

"Sky Blue?" he asked.

No one spoke to him. One did not expect emotionalism from Larribee, his sleek face was generally so filled with a sort of animal content. But now there was anguish in his voice. So no one answered, just as men are hesitant when a father asks after a dead child.

Then Larribee saw Gurry and made a gesture toward him.

"Gone," said Gurry hoarsely. "And how are you, my boy? How's that back of yours? I thought I seen it busted in the center. How's the feel of your spine?"

"Gone?" said Larribee, clinging to that word, and understanding nothing else. "Did you say that Sky Blue is gone?"

"He's gone," said Gurry in the same husky tone, "as sure as a rocket is gone, except that the fire burns out in a rocket and the fire'll never run out of Sky Blue, till a bullet or a fall puts it out. He's gone, and the fools have gone ridin' after him."

Larribee sprang to his feet, staggered a little, and put out both his hands to steady himself.

Now, bare to the waist, one could see the source of his strength of limb. It was not the sleek fat that covered him, but the flow of smooth muscle, like water that slides over small stones. When he extended his arms, now, in that balancing gesture, long lines were seen, intertwisting from shoulder to wrist.

Arabelle Ransome caught him under the pit of one arm. "Steady up," she said. "You'll have Sky Blue again, one day. You'll ride him. D'you hear? You're not done for. You're all right."

He was still half dazed, otherwise he would not have brushed her away as he did. Then he walked slowly, uncertain of foot, toward the spreading low tree. When he stood under it, his head almost grazed the branches. It was a triple wonder, seeing him, that he could have escaped without a ruined body, if with life.

The saddle lay well out to the side, a twisted and a crumpled heap. Larribee kneeled beside it and put out his hand to it. He was yet more than half dazed. His brain was refusing to work, except by fits and starts—syllable by syllable, as one might say. So he turned the saddle. "He went off free," he said to himself, although others heard the words. "He seemed to turn mad, all

76

at once. I thought I had him. I thought that he had me, I thought that we were friends to the finish . . . then he exploded and the reins broke. I remember patches of things, now."

They stood about him in awe. A patch of sunshine fell through the branches and struck on his naked skin. It shone crystalline as snow, with a stain of rose under it.

"The reins broke in your hands," said Colonel Pratt briskly. "That was all that happened. The reins snapped. Otherwise, you had him beaten. He was in the palm of your hand."

Larribee looked up to him with dim, bewildered eyes, and rubbed his knuckles across his forehead. "You wouldn't want to beat a horse like that," he said. "You wouldn't want to have him in your hand. You'd want him in another way." He could not think of the right words.

The colonel leaned and examined the saddle. "It's smashed to a pulp," he said. "It's smashed to bits, and. . . ." He paused, and, slowly straightening, he presented to them a spot of red on the blanket of the saddle, a spot that was like an accusing eye. "Look," said the colonel.

They rushed in to stare. It was clear enough now. The thorns of the bur stuck out an inch or more, and they were stained all over with blood. One half of it was buried in the tangle of the blanket, but the rest of it was in clear view.

"So," said Colonel Pratt. He gave the blanket into the hands of Larribee, who stared at it, then raised his great head and looked about him. He shook that ponderous head of his, but understanding, it appeared, would not come to him.

In every gathering there is a fool. There was one present in this crowd, and his shrill, squeaking voice, half throttled by a sense of his own importance, cried out: "I seen young Josiah Ransome pick up a bur like that, and then I seen him fooling around Sky Blue's saddle, after the second ridin'."

"You yellow sneak," said some unnamed man of sense. He

turned, and with a hand of steel he smote the fool fully in the face and knocked him headlong in the dust, rolling over and over.

No one stooped to pick him up. He got to his knees, whining and whimpering. Then he found that Larribee was standing over him on one side and Dan Gurry was on the other.

Larribee was quite recovered now. He was lifting the informer to his feet, and saying in his gentle, rather husky voice: "You saw Ransome do it?"

The fool looked up at the still face and the still eye of the big man and suddenly he realized that he was speaking life or death for Josiah Ransome.

He quailed. "I mean," he said, "that I seen him, only, picking up a bur . . . like this one . . . and I sort of thought. . . ."

The hands of Larribee released him. "Thanks," he said. "That's all that I need to know." He turned straight about. "What do you think, Marshal Hannahan?" he asked. "Would you ask for anything more than that as proof, outside of a court of law?"

Now, the marshal was a brave man, and, in a pinch, a fairly wise one. He showed his courage by coming out to face the crowd on this day, and now he answered: "Larribee, be sensible. No horse in the world is worth a murder, and I'm afraid that that's what you have in your head."

Larribee smiled at him, and his smile was not a very good thing to see. He looked at Gurry, and Gurry nodded back at him. "I'll be going along," he said. "Are you coming, Gurry?"

"I'm coming, Larribee," said the other.

They started off through a silent crowd. Every man there knew what would happen next. And there was no one who blamed Larribee for what he had in mind; although every one of them understood that he would have to hang for it, later.

A third man joined the first two. It was little Colonel Pratt, moving with a brisk and business-like step. His mare followed behind him, like a well-trained hunting dog, heeling its master. "If you don't mind, Mister Larribee," he said, "I'll join you. There is such a thing as justice, I believe, above the law. Will you permit me to be your assistant, your second, in a manner of speaking?"

"Of course," said Larribee.

And so they walked off the field together, shoulder to shoulder, with death in all three of their hearts.

CHAPTER THIRTEEN

The three men walked along grimly, silently for some time. It was the colonel who spoke first, saying: "As a friend, if I may call myself that, what is your method of procedure going to be?"

And Larribee answered: "I'll proceed to wring his neck, if you don't mind."

"Not at all," said the colonel. "When a man has degraded himself as Ransome has, it is better to take bare hands to the rascal. However, there is a certain amount of respect due to the blood that runs in his veins. The Ransomes, I dare say, are not the oldest of families, but they have been known here for three generations. The other side of the affair, if it is worth a word, is that you will most certainly be hanged, if you kill young Josiah with your hands, whereas with a gun, a rifle, or a revolver. . . ." He paused and looked aside at his bulky companion. Then he added: "You handle such weapons, Mister Larribee?"

"I don't know a rifle from a walking stick," said Larribee. "But I've used a revolver." There was a note in his voice that made the colonel smile, suddenly, though his eyes were fixed straight before him as he did so. "Very well, then," he said.

They went on to the heart of Fort Ransome. They climbed the gentle slope to the eastern rim of it, and there they came to the Ransome house itself, sitting back from the street and surrounded by a hedge of great size. It had grown so tall that small boys and dogs found no difficulty in creeping through between the evergreens.

As they walked down this hedge, they could see through the greenery the white front of the Ransome house, the narrow white columns of wood that held up the verandah roof in front of it. Then they turned in through the gate. It had a slip-latch that allowed the gate to swing back and forth behind them with a light, musical clicking. Larribee wondered mildly whether there ever had been a more important mission to pass through that swinging gate and approach the mansion.

He had stopped in a Fort Ransome store to get a shirt and a coat, and now he was fairly respectable to the eye, although his trousers were still the tattered ones that he had been wearing in the morning of this day. His hat was badly battered, also, but that made little difference, since he carried it in his hand as they stood before the house.

Major Ransome came out from the house at once, looking very grave.

Colonel Pratt advanced before the others, giving them a gesture that bade them wait behind. They heard him say: "We have called to see your son, Major."

And they heard the major answer: "You can't see my son, Colonel. I've heard of the ridiculous charge that is laid against him owing to the chattering of some nameless fool in the crowd. I won't have my boy appear to answer such a remark, no matter to whom."

The colonel bowed a little. "I have come," he said, as though he had not heard the major's remark, "to represent Mister Larribee, who is waiting here."

"Mister Larribee and all his vagabond kind may take themselves off to the infernal regions," said the major, who had one of the quickest tempers in the world.

"I am flattering myself," said Pratt, "that I belong to Mister Larribee's kind. Not as a horseman, but, I hope, as a man."

"You can fit onto your foot any shoe that suits it," said the blunt major, "but I'd like to know what the mischief has mixed you up with the affairs of hoi polloi."

"In the meantime," said the colonel, "we are waiting to see your son, Josiah."

"You can wait till you put out roots," said the major. "But I'll not let my son leave the house. I've forbidden him to go out of his room."

"This will have an odd sound when the people of the town hear of it," said the colonel.

"You'll tell them, of course?" said the major. "As for what the other precious pair say, it's of no consequence. But if you make yourself responsible for such yarning, you'll have to answer to me for it."

"I stand ready to do so," said the colonel.

"I will send a friend to visit you," said the major.

"I shall be ready," began the colonel, "to see him at. . . ."

But here Larribee stepped forward and stood beside the colonel. "There won't be any duels and such rot out of this," he said. "I want to see your boy, Ransome."

"I don't know you," said the major. "And I don't intend to know you. You're an intruder on these grounds, Larribee."

The major was as hot as a stove. He glowed with courage and with irritation.

But Larribee said: "Your precious boy has done worse than murder. And it might have been murder, too. I'm going to see him if I have to break every door in the house."

"You'll never enter it," said the major, "until you're an invited guest. If you try force, my heavy-handed friend. . . ."

Larribee stepped a shade closer. The major did not flinch, but he could not help feeling something like a shadow of strength that fell from the presence of the taller man.

"Look here," said Larribee. "If I want to call out your son, or you, either, I'm of a dog-gone sight older family than yours, and one that's just as good. If you know salt from sand, and read as much as a daily newspaper, you know the Larribees. And I come from the Larribees that you've read about. It doesn't make a rap of difference to me, though. I'm not here as a name. I'm here as a man, and I'm going to have out your Josiah Ransome, the third. Stand out of my way, Major Ransome."

The major did not stand out of the way, but he took a step backward, and he passed his hand inside his coat.

Larribee jerked his own hand backward. "I'm going to talk like a book," he said, smiling. "I'm going to count to five, Major."

"You can count to five million, you ruffian, before I'll budge an inch," said the major with murder in his eye.

The lightning had gathered in the air. Colonel Pratt made no effort to intervene. He was a military man. He was accustomed to bloodshed. In fact, he loved a fight better than a round meal and a bottle of wine, any day of the month. So he merely curled the ends of his short mustache and waited.

Then the front door opened and Mrs. Ransome appeared. "There's no use fighting about it," she said quietly. "Major Ransome, your precious boy has run away."

The major actually tottered. He had to draw his hand from beneath his coat and put it against the wall behind him. "My dear," he said, "you're mistaken. Josiah is my own son."

"Josiah is my son, also," said Mrs. Ransome, "and I say that he's run away from trouble like a. . . ." She stopped, some terrible word forming in her throat and dying before it issued from her lips.

Larribee took the colonel lightly by the arm. "Missus Ransome," he said, "in a question like this, I think it's a good deal better if the affair is kept between the families concerned, and, unless the Ransomes feel like speaking of it, nothing will be heard from Colonel Pratt, or from Mister Gurry, or from myself. Good bye, Missus Ransome. Good bye, Major Ransome."

So he took his companions, one under each arm, and the Ransomes, half choked with surprise, were actually not able to utter a word.

When they got to the street, Gurry exploded. "You can talk for yourself!" he said. "But you can't talk for me. I'm going to let the whole district know what's happened here. Sky Blue's gone. And I'm going to rub the name of Ransome in the dirt for the loss of him."

"Man," said Colonel Pratt, "you'll do what I'm going to do. You're going to take the good advice of Larribee and let this matter rest here. The Ransomes are honorable people. Did you hear the major talk? You'd think him a boy of twenty, trying to win his spurs. But he knows, and I know, that he's got a bad eye, and that he hasn't hit a mark in eight years. Yet he was ready to fight at the drop of a hat. It's such men as the major that make the world spin around. The thing for you two gentlemen to do, I should say, is to get on the trail of the big horse. I've seen horseflesh, in my day, but I've never seen anything worthy of being mentioned in the same breath with Sky Blue. I've seen horses and horses, my friends, but he is apart from them all. I've never seen his color . . . I've never seen his like." He paused, as though unwilling to exaggerate. "When he went past me on my good mare, today," he said finally, "I thought that I would give the last years of my life . . . there may not be so many . . . for a single day on his back."

The others nodded, as though there were nothing extravagant in this remark.

Then Gurry suggested that they should get to the center of town, and find out what the hunters of the horse had learned. Not one of the three had any hope that the big fellow could have been captured. They merely trusted that something could be learned about the general direction of his flight.

So they went back to those few short blocks where the trading stores, the fur buyers, the outfitters of caravans, and the saloons were congregated. The moment they entered this district, which seemed to be surrounded by an intangible deadline, they found themselves objects of general interest. Gurry was noted for one, as a half owner in the horse, and the colonel because he was always noticed, and Larribee because of what he had done in the saddle and out of it, that day.

They had not gone a block, before a troop of half a dozen on sweating horses with drooping, tired heads drew rein near them. A grave old fellow with the color and the look of sun-dried rawhide said to Larribee: "If you and Gurry want to get Sky Blue back, you'll have to hire a set of wings. Horses will never land him. He walked away from us. He left us standing. We come up with him again, and again he goes and dissolves himself on the edge of the sky. You take that color of his, you can't see him till he's a quarter of a mile away. He sort of melts into things. I wish you all the luck, because it's luck and nothin' but blind luck that'll help you. He's gone, and the looks of him as he faded out seemed to mean that he wasn't comin' back this way in a hurry."

CHAPTER FOURTEEN

They learned all about the probable location of the stallion. He was out between the Muscle and the Thomas Sloughs. Then Colonel Pratt offered to mount Curry and young Larribee and to accompany them himself. They accepted the offer gladly. Larribee, meeting Wilbur Dent in the street as the three of them set off, merely leaned from the saddle to shake his hand, and smile at his condolence.

Going on, something made him turn again in the saddle and wave his hand at Dent, and he found his cousin standing rooted in the street, staring after him. It gave Larribee an odd twinge, but how could he guess that he would never lay eyes on Wilbur Dent again?

It was dusk when they got out to the region in which the stallion had last been seen. It was too dark for them to hunt any farther, so they made a camp, and ate the crackers and cheese that the forethought of the colonel had equipped them with. All that night, none of them slept long at a stretch, for the thought of the stallion, wandering unmastered, was like the thought of a great diamond unguarded in the streets of a city. Like a jewel he shone, too, in their minds.

And Gurry expressed it in the morning: "He'd make a hoss thief out of an archangel."

That was in the coldest gray of the morning and before the eastern sky was touched with pink they were in the saddle and under way. In fact, the rose of the morning had hardly commenced when, on the frosting of the dew in the long grass, they saw the dark streak of some animal's trail. They went to it and found the sign of a horse. Curry did not even have to dismount, he knew the hoof prints so well.

"Sky Blue," he said.

All three of them laughed in sudden relief. It seemed a promise that the diamond had not yet been picked up by some covetous hand.

They came through a soft marsh, through a scattering of trees on the farther side. As they left the screen of timber, Sky Blue suddenly appeared before them, standing on a hummock against the blue heavens. He turned his head toward them. An inhuman cry came out of the throat of Gurry, and then the stallion wheeled and fled at full gallop.

For five minutes they spurred foolishly after him. At the end of that time, he was a glimmering shape in the distance. A short way off, he was the blue of a mirage, outlined against the ground or dissolving in the sky, just as the other horse hunters had reported.

They drew in their mounts.

"Oh, it's all right," said Gurry. "We've got his trail, now."

"It's all right," said the colonel, "unless some horse-stealing Indians get sight of him."

"Are there many this far east?" asked Larribee.

"This far east? How far east do you think you are?" said the colonel. "We have Indians almost as thick as coyotes on the outskirts of the fort. If they should see Sky Blue, a whole tribe would travel clear around the earth to catch him."

The colonel had a good pair of glasses, and with these, after traveling three hours more at a jog, they picked up Sky Blue again on the rim of the world. So they turned to the right and made a great detour, which cost them three hours more. At the end of that time, they figured that they were well to the west of the big horse, and they spread out to quarter-mile intervals and worked gradually in on the line of his travel.

It was noon. The sun was high. And the heat waves rose like a dancing mist off the softly rolling prairie. Such grass! Larribee felt all the hoofed and horned cattle of the world could graze within the reach of his eye. But when the glasses found the stallion again, he was to the north and west of them again.

"He's changed direction," said the colonel. "What's in him? You'd think that he had a goal in mind and was traveling toward it, shifting now and then to throw us off. What keeps him headed so steadily west?"

They found a small stream of water and made a midday camp there. For their meat, they had one rabbit, a small portion to divide among three very hungry men. But they were cheerful.

Gurry said: "Sometimes I've got an idea that he's gone for good. That's only because I want him back so bad, I suppose. Only, you take the size of things out there, there's plenty of room to lose a horse, even a Sky Blue."

They let their mustangs graze for a full hour and a half. Then they caught up the animals, resaddled, and voyaged on across the green inland sea. They headed straight on the last course of the stallion, but spread out a full four or five hundred yards apart. They had gone on an hour, when Larribee found the trail of Sky Blue as clear as print. Ten minutes later, he found something else that made him throw himself from the saddle and bend over the ground. It was the trail of a smaller horse, a horse stepping hardly two-thirds of the walking stride of Sky Blue, an unshod horse, whose easy step hardly crushed the grass. Already it was springing up where the animal had trod.

A rapid thudding on the ground made Larribee rise, and he saw Colonel Pratt galloping toward him, as though bent on serious business.

"What's up?" demanded Larribee.

The colonel pointed a stiff arm ahead of him, and then waved his arm to include half the points on the horizon.

"Indians," he said, "and trailing Sky Blue. Some brave is after him. We'll have to watch the skyline now for smoke, because, when that brave finds that he can't catch the stallion by himself, he'll call in his tribe, if their teepees are anywhere near."

"And what's this?" asked Larribee, pointing to the new-found trail.

The colonel gave the thing one glance. Then he straightened in the saddle and shook his head. "More than one Indian. That's what it means, Larribee. If you're a sensible fellow, you'll turn about and head for Fort Ransome straight off."

Gurry came hurrying in. "I've found a trail . . . ," he began.

"Of an unshod horse, eh?"

"Of three of 'em," said Gurry, "and half a dozen more going ahead, crookedly, like three men were driving half a dozen spare horses."

"They are," said the colonel. "And they're Indian horses. What's more, if Sky Blue is ever broken, it will be under an Indian saddle. My friends, we'd better go back of our own accord before we're sent back. Mind you, you have a claim to the stallion, but no Indian gives a rap about claims to a horse found wandering freely over the plains. Even if they did have laws about thefts, they'd unsay the laws for the sake of Sky Blue and cut the throats of the whites they found riding behind the horse."

Gurry looked not at the colonel but at Larribee, and Larribee looked mildly back at Gurry, as though waiting for him to give the answer.

Gurry said at last: "You've said a true thing, Colonel. But lemme pay you for these horses and saddles. You go back to the fort. But Larribee and me have got to go on."

"Is that it?" said the colonel. "Abandon the pair of you in the middle of a march? I think not, my friends. Besides," he argued against himself, "we're still close in toward the settlements. Here and there, a few of the red demons know me. And we might claim the stallion after they've caught him."

"And suppose that they don't catch him?" asked Larribee.

"Not catch him?" said the colonel, lifting his eyebrows with a smile. "Oh, the Indians catch any horse. Indians, for the sake of a good horse, could walk the air for ten miles, or hide in grass as short as a wolf's fur. They will rise up out of the ground all about Sky Blue and swallow him in the nooses of a hundred lariats. No, no, don't doubt it. They'll have Sky Blue. But perhaps we can buy him back, before they have a chance to try his speed."

That seemed the likeliest chance to ride straight on in the trail of the Indians and, when the red men had caught the big horse, to come up with them and buy Sky Blue.

The colonel would go on with his friends as much as two whole days, in the effort to get the stallion. After that, of course, he would have to turn back to Fort Ransome, where his affairs would be requiring his time.

When this agreement was arrived at, they struck out on the second half of this day's march and traveled now a full half mile from each other. The colonel, with his glass, was between the two, so that he could pick each of them up the more readily. Spread out in this manner, they would be far less likely to miss any swerving of the tribe's course in pursuit of Sky Blue.

They went on quietly until they came to a rolling country in which they lost each other repeatedly, and it was only when they climbed to the top of some higher hummock, here and there, that they had sight of their companions.

Larribee, on the left wing, had the most southwesterly position, and he kept his attention toward the outer flank, scanning the ground there. The colonel, in the center, was following the main trail that the Indians made. His eyes were most experienced in following prairie sign, and they could trust him to keep them on the right course.

The country now rapidly grew more and more broken. A small dry draw turned Larribee a little distance out of his direction, and, when he had crossed the steep banks, he found himself in an exceptional growth of brush, half the height of a mounted man. The grass was more sparse, and patches of red clay looked through here and there.

He started, now, for the top of the highest place that was near him, to relocate his companions or the colonel at least, for he began to be a little worried because of the distance he had gone without sight of his fellows.

He had to cross one low hill and then a swale, before climbing another hill, fairly considerable, beyond, and it was in the midst of this brushy swale, as he pressed the sweating mustang on, that a pang of red fire darted through his right thigh, and at the same moment he heard the loud twang of a bowstring.

He looked down, bewildered. The little bloodstained, triangular point of an Indian arrow protruded through the front of his trousers, and the feathered haft of it stood out behind.

Chapter Fifteen

After the first stroke of pain, Larribee was numb down the length of his leg. He snatched out a revolver and turned in the saddle, kicking the mustang to speed with his left foot. He fully expected to see the feathered head and the long hair of an Indian above the brush, somewhere to his right, but he saw nothing except the heads of the shrubs, bent by the wind, with the sun blazing above.

The mustang answered the urge of the kick with a half buck and a lunge forward, but its next stride seemed to stop in mid-air. So hard was the second arrow driven that, although it struck the horse, Larribee felt, or thought he felt, the shock of the impact, one instant before the twang of the bowstring smote on his ear with a sense of horror.

But the mustang, falling, shot through just behind the shoulder, cast Larribee, heels over head, away from him. And Larribee, flung to the ground for the second time that day, lay flat upon his back with his arms outstretched, the revolver still gripped in one hand. He felt a great pain at the base of his skull. A cloud of black covered his eyes, and through it, dimly, he saw the broad red disk of the sun.

The cloud lightened a little. It was as if through a parting fog that he next saw the face of the Indian running in at him, the flicker and sweep of the long hair blown back across his shoulders that gleamed coppery bright. And what a mighty out-thrust of the chest beneath, what a sweep of sinewy arms. The knife that the red man carried seemed an insignificant spark of light in the grasp of his powerful hand.

Larribee pulled himself together, or tried to. But his sluggish body would not respond. His brain spoke, and the nerves strove to carry the message of command, but the muscles would not answer. He saw the handsome face of the savage stoop above him, the hand jerk up, and the arm tense for the blow. Then desperation gave Larribee strength in his right arm. He struck blindly with the revolver weighting the stroke, and the red man disappeared from his view.

Perhaps he had stunned the Indian, but he knew that that blow could hardly have been fatal. He told himself that he must sit up. He must strike again. He must level the gun and fire.

His brain was crystal clear. The cloud was gone from his eyes. He could even feel the warm trickling of the blood from about the ends of the arrow, but still he could not force his body to stir.

His right arm alone seemed to have life in it, and on this he finally thrust himself into a reclining position.

Then he saw that the Indian had fallen at his feet and was now making blind struggles to rise, his head wavering from side to side. He was still stunned by the force of the blow.

Larribee pushed himself into a sitting posture. He raised the revolver and fired at the same instant that the red man gained a crouching position and sprang at him with the knife. He knew that that bullet had struck home, somewhere, but he also knew that the shot had not passed through either head or heart.

The knife flashed before his eyes. The keen pain of it darted into his body, and the whole driving impact of the Indian's body struck against him, throwing him back to the ground.

A strange disgust and horror came over Larribee. He told himself that he was like swine in a sty, being butchered. The revolver had fallen from his hand, and he had only those hands to help him. He thrust out his arms and gathered the Indian to his bleeding breast with a force that would have shattered the ribs of a common man. But here was no ordinary figure. It seemed to Larribee that he had thrown his arms around the staves of an oak barrel, so stiffly did the body of the Indian resist him. And there was that armed hand tugging, straining, wrenching to be free.

It jerked away; the knife gleamed in the sun, rose, fell, and thrust deep through the muscles at the base of Larribee's neck.

Like swine, Larribee thought to himself. *I'm being stuck like a pig in the butchering season. I'll bleed to death, squealing the same way.*

The knife flashed upward again. A stream of red drops fell from it into the face of Larribee, and he caught blindly at the knife itself, at the glitter that was dimmed by crimson. It was not the knife that the left hand of Larribee found, but the sinewy wrist of the Indian.

With all his might, the red man sawed his arm back and forth, striving to free the armed hand. But the grip of Larribee was like the grip of ten. He felt the life running like a river out of his body; before the tide was out, he would, nevertheless, have existed long enough to end the days of this murderer from ambush. A high disdain for his own fate seized on Larribee. He thought not of his death, but of the wretched creature with whom he fought.

Pride is nine-tenths of a brave man's strength. Pride raged in the heart of Larribee as he closed his iron grip over the wrist of the Indian. He would put out the light of hate in the red man's eyes. He would still the teeth that gnashed in his very face, and the voice that, to his amazement, said in perfectly good English: "White dog. White coyote." The last word disappeared in a gasp.

For Larribee, sinking his fingertips deeper, was turning his hand slowly and burning the tendons of the Indian's wrist against the hard bones. It was not a matter of endurance. The nerves in the Indian's fingers grew numb and refused to control the muscles. The knife fell. By a freak of chance, it landed point down in the grass beside Larribee. At first, it had threatened to enter his very eye.

But the Indian was disarmed. It was man to man and hand to hand, now. And what man had ever been able to hold Larribee?—this one more than all others.

He could tell, as they twisted, breast to breast, that to the red man it was utterly amazing to find such strength as this. No doubt, in the Indian camp, his arm had been the strongest, his hand the quickest and surest. With the might of a great body, an unconquered will and pride, the Indian fought back.

Larribee felt the resistance of the red man gather, reach its climax, and then, in the full power of a glorious exertion, a tremor struck through the whole body of the Indian. And Larribee knew that the fellow was his. He smiled up into the face of the barbarian, and said: "Now, you sneaking bush master, you've sponged on the whites long enough to learn their talk, so you can listen to me. You've sponged on them, and you've probably cut the throat of the poor fool who took you in, gave you a home, and treated you like one of his family. But now I'll put an end to you. I'll leave you here dead as charred wood. D'you see? Now I'm the underdog. But I'm going to turn you. The arrow you put through my leg has caught its heel in the ground, and I feel it tearing my leg, but still I'm turning you. Fight like a demon, my friend, but, no matter how hard you fight, I'm going to last long enough to throttle you. Fight, my friend."

He laughed. With a great, but slow effort, he turned. He felt the end of the arrow snap, with a gush of hot blood following it. But the weight of the Indian had turned with him, and that great, writhing, plunging, twisting, powerful body was now pinned beneath him on the ground.

A wave of faintness rushed over the brain of Larribee. He cast it away from him, as a man beats back spray, with a gesture of the hand. Then, in the clasp of one hand, he placed both the wrists of the Indian.

Mightily the other strained, thrusting his elbows out, tugging with all the force of his big broad shoulder muscles, but the fingers of the white man held like lashings of stout rope.

Larribee plucked the knife out of the ground. "D'you feel the point of it?" he said. "The same point that you ground to a needle on a stone, some evening in your teepee? You rat-catching dog!" He flicked with the point a cross on the brow of the other, and the blood sprang out, painting the line a broad crimson.

The other suddenly lay still. "So, then," he said, "strike. You are strong. You are stronger than I am. I would have taken your scalp and dried it over the fire in my teepee, but you will never live to dry mine. Death is making the eyes jump out from your head. I have not died for nothing. My people will find me here and the scalp still on my head. They will bury me. But they will count the coups on your body, and rip the scalp off the bones of your skull. May you wake up long enough to feel them tearing. May they take that scalp with dull knives. But me they will bury properly. They will raise a platform. They will wrap my body in their best robes. They will lay their best weapons beside me and kill their finest horse under the platform, so that my spirit may ride hunting through the fields of the happy sky forever, while your soul rots with your body and moans in the wind on black winter nights. Strike, now, white man. In my lodge, there are seven scalps. They are all of your people. Strike surely. You have only a moment left to live."

Larribee raised the knife to strike, raised it high, and with an arm stiff with power. But, as he looked down into the proud, confident eyes of the red man, he thought of other proud eyes that had stared into his—the stallion, Sky Blue, equally strong and brave. In the world where would one find another horse like that, and in the world where such another man as this?

Suddenly he released the wrists of the Indian.

"I wish," said Larribee, muttering slowly, "that I'd killed you in the middle of the fight. But I can't murder you, man. Put my scalp with the others. I'm going into the dark, but that's no reason why I should take a fellow like you along with me. You wouldn't," said Larribee, laughing faintly, "be fit company for a man who. . . ."

So, his laughter trailing away, he slumped down upon one elbow, and then fell limply along the ground.

Chapter Sixteen

The Indian had had death hanging in the air above him one moment, and the next he found himself free, with the loose bulk of the white man pressing upon him. He rolled from beneath the burden, and, resting upon one hand, he looked upon the face of his late enemy. With the other hand, he tried vainly to stop the blood that flowed from his body, where the revolver's bullet had torn its way through his flesh.

He could not stop the passing of that blood, and he could not stop the great aching that possessed all his vitals. He looked down at the mouth of his wound. It was small, purple-rimmed, and the blood welled from it with a steady pulse. Already half his body was smeared with the crimson. He raised a hand behind him and felt the spot where the bullet had issued from his body, and that aperture, he could estimate, was four times as large as the one made by the entrance of the lead.

So he looked up to the sky and the white clouds that drifted there, and he thought to himself: *Now I am about to die. The gods of my people receive me. May my friends lay a good rifle beside my body, and kill a fleet horse under the platform that supports my dead body, for men say that the buffalo who run in the blue fields of the sky are far fleeter than the buffalo who run over these plains. It may be that my comrades have snared, by this time, the strange-colored stallion we hunted today. If that is true, then they will surely sacrifice him in my honor, for only the best can be given to a dead chief. On the back of the ghost of that horse, I shall pluck the very eagles out of the sky and overtake the hawks. They must give their best to their chief, when at last he is found with the scalp of a dead enemy in his own strong dead hand.*

So he mused to himself, and he picked up the knife with which he had twice wounded Larribee, and which Larribee, in turn, had poised above his breast, holding him the while helpless. He caught the hair of Larribee's head and prepared to cut and tear the scalp away, but, as he did so, a faint murmur came from the lips of the unconscious white man, and the heart of the Indian stood still. An unseen power stayed his hand.

He remembered, then, how his enemy had held him powerless. He dropped his hand to the ground and looked around him. His code told him to slay, to count the coup, to take the scalp, which would be treasured in his nation after his death. Death itself was not bitter or painful, since it had come so gloriously.

When had any of his nation seen so glorious an enemy as this white man, who lay there on the soft grass with his arms thrown out, crosswise?

He thumbed his sore wrist. The flesh was bruised to the bone where the gigantic grasp of the other had lain upon it. Then he looked at the loosened hand that had hurt him so and numbed his own powerful hand and half his arm with the pressure.

We are as two brothers, said the Indian to himself. *Except for the color of his skin, we might have been born of the same mother. Here we are to lie, dead by one another's hand, for no medicine man can heal the white man, and no medicine man can heal me. The sweat of death is on my face. But this man fought with me honorably. Like a brother, he gave me my life . . . he left my scalp on my head, and, therefore, my soul shall be an entire soul.*

When this thought had come to him, a sort of pity arose in his fierce heart. The more he looked down on the white man, the more it seemed to him that, if they two had been joined together in any undertaking, a hundred braves could hardly have stopped them.

Then a dizziness came over the red man. When he recovered from it, he found himself lying face down in the cool grass. He was breathing with difficulty, and he could only, by summoning all his strength, thrust himself up.

I am about to die, thought the brave. *If they find me here with the white man, they will take his scalp in my name and give it to my squaws. This should not be, because he gave me my life, and spared my soul. Therefore, I shall spare his soul. We shall stand up together among the Sky People. If there is but one horse between us, I shall run on foot and he shall sit in the saddle.*

So he went through the ceremony of blood brotherhood. With that keen knife he made a cut on his arm and through that the blood ran lazily out from the wound. In the arm of the white man, he made a similar cut, and, laying the two wounds together, with a strip of Larribee's shirt, he bound them closely together.

As he was doing this, his head was filled with ringing, as though a bell were sounding in the distance. When he had spoken the words that ended the ceremony, he sank down on the ground beside Larribee, and he, too, became unconscious.

The bright sun flared in their faces, as they lay side-by-side. The prairie wind ruffled their hair. High above them appeared a buzzard, which began to circle leisurely toward the ground. Then, to its right and its left, many dim specks appeared, others of its kind dropped into view, settling likewise in the same direction.

It was the buzzards that showed the Indians the way. Eight of them came up, carrying with them something better than scalps—two white men, bound with their hands behind their backs, their feet lashed together under the bellies of their horses, their horses, in turn, tied bridle to bridle and led by the youngest of the party.

So they came up at a gallop. The leader, seeing the two men lying side-by-side, leaped from his pony first of all, threw the rawhide lariat on the ground so that the horse might be more easily recaptured if it strayed away, and, snatching out his knife, he laid his grip on the hair of Larribee's head.

The second brave had been only a stride behind the other and was on the ground only a second later. As he stooped over the enemy, he saw something that made him cry out and catch at the hand of the leader. The latter paused, angry. "But look," said the second man. "These are blood brothers. The rite has been performed. Their arms are bound together. They are dead, but they are dead as brothers."

Here the Indian stirred, groaned, and laid a hand upon the bullet wound.

In an instant, the party was in confusion. As for a dead companion, seeing that he would have fallen in honorable battle, hand to hand with a brave enemy, he would have gained envy rather than pity. But a wounded brave was another matter, a thing to call for effort from all of them.

They undid the bandage that bound the two arms together, untying the cloth with a certain reverence. The oldest member of the party then took certain herbs from his saddle pouch, ordered the lighting of a fire, and heated water poured out of the water skins. In this he steeped the herbs and made a dressing that was carefully bound over the hurts of the fallen companion.

For he made sure that the brave breathed, though faintly, but he did not stop there.

"He who is the blood brother of Shouting Thunder," he said, "is likewise a brother of our tribe. Wash the blood from his body. Take my own robe from behind my saddle to wrap him in. I give my lance to help support his body."

There were half a dozen knives itching to get at the scalp of the white man, as he lay there in his blood, but the force of the custom was stronger than their hands.

They set about cleansing the body of Larribee, but they had not gone far with their work when the same boy who led the horses of the captives uttered a sharp cry. "Look," he called, "he lives, also!"

They came, gaping. They said that there were enough gates open in his body to let out half a dozen lives.

The old man reproved them sharply. "It is my fault," he said. "The Sky People were always gracious to Shouting Thunder. They will be gracious to his blood brother also, will they not? Both of these men will live and be a power to the tribe again. Treat him, now, as though he were your own father, a poor but a very honorable man and the first voice in the assembly. Rebuild the fire. There is life in him. It is not his own life, perhaps, but a second one that the Sky People have given to him."

And he set about, with all care, dressing the wounds of the stranger. As he worked, he gave orders. He sent the boy to ride in the direction of the marching tribe. "Tell them," he said, "that we have found wood and water, and that Shouting Thunder lies here, too weak and ill to be moved. Let them say whether or not they will march here. The rest of you take all the horses and ride on north and west in the direction of the horse that is the color of the summer sky in the evening. I have made no medicine, but my heart tells me that the horse came to show us the way to this man who lies here. Much good or much evil will come to us out of him. Ride hard. Be as cunning as foxes and as wise as the Pawnee wolves when they come down on us to steal our horses. The man who brings the blue stallion back to the tribe will win honor more than the winning of a Pawnee scalp."

They went off in a flash, without question. They were glad to be free from the care of the two wounded men, which meant labor like the labor of a woman.

But the old brave sat down and lighted his pipe. He blew a puff toward the earth. He blew a puff toward the sky. He blew smoke into either hollowed hand, releasing it to float upward and carry his prayer, which was not for himself, but for the wounded men at his feet.

And all the time the captives sat on their horses and said not a word, but looked steadily at the waxen face of Larribee, doubly pale against the green of the grass.

CHAPTER SEVENTEEN

In a very strong man there is not only much blood, but a certain excess of the vital spirit that is as important as the life fluid itself. So Larribee did not die.

He lay as close to it as a man could. For a week he was in a coma on the spot where he had fallen, only raised from the ground by the soft comfort of an Indian bed of willow slats and deep Indian robes. His wounds were dressed with a good deal of practical skill. But his recovery was delayed by the powwows and smokings, infernal noise and ceremonies which took place, night and day, in the hastily constructed lodge of Shouting Thunder, where the white man lay ill.

As soon as it was possible, he was given herb concoctions to drink, but he would have died beyond a doubt had it not been for the intelligent care that the colonel and Gurry gave to him. They had an added reason for their careful nursing, if they needed one, for they had been told by a chief of the tribe that their wretched lives were only spared until their white companion should recover his senses long enough to tell the Indians how much they were his friends. If he died, they would die on the same day, and with as much long-drawn-out pain as the Indian women could devise. So they relieved one another in watches, and it was particularly the wisdom of the colonel that saved the life of Larribee.

For a week, the section of the tribe, from which those hunters had been detached, camped by the two sick men. Before the end of that time, Shouting Thunder was greatly improved. Though poor Larribee was still out of his head, a callous medicine man declared that he was fit to travel.

So travel they did. Larribee would have been put on a bumping travois like a bundle of household goods, had it not been that the colonel solemnly swore that half a day of such conveyance would most certainly jolt the life out of his body. Then Shouting Thunder intervened, and the white man was carried in a more comfortable horse litter, swung between two ponies. Shouting Thunder even had a little canopy made to shield the face of his white brother from the rays of the sun.

For ten days, Larribee went westward and northward with the Indians. He should have been killed by that arduous journey, but he was mercifully out of his head most of the time. Meanwhile, that mighty constitution was working for him like a day laborer, husbanding new strength and healing his wounds.

When his full wits came back to him—that is to say, when he was drugged neither with fever, weakness, nor sleep—he opened his eyes and raised before them a narrow, wasted hand that he could not recognize as his own. He could feel, also, the sagging of his cheeks, and, when he rolled his eyes, he saw the smoke rising in the center of the lodge and passing slowly out of the smoke hole above, where the poles crossed.

He looked at this for some time, with a frown as if puzzled. Then, glancing aside, he saw the colonel. "I'm glad to see you, Colonel," he said. "Otherwise, I'd say that I've been dreaming, and that I'm still dreaming."

The colonel had altered, also, and not for the better. He was very thin, and his cheeks, also, sagged. But now he leaned forward, his eyes brightening. "Good for you," he said. "We'll shake hands on this. Wait till I call poor Gurry. It'll most surely be a weight off his mind. Gurry, come over here."

Gurry started out of a sound sleep and rushed over to look.

"Is he worse?" he asked grimly.

"See for yourself," said the colonel. "His eye is as clear as a baby's. This is the first time that he's noticed us. You've been confoundedly aloof, Larribee."

Larribee frowned a little as he looked from the colonel to Gurry, whose anxiety had left its mark upon his countenance. "Suppose you tell me what's happened," said Larribee. "I don't even recognize my own hand."

"Happened? We're still in it," said the colonel blandly. "That red-skinned thug you'd been fighting with made you a blood brother. Were you awake for the ceremony? You've been sleeping . . . mad or only half sane . . . ever since, I should say. And you can thank Shouting Thunder for it. Gurry, you answer his questions. I'm half dead and I'm going to sleep the clock around. Not even the Indian dogs or the howling Indian serenaders can trouble me."

He retired, and Gurry sat down, cross-legged, by the bed of the sick man.

He began with the tale of how the two bodies had been found, and he followed with the story of Larribee's long fight against death.

"Where's Shouting Thunder, if that's his name?" said Larribee. "I've got something I want to say to him."

"You couldn't've missed him any day but this," said Gurry. "He's been draggin' himself out of his bed when he was more'n half a corpse himself, and comin' over to have a look at you. He's got an idea under his red skin that he lives and dies about as you live and die. He's been holdin' out to the medicine fools that half of his soul is your soul, and half of your soul is his soul, something like marriage, but a lot more. He's more'n half white, that thug." He paused, then added: "But he's still got some of the ideas of his tribe, you see." He pointed to certain grisly ornaments that were strung between two of the poles of the teepee. They were scalps, and at least two of them had not yet been so smoke-darkened that the blond of a white man's hair was concealed.

"He told me," said Larribee. "I remember something about that, but the last word was that he was going to add my pelt to the lot. He must have changed his mind. I was about to knife him and I changed mine." Then he asked: "Where are we?"

"At the tail of Sky Blue," said Gurry.

"At Sky Blue?" cried Larribee. "What do you mean by that?"

"Lay easy, and don't get worked up," said Gurry. "We been drifting all this time, with the tribe usin' its left hand to hunt venison and buffalo meat and having pretty good luck, at that. But the right hand, the cream of the horses and the cream of the young men, are always out circling along the trail of Sky Blue. They've had five ropes on him. They got two around his neck at one time, but he yanked them ropes out of their hands. I seen the hands of Little Beaver with the flesh burned off pretty near to the bone.

"They've even had ropes on his legs. But that time, he rolled himself down a little slope and right in among them, and he busted the neck of one of those Cheyennes with a kick and near tore the arm off another with his teeth. Then he shook those ropes off and trotted away. That's the nearest they've come to luck with him. They say that he's a medicine horse and that he's leading them somewhere. A pretty hot road he's made for them and their hunters." He stopped and shook his head.

"Still after Sky Blue," said Larribee. "I've dreamed about him. I've dreamed that he had me by the body and that he was crushing the life out of me with his teeth, shouting like a man while he did it."

"You might've dreamed pretty near anything," said Gurry, "and pretty near anything would've been right."

"What's the tribe?" asked Larribee.

107

"Cheyennes."

"I've heard of them."

"You better had heard of them. They're worth hearing about. Six foot is sort of short in this tribe, Larribee. You take yourself . . . you'd make only a fair to middling buck in this outfit, for weight. Well, you've seen Shouting Thunder, and he's a long shot from their biggest man. These fellows are dry powder, too, and, when they blow up, something has to break. I'd stack a hundred of 'em against any two hundred cavalry . . . training and guns all against 'em, too, modern methods and all that. They fight like terriers. They've got the instinct. This is only a flying wedge of the whole outfit, and Shouting Thunder is the head of the lot, except for one hatchet-faced old medicine man who outtalks him. You'd've been nearly well a week ago if that old fool hadn't been in here raising a racket and a smoke nearly every day. Cure or kill. That's his motto. But, here you are, all right again, Larribee, and thank goodness for it."

"The poor colonel," said Larribee. "What will be happening to his affairs?"

"There ain't any affairs that matters much to him," said the other, "outside of Sky Blue. He stewed and worried for the first ten days, and after that he sat down and read the paper every day, and didn't care."

"Read the paper?"

"I mean that he listened to the yarns of the horse hunters," explained Gurry. "Every day, they come traipsing back and tell something about sighting the blue stallion somewhere on the edge of the sky. But I'll tell you, old son. There's a kind of a luck in this. Sky Blue, he's meant for either you or me, and out here in the open is where we're going to catch him. Only hurry, hurry. Get your legs under you, so's you can set up in a saddle. Sky Blue belongs to you and me."

Larribee lay back on the Indian bed and felt the comfortable give of it under his weight. "Where are we now?" he asked.

"I don't know. I only know that we're on Sky Blue's trail. That's all the whereabouts that I care for, anyway. What about you?"

Larribee, making no answer, drew a long breath. From all his wounds, distinctly, he could feel a separate pain, and he told himself that this was a sort of second payment for Sky Blue. The first had been when he was smashed out of the saddle and left senseless upon the ground. Would there be a third and final payment?

And he heard Gurry saying: "You'd better hurry, though. There's a pack of Pawnee thieves out on the trail of the stallion . . . and there's a few long-haired Crows, too, they say, with a white man at the head of them. We've got competition, old son, and we need to ride soon."

CHAPTER EIGHTEEN

Larribee did not ride soon. It was another month before his strength was fully restored. Long before that, however, he was able to sit in a saddle and jog quietly with the train of the women and children, the tough little Indian ponies dragging the travois behind them and raising a dust above the dry grasses.

It was the sort of life that he loved. He could loiter and linger and loaf without drawing a reproach. He was a man without dignity and, therefore, as likely as not he would be sitting, cross-legged, in the camp, chattering all the Cheyenne he had learned with a number of children, picking up new expressions from them, and joining them in their games so far as his activity permitted.

It was very well known that this white man was a terrible fellow, a great brave and champion, because he had fought Shouting Thunder to a draw, at least, and some whispered that he had done even more. He was the sworn blood brother of that great chief. Finally, perhaps above all, he was the only human being who had remained more than some sixty seconds upon the back of Sky Blue, the great stallion who the horse hunters were following with such eagerness, that already famous medicine horse.

Nevertheless, in spite of his prowess in the past, it was surely apparent that the Cheyennes of that encampment could not retain any particular respect for the man. He had no dignity. He hired small boys to fan the flies off him, and then lay with his face in the shade and his large body sprawling in the sun, and slept for hours at a time. Doctors of another age might have told the Indians that there was no better way to cure old, aching, half-healed wounds. But there were no doctors of that kind among the Cheyennes. Instead, they had medicine men. And here Larribee was even more seriously in the wrong. When the medicine men donned their most horrible masks and raised their most frightful stenches with burning herbs, when they danced and pranced and sawed the air to call up demons or draw down the spirits from the sky, then Larribee yawned in their very faces.

He was actually fond of mimicking the great magicians, and he would go dancing and prancing in the presence of the children, with a cow's tail fastened to the tail of his own coat and a horned buffalo skull for a mask. He would caper low and caper high, until the children screamed with amusement and their angry mothers came and hurried them off to their teepees. But even the mothers were hardly more horrified than they were amused.

They used to whisper together, now and then, and wonder why the miracle workers of their tribe did not blast the white stranger with thunders from heaven. Concerning such a feat they had often spoken with the utmost confidence. But nothing happened to young Larribee except that the medicine men no longer were aware of his presence, when he came among them, and the warriors began to feel that there was something almost half-witted about the pale face.

It might be true that he had done great things in the past, and, possessed by some great spirit, he had actually ridden the great stallion. Was it not true that the spirits were more likely to enter the minds of the weak-witted?

For the present, however, was there grace, energy, pride, or dignity about the man? There was not a trace of any of these essential qualities. He would not even spend his time at the feasts, for, when the most enchanting storytellers of the tribe began their narrations, Larribee went sound asleep. Three Black Spots, that grim and famous fighter, was interrupted one evening by the loud snoring of the guest of the tribe.

Sometimes the superior warriors ventured to bring up the subject of the guest with Shouting Thunder himself. They did it tactfully. But they could not help wondering, they said, whether such a man would strike a blow for the Cheyennes, when he was always lolling and sleeping about the camp, even now that his wounds were healed? He was sleek and smooth, like an overfed dog, in the height of the buffalo hunting. And of what use would he be, either to hunt or to entertain in the long evenings of the winter? Above all, what sort of a moral influence would he exert over the minds of the youth of the nation?

That was the moot point. Shouting Thunder could only fall back upon a serious reserve and a frown worthy of his chieftainship. But he had nothing to say. It was quite true that this man lured the boys away from their manly games and sent them into fits of laughter with his nonsensical imitations of the medicine men and the droll stories of men and beasts, which had no point to them at all, except to the ears of children, because they never celebrated the feats of any heroes.

If heroes entered into the tales of Larribee, it was generally when he described how some great man, some hero of many coups, went out into the dark of the winter night to do famous deeds, and how valiantly he walked along until he slipped in the mud, fell, and lost his pocket knife, then had to come back and sit by the fire to nurse his chilblains, and comfort the cold in his nose.

These stories of mock heroics used to send the Cheyenne youngsters into peals of merriment. Sometimes young bucks of fifteen and sixteen would creep up and enjoy the tales, and fairly stifle and choke themselves trying to keep the laughter back. For every one of these heroes of the storyteller was really a fairly close parody of the features, the voice, and the manners of some celebrated hero of the tribe. The women, too, used to come as near as they could, and broad imitations of the narratives used to be breathed about the camp on the following day.

Now, a hero will stand practically anything except jokes based upon his heroism. It was inconceivable that the mightiest of all the Cheyenne horse thieves could endure the tale that Larribee told of how this celebrated man had gone to the camp of the Pawnees and taken fifty horses, dragged them all safely away by their tails, twenty-five tails in either hand, until, going up a hill, the heel of the brave stuck in the brush, the tails of the horses, unluckily, all pulled out, and the horses galloped to the bottom of the hill and so, all of them, got back to their proper masters.

How could this hero endure such a story, told with a good deal of snoring and snorting noises such as he made in speaking, for the reason that a horse one day had kicked him in the face and badly smashed his nose?

No, such things could not be endured, and, although the broad shield of the blood brotherhood protected Larribee, he was half a dozen times within an ace of having a knife driven into the hollow of his throat to stop that annoying voice of his.

But he seemed not to care. He wandered about the camp, or else, when they were on the move, he would be content to ride a mule, humped over, his legs dangling, and perhaps a saucy boy sitting across the animal's neck, facing the man, bantering and laughing with him. Still another youngster, some naked, quarrelsome brat, would perhaps be seated slantwise on the hind quarters of the mule, kicking it with bare heels and shouting at Larribee to hurry. Dangling from his saddle, there might be a bundle of household goods.

What manner of warrior could such a fellow be? No, he was

too much like a squaw. In fact, next to the children, he seemed to prefer the company of the women, not the girls—they were prouder than the men and would have scorned to be seen in the company of such an unheroic hero—but the old, deformed, labor-branded squaws. When they had tales to tell, stories of the early days of the race, or legends of the underwater spirits, or the Sky People, then Larribee could loll in a tent for hours, only rousing himself, now and again, to go to the meat pot and copiously help himself.

For another thing, the man had no shame in the way he wandered uninvited into every lodge. Welcome or silence made no impression upon the fellow. He cared not where he lay—any place was good enough for him to sleep in. That lodge that had the freshest venison could be reasonably sure of a visit from the glutton who could swallow down three men's portions without an apparent effort and be ready to eat again in an hour or two.

If he went to a feast, it was only to eat and to leave when he was full. Shouting Thunder made half a dozen attempts to explain—this might be good manners among the white men and he knew his brother could do no wrong. Still, the ways of the Cheyennes were the ways of the Cheyennes and it might be as well to observe some of them. On such occasions, Larribee had an annoying way of pretending that he could not understand the words that were spoken to him, although at most times he was fluent enough in the new tongue. Neither did he seem able to comprehend the perfectly good English of his blood brother, but was always interrupting with foolish remarks that diverted the chief from the point and left him groping about, so to speak.

The discontent of the Cheyennes grew. Even Gurry and the colonel began to blush for their friend. Disgust and open scorn showed in the faces of the Cheyenne warriors of state, when the white man came among them.

Finally Spotted Bull, a giant who was taller than most of the tribesmen, with a face hideously scarred from smallpox, in casting the stone for distance, seemed to make a mistake and shot the stone with a mighty heave within a foot of the white man, as he sat squatted in the dust and sleepily stared at the big braves competing in that test of strength.

Then Larribee got up, half yawning, and he called out: "You would have won with that cast, Spotted Bull, if you had thrown it straight. Try again!" So saying, he heaved the ponderous rock with such incredible force that it shot back at Spotted Bull and landed, not at his feet, but actually drove straight at his head. Spotted Bull had to dodge to keep his brains inside his skull. When he realized that he had almost been killed on the spot, he let out a roar and leaped at the white man.

Shouting Thunder roared in vain that the peace must be kept, but Larribee merely laughed and, meeting the big warrior in mid-career, he took him by either hand and held him.

"Don't be alarmed, Shouting Thunder!" called Larribee. "Spotted Bull and I are the best of friends. See . . . we are shaking hands and vowing friendship."

Spotted Bull did not speak. His face was contorted with pain, and, parting from Larribee, he hastily concealed his hands under the robe he was wearing and strode away.

But no one cast the stone again that day. Half a dozen of the boys stepped off the distance from where Larribee had stood to the spot where the missile had landed. They paced the distance, and the paces were ever more remembered.

CHAPTER NINETEEN

If the circumstances had been a little different, the feat of the stone casting would have been enough, together with the blood brotherhood with Shouting Thunder, to make the white man forever an honored member of the tribe. But too much bad feeling had grown up against Larribee. There were the bruised hands of Spotted Bull, for instance. Instead of admiring Larribee for mere strength, the medicine man of the party ascribed this work to sheer black magic, not magic of a good kind. The result was that Larribee got blacker looks than ever. But even he was not prepared for what followed.

He had been sitting idly in the teepee of Shouting Thunder, talking with Gurry and the colonel. They were talking, as usual, about Sky Blue, and they were chiefly concerned about some new device for trapping him. The matter was really less difficult, now, than it had been before, for the stallion had picked up a number of mares and young horses, which followed him as his herd, and over which he ruled like any wild king stallion of the plains. Since he had assembled followers, it clearly would be easier to take him, for now he could be driven with his herd. But, even so, it was not a simple matter; otherwise, the Cheyennes or the Crows, expert horse thieves, would have had him long ago.

They talked with one another of various devices. But that which was most favored by the colonel and Gurry appeared to Larribee far too difficult. What the colonel and Gurry agreed upon was that the stallion should be driven on toward the west. It was already apparent that they were close to the foothills of the Rockies. Once in a region of cañons and narrow valleys, if the great horse settled down, as he was sure to do, as the lord of some special domain, they could study his ways, fence in some gorge, and then make the drive that would bring him into their power.

Larribee pointed out that this would be a matter requiring months, with a long chance besides.

"Well," said the colonel, "you are younger than we are, Larribee, and therefore time seems invaluable to you. To me, it's the cheapest stuff in the world. Gurry is willing to wait, too, if Sky Blue is at the other end of the line."

"Look here, Colonel," said Gurry, "there's one thing that I can't make out. Larribee and me, we've got half shares in Sky Blue. But there's been no share in him offered to you, and yet you go along hunting him."

"Well," said the colonel, "suppose that you look at it from this angle . . . a good many men have gone clear to Africa to shoot big game. What do they get out of it? The mask of a lion or the tusks of an elephant? No, they get the pleasure of the hunt. And what lion hunt was ever as much sport as the trail of Sky Blue, even up to this time? Who can tell where it will lead later on? We have Cheyennes and Pawnees and Crows already after him. You two may have the horse . . . give me your companionship on the way."

They both looked curiously at him. His manner was always quiet. His air was the most modest in the world.

But the little gray man now spoke with a gleam in his eye. He added: "I knew a fellow who spent three hot seasons in India trailing a man-eater, a tiger with a twisted forepaw. He never got the tiger. The fever ate the man, instead. But he had three happy years, in spite of fever, mosquitoes, flies, dysentery, and all the rest. Well, my friends, don't you think that Sky Blue is worth half a dozen tigers with twisted paws?"

"And your own affairs, your business?" ventured Larribee.

The colonel's mouth pinched together. He shrugged his shoulders. "Business has to be kept in its own place," he said.

Then Shouting Thunder came in and gave his wife a look. She was a shovel-faced woman, long and wide in the chin, almost noseless, with receding brow. Shouting Thunder wanted strong hands more than pretty faces in his lodge. When the squaw received the glance from her lord and master, she picked up a three-year-old child, a basket of bead work, half finished, a hatchet, some deer tendon to be unraveled into strong thread, and ducked out through the entrance flap. Shouting Thunder dropped the flap behind her, because her hands were full. Then he came back to his own backrest, settled against it, screwed the long stem into his pipe bowl, filled the bowl, and lighted the tobacco with a coal. He began to smoke ceremoniously, with the exhalations to the various winds and spirits.

The three white men, falling silent, looked at one another. They knew that something important was about to be pronounced.

Then the chief said: "What is in the mind of the Larribee?"

For the tribe had turned Larribee's name into an epithet. Usually they furnished names of their own to strangers, but the sound of this word had tickled their ears as the ears of children are pleased by sounds that they do not understand. They kept it, merely turning it into an impersonal, mysterious noun, as it were.

"The Larribee," said the colonel, "is thinking of going to sleep."

"He must sleep far away to the west this day," said Shouting Thunder. The three watched the Cheyenne. His brow was furrowed. He explained: "I have sat in the council and listened to many speeches. The warriors have turned into women. They are all terribly afraid." He began to smoke again, puffing slowly, with the same ceremonial detachment. They could hear the gritting of his teeth against the thick stem of the pipe. And still the white men knew too much to interrupt with hasty questions.

Said Shouting Thunder: "They are afraid of the blue horse, and they say that he is not a horse, but something that has fallen out of the sky, like a cloud. They say that the horse is leading us to danger, and that the horse is drawing the Larribee, and the Larribee is drawing me, and all the rest are taken along with me." He paused again. He had made himself clear enough.

"Well, brother," said Larribee, "you and the tribe turn back and go where you ought to go. You've come closer to the mountains than you usually range. It's high time for you to turn east again. But the three of us will go on toward the setting sun. We understand your trouble. We're getting into the land of the Crows, and those long-haired demons are hard fighters and there are plenty of them. Of course, your people want to turn back."

"My people wish to turn back," said Shouting Thunder, scowling at the low-burning fire.

"Take them, then," said Larribee. "And take our thanks along with you. Not one of the three of us would be wearing hair, except for you, Shouting Thunder."

The chief shrugged his great shoulders. "The children will make a great deal of noise when they learn that you are going away," he said.

"Well, I'll slip away at night," said Larribee. "The three of us will get out of the camp after dark. We want to buy some horses out of your string, if you'll sell 'em."

"Sell?" said the chief. "To my brother?"

The ring in his voice put Larribee to shame.

Said Shouting Thunder: "Many of the warriors and the medicine men, they will be glad when you have left us, of course."

"Because I've set the children laughing at them," said Larribee.

"Laughter," said the chief, "is like the bite of the snake. It feels like the prick of a needle, but it kills after a long time."

Larribee nodded. "I've said too much," he agreed.

"Not for men to bear," said the chief. And again they could hear the gritting of his teeth on the stem of the pipe. Then he said: "My friends, I have been so close to the great horse, that I have almost felt the wind of his passing."

The colonel suddenly smiled and leaned forward.

"And if the blue horse is leading me," said the chief, "to my fate, that is a thing that cannot be escaped. He who runs away from trouble takes the arrow through the back and dies like a coward."

"He'll go with us," murmured the colonel. "He's got the poison in his blood."

"Let us," said the chief, "make no great talk. Let us ride out to hunt, with the best of the horses and our weapons. That will be no lie, for we will ride to hunt Sky Blue."

Still he had not finished what he had to say, for he did not knock the ashes out of the pipe to terminate his words and give them a period. Instead, he went on, after a little interval. "Great treasures cause great crimes. For a hundred robes, a life can be bought. Then for such a horse, what would not a man pay down? Only to be sure that after death his soul would be mounted on the stallion, would not a man cut the throat of his brother while he slept? Now, I, Shouting Thunder, wish to give you my hand and to swear to you that I shall work for you as a squaw works for her master. And you will work for me, and each of us for the other. Four men are forty times the strength of one man. Is that truth?"

"That is truth," said the colonel.

"But one hurt man or one weak man," went on the chief, "is a burden on all the others."

"True," said the colonel. "You speak like a great chief, Shouting Thunder."

The Indian raised his hand. "We ride out together," he said. "We give ourselves to one another. And the first man who finds his brain dizzy with the fever, rides out of the camp that day and loses himself from the rest. The first man who is bitten by the arrow or the bullet of an enemy, leaves the others and turns back to die by himself. He rides out of the minds and the thoughts of his friends who are left. For in this way, some one of us may come to the end of the trail. But not more than one of us, I think, will find it in his fate to come to the blue horse at the finish. Here is the hand of Shouting Thunder. Which of you will take it?"

CHAPTER TWENTY

So four men rode out of the Cheyenne camp. The warriors watched them with sour looks, but the boys ran barefoot at the sides of the horses, or, springing onto their own ponies, careered in a cloud around their favorite, the Larribee. For it was the first time he had left the teepee or the marching column of the tribe, and it was probable that he would do some great thing.

But the chief ordered the youngsters back, and the four men went on alone. They had with them the three horses that the whites had been riding when Shouting Thunder and his party surprised them. They had a round dozen of the toughest and fleetest mounts in the big string of Shouting Thunder, who was particularly rich in horses. If ever they straightened out after Sky Blue, they would need all the leg power they could press into service, but a larger herd than this would be too bulky for their handling.

They struck out to the southwest over the prairie, but, when the cluster of the teepees had drawn together and the smoke from the fires had become a single mist standing in the sky, they swerved to the north and went onward at a brisk pace.

Even after it had grown dark, they kept on their way, until Larribee was cursing at every jar of his stiff-legged horse. But he did not request an earlier halt. It was best, he knew, to leave the guidance and the command of the party in the hands of the Cheyenne chief. Not until he gave the word, did they halt to make camp.

Their food was parched corn; their drink was water out of a muddy pool with green slime at the edges of it. But they did not complain. Each wrapped himself in a blanket; three of them lay down to sleep. The colonel, chosen by lot, watched half the night, and then roused the Cheyenne to take charge of the second watch.

In the dawn, they were riding hard again.

They knew, from the last reports of the horse hunters, just about where the stallion was ranging with his newly gathered herd. He had gone off into the northwest, in the direction of the Camerons, whose ragged peaks were blue in the sky. Those peaks turned to brown in the course of the day. They rode through the rolling foothills, and before night they were under the knees of the mountains.

They held a council, and the chief expressed his ideas with much clarity. There were half a dozen possible trails through the low but rough-headed Camerons. Four of these were much more practicable than the others. Each of the men would take one of these trails. Issuing on the somewhat higher plateau on the farther side of the little range, the four would find, in the distance, the flat head of a mesa. Under the eastern lee of this they should reassemble.

It might be a dangerous business to pass through the range, as the Cheyenne pointed out. They had found the prints of a herd of horses the day before, headed toward the pass, and, although there was no proof that Sky Blue traveled with that lot, still he might be among the number. If so, then the Pawnees and the Crows were as likely as not to be riding in the same direction. And there was no doubt that they would murder their rivals in the horse hunt, if they could.

So they slept once more, wrapped in their blankets, and Larribee, keeping the second and most difficult watch, saw the stars at last grow slightly dimmer in the east, as though a pale mist were rising from the earth to obscure them.

At this first token of coming day, he roused his companions; before the pink of the morning, each was entering the pass that had been assigned to him, and Larribee, riding a low-built, mouse-colored mare—built rather for the rider's weight than for speed—profoundly hoped that he would not see the stallion on this day, when his mount was such a dull one.

The pass upon which he entered twisted like a snake's course through grass, for it doubled back and forth. It was fenced in by bright-faced cliffs of solid rock a good part of the way, but at times softly rolling slopes went up toward the higher peaks. Coming around one elbow turn, Larribee found before him a natural amphitheater that spread out a full mile from side to side. A small stream flashed in the center of it, and at that stream a little herd was drinking, or standing in the middle knee-deep.

There were a score altogether, but there seemed to Larribee to be only one—a gigantic blue stallion, standing on this side of the water and grazing. Now and again, as some cloud shadow flicked across him, he raised his head and looked back—always to the rear and down the cañon, as though he knew that from this direction danger, if any, must be approaching.

Larribee slid from the back of his horse. He wanted to see if there were any possibility of sneaking up on Sky Blue through some side pass, or by taking advantage of shrubs and rocks, here and there. But as he crouched behind a nest of big, naked stones, he realized that there was no hope. He never could manage to steal close enough to send the forty-foot rope and its noose over the head of Sky Blue. So he crouched there and stared and fed his eyes full.

The stallion was much altered. At that distance, even, it was possible to see that the body line was more finely drawn; the neck seemed thinner and arched like a steel bow. He had looked, in the old days, a little too heavy for speed; he looked now as though he could gallop away from a tornado. There was a gentle wind and his tail streamed behind him and lifted his mane. The heart of Larribee quaked within him, so great was his desire to get possession of Sky Blue.

Yes, Sky Blue had been run and hunted into the pink of condition. They had worn out their mounts, the Cheyennes and the other hunters, but all they had managed to do was to take the superfluous flesh from his body. He was ready now. He was ready for the supreme contest, which Larribee told himself, was about to begin. He remembered what the colonel had said about the tiger hunter and the three-year trail. It seemed to him, now, the most reasonable thing in the world. He himself would spend more than three years. He would spend his life in such a quest. It seemed to him that nothing in life could compare with mastery over that great horse. And he, alone, of all men, really knew what it meant to have that glorious power taking wings, as it were, beneath the saddle. The others had hope and a dream before them; he had tasted of the actuality.

Suddenly he hated them all—the colonel, Gurry, and even his blood brother of the Cheyennes. They were his rivals in the hunt. They could call themselves friends, but they were no friends of his.

Now he told himself savagely that, when the time came—if ever it were to come—when the stallion was in their hands, they would have to deal with him, with Larribee. Then let them look to the safeguarding of their lives. In the meantime, let them work. Let the fools struggle and strive for the prize jointly. He, Larribee, alone would enjoy it.

His eyes narrowed and squinted in the viciousness of his determination. He remembered what the Cheyenne chief had said. Throats cut at night—yes, even that was conceivable. He moistened his white lips with the tip of his tongue. He closed his eyes and breathed hard and deep. Then, twisting his head about, he looked eagerly down the ravine. For others might come—not from his own party, but from the Crows or the Pawnees. Of the other Indians, he had the Crows more continually in mind, for he remembered that at their head they had, said report, a young white man as a leader. Indian craft and white man's brain power and patience made a combination terribly hard to beat.

He could see nothing behind him except the gleam of the rock faces in the lower ravine. When he looked back toward the herd, however, he saw enough to make him stare.

For out of the defiles of the upper gorge came a galloping horde of wild horses. No one needed to be told that those ragged manes had never been touched by a human hand. There was something about their goat-like surety of foot among the rocks and the carriage of their heads that spoke for their eternal independence.

In the front came the young stallions, behind them the mares and the colts, and behind these the brood mares, running lower, as it seemed, with their heads rather down and their foals beside them. Last of all, out flashed a black horse, a glorious, wind-footed stallion. He was the master, no doubt, the king of this fine group of threescore wanderers. He was herding them out of the upper entanglements of the pass, and now he was running them out into the open, toward the water. Or were they pursued by some enemy from the rear?

When the two herds sighted one another, they spread out. The newcomers stopped short. Then, from the rear, the black leader shot around the flank and came surging to the front. More beautiful than Sky Blue, he seemed to the eye of Larribee, at that first flash of the eye, more beautiful and almost as huge.

No, as he came closer, he had not the full commanding presence of the thoroughbred. But he was one compact mass of speed and power. For sheer beauty, for exquisite symmetry, he was surely the match of Sky Blue. In height, perhaps, he was a few inches shorter, but no vital difference.

Then the heart of the watcher jumped into his throat as he realized what was about to happen.

From behind his own herd, galloping, Sky Blue swept forward, cleared the stream with a single bound, and rushed onward against the foe. It was what Larribee had heard of before. It was the meeting of the masters of two wild herds, and now they would fight for supremacy and leadership—Sky Blue against a horse that all its days had wandered through the wilderness, the veteran of a score of battles against his kind.

Larribee slid his rifle from its saddle holster and leveled it upon the advancing black.

127

CHAPTER TWENTY-ONE

The very sight of a rifle is like a focused telescope that draws its object nearer and casts, as it were, a greater light upon it. In the circle of the peep, Larribee saw the stallion come shining into view, wavering with his gallop. He could even see or thought that he could see the gleam of a white star on the forehead and the white splash of the long stocking on one foreleg.

No, for sheer perfection, for statuesque and dazzling beauty, the black stallion was as far beyond the blue roan as a painting is beyond a rude sketch.

When, once, the stranger stallion had come flush upon the imagination of Larribee, he could not shoot. He could not dream of snuffing out that torrent of magnificent life. So he lowered the gun, and then he saw the blue roan cantering forward on the farther side of the creek. And it seemed to Larribee that the mares had ranged themselves in semicircles behind their respective champions, to view the battle that was coming.

The black, having advanced in the center of that great, green arena, paused there and seemed to say that he had gone far enough and that he would await the charge of his enemy on this spot. But the roan plunged straight on. No, he was not as beautiful as the black. His head, by contrast, was too big. Even from a distance, one could see the upward projection of the withers and the slight outthrust of the hip bones. One was a picture to fill the eye. The other was the perfect machine, flowing over the ground, as effortless as wind.

Sky Blue did not pause. He rushed straight in on the black, and, as they came together, the difference in their size seemed less and less, for the exquisite symmetry of the black had made him appear smaller than the fact. He stood on braced legs, with high head awaiting that attack. As the blue roan rushed, the black leaped to the side, let the roan shoot past far enough to miss the target, and then rushed in on the exposed flank, rearing to bite and strike.

At least one or two blows from those powerful forelegs must have fallen upon Sky Blue as he shot past the wily black. Larribee snatched up his rifle once more, only to lower it again. Now that they were so close, he could not risk a shot, since he might strike the one in aiming at the other.

Sky Blue wheeled, when that first dash failed to find the mark. As he wheeled, he came erect upon hind legs and met the black with striking forehoofs. Reared opposite to each other, there was not much advantage in sheer inches in favor of the roan. Yet he seemed towering above the black, by the excess of his fierce spirit.

They closed very much as two striking warriors might have come hand to hand in the old days, belaboring each other. And the black, lowering its head, made a long lunge for the throat of Sky Blue. If it had reached its mark, Larribee knew very well that the powerful teeth would have ripped open the windpipe of the roan more easily than the teeth of a tiger. But it seemed that Sky Blue reared himself to a greater height and redoubled his strokes.

The black, staggering suddenly, gave back and dropped to the ground on its forehoofs. It was badly hurt, but not yet beaten. For it reared once more to meet the continuous charge of Sky Blue. Only, this time, it could not keep its ground even for an instant. As a superior prize fighter takes advantage of an opponent's daze, so the roan pressed in, dealing lightning blows with both forehoofs.

The black was forced back. Then he swayed to this side, and next to that. He sprang away, shaking his head in a human effort to clear his dazed wits, but the roan was still at him. Now, like one sure to fall, but unwilling to surrender, the good black reared a third time and met that overmastering attack. They closed, and, at the first stroke, so it seemed, down went the black and lay limply upon the ground.

Brained, this time, said the watcher to himself. *And a mighty pity. He stands second only to Sky Blue among the horses that I've seen.*

Sky Blue did not trample his fallen adversary. Instead, he walked once or twice around the motionless black, then, erecting his head, while the sun flashed on a new flow of crimson that stained his shoulder and half his side, Larribee could see the big fellow's mane shake and his tail arch, but it was a second or two before the trumpet note of the neighing came down the valley to him.

The black being beaten, the herd, which had followed him faithfully so long as he was the conqueror, went instantly to the new and greater hero.

Larribee watched with the most intense interest. With the old leader down, some half dozen younger stallions, or those previously vanquished, gathered together, shoulder to shoulder, as though they intended to rush in one mass upon the already wounded victor. And Sky Blue, dauntless, pranced toward them to receive their attack. When he came nearer, they melted to this side and to that. They sniffed the air and seemed to find welcome news in it, for their flattened ears pricked forward. As they scattered, some of them carried out their pretense of disinterest in the political change by beginning to crop the grass.

Sky Blue went through the gap in the hostile ranks as though it were a mere rolling mist that surrounded him. He encircled the rest of the group at his matchless, long-gaited gallop, and the mares and their foals, after regarding him for a while, allowed him to go prancing ahead of them down toward the water of the creek.

It was a very odd sight. Sky Blue, whinnying loudly, called his former band forward and brought the new recruits into the water. There they drank, the youngsters throwing the water with their muzzles, after the first long drafts, and the mares more quietly and thoroughly taking their fill of the precious stuff.

They were drinking, or wading in the water, or cropping the good grass along the banks, all except the prostrate black. Now he stirred, and Larribee watched with relief and a sigh of pleasure as the big fellow heaved himself to his feet.

He staggered for a few paces, and then went slowly down the valley. His black satin coat was stained with red, his head was down. He moved like an ancient and weary nag, yet he had entered that arena like a king.

The wind, coming down strongly behind him, blew his long mane over his head and fanned his sweeping tail along his flank, so that it seemed as though invisible hands were whipping the big fellow forward.

Pity filled the heart of Larribee. It seemed endlessly cruel that such a magnificent fellow should have been cast out and a stranger put in his place. How many times had he brought his herd through dangers, rallied them across the path of storms, run to the rear to beat up the weary, run to the van to face the first danger. How many times had he given the signal of hunting wolves, or for stalking mountain lions. Yet, now, in an instant, he was discarded. So, broken-hearted, he stumbled down the ravine, while the victor, after his winning, gathered his enlarged herd about him and, with them at his heels, cantered forward toward the upper pass.

The last of them passed from view, before the black stallion was near to Larribee, and it was the idle rope in the man's hands that put into his mind the thought that here was a mount certainly worth capturing.

The dethroned king, drearily passing down the valley, came close by the rock pile behind which he was concealed. Larribee was but a green hand with a rope, but he did not require skill in this instance. He made the cast just as the black passed by him, and, as the noose flicked over the head of the horse, he attached a running knot around a smooth projection of stone.

The stallion, as the long, flexible finger of the rope slapped him, came out of his lethargy with a squeal and a plunge that burned the rope tautly about his neck. Perhaps the rope would have parted under the shock, but the slipknot gave it just sufficient play.

The black was stopped. He reared in an effort to get to the side, lost his footing in the loose, small stones, and fell heavily on his back, with his four legs wildly striking at the air.

Larribee ran in on him. He was rather more lucky than skillful here, also. As he ran in, the circles of rope that he cast in the air ensnared a forehoof and a rear leg. The moment that happened, the black was helpless and he seemed to know it. He gave up and lay still, with his small velvet ears flattened against his head. His reddened eyes turned dull, as the eyes of a fish film over when it lies upon the bank having struggled its last.

Larribee sat down upon a stone and laid his hand upon the head of the beaten warrior. It was gashed and torn in half a dozen places where the slanting blows of Sky Blue had glanced from the flesh. In other places, where the strokes had fallen solidly home, great bumps were rising. Over his shoulders, even, the silken skin had been ripped by the forehoofs of the victor, and the blood was still trickling. But he was not badly hurt. He had been, in ring parlance, knocked out and could not come to time, but he was perfectly sound.

Legends rang dimly in the memory of Larribee about wild horses that never could be tamed. Even the mares might be worthless, and the stallions almost always. But here was a champion given into his hands at a lucky moment, already three quarters subdued by a power greater than the hands of man. So he set instantly to work, stripping the saddle from the back of his own mustang and working the stallion next to its feet, giving it just enough rope to stand if it was steady, but checking it closely enough so that it fell if it pitched and struggled. That accomplished, he cinched the saddle on its back.

It was not so simple as the telling. He worked for two whole hours, and by the end of that time he was wet with perspiration. A steady stream of sweat was dripping from the stallion and it was trembling with exhaustion. But the first horror of man had passed from it, and the magic of Larribee's voice and touch had begun to work upon that wild nature at last.

CHAPTER TWENTY-TWO

They were gathered on the eastern side of the mesa of which the Cheyenne chief had spoken. Gurry, Colonel Pratt, and big Shouting Thunder himself. They had gone through their separate passes, and now for well over an hour they had been waiting. They were slightly anxious about Larribee. Then, they saw, well to the north of them, a dim cloud of dust.

"What could that be?" asked the colonel.

"A war party or a herd of horses," said Shouting Thunder. "We should be off after it, except that we must wait for my brother. However, the tracks they leave will not be covered soon. Where is the Larribee? Where can he be? The cunning Crows may have found him in the pass. You go forward after that dust cloud, brothers, and I'll go down the throat of the pass where the Larribee rode. Afterward, I'll come back to you."

"I'm fond of Larribee," replied the colonel in a sharp, cold voice. "I'm very fond of him. He's a man. But those who linger and fall back on this ride must make up the lost time and find their own way back to us."

The other two looked suddenly at the colonel, with something like alarm in their faces, as though this speech of his brought home to them vigorously for the first time the full danger to which each of them was subjected.

Suppose, for instance, one of them were cut off from the others, what would be his chance of returning safely? The danger of the prairies, like the wide danger of the seas, lay behind them, filled with many enemies.

So the two looked at the grim colonel, but each of them, at length, nodded. The fever for horses is greater than the fever for gold. It is very nearly the root of more universal evil. So the three suddenly and in silence mounted their horses again and rounded up their little herd of remounts, striking out, northwest, on the trail of the fading dust cloud.

It was the Cheyenne who hung to the rear most and who twice dismounted on the plea that the saddle girths needed attention. It was, therefore, the Cheyenne chief who suddenly called out and waved his hand.

His two companions turned and, following the direction in which he pointed, their straining eyes at last made out the loom and then the gleam of some approaching object. At length, it developed into a mounted man leading a horse.

"It is not our friend," said the colonel. "For he went off with only his mount. We took the trouble of the rest of the herd off his hands."

"Because he had the trouble of the second watch last night," corrected the Cheyenne severely. "Whoever this rider is, it is worthwhile to see him. For he comes straight on, though he must see the three of us as clearly as we see him. One hawk does not fly close to three strange hawks in the sky," he concluded wisely.

And so it was that the trio waited, until out of the distance the rider came nearer, and they were able to recognize the familiar, wide-shouldered silhouette of Larribee.

Shouting Thunder was now the quietest of the three. It was Gurry who shouted and waved his hand, who cantered a little way to meet their comrade. Then, all three suddenly spurred out and swooped down on the truant. They did not even ask what had delayed him, for the proof was there under their eyes.

The wounds of the black had been washed clean in the creek

as Larribee rode him across it. Then, after the third frantic and vain burst of pitching beneath the saddle and the horrible weight of man, the wild black, guided by a gentle hand, had become more than half tamed.

Larribee merely shouted to the others to keep their distance, and so the black was contented merely to dance sidewise a little, shaking his proud head and glancing at the others with his fiery eyes.

Behind him followed the down-headed, mouse-colored mustang, looking like a little dog behind a greyhound. The three friends of Larribee regarded this phenomenon with amazement.

"Look," said the Cheyenne. "There is no sign of harm on our friend's body. There is not even a rent in his clothing, but the stallion has been badly hurt. Such is the strength in the hands of the Larribee. He takes horses and fights them, hand to hand."

"Stuff," said the colonel. But he stared with a fierce interest at the black.

Gurry was bewildered. "How's this?" he asked. "Do the plains and the mountains give up their thoroughbreds like this, or is this here another hot-blooded one that's escaped from the east and come a thousand miles vacationin'?"

"It's not a thoroughbred," said the colonel. "But it has plenty of hot blood. It's an older and a purer strain than any thoroughbred, though. It's the true mustang stock, which is the pure Arab and barb of the Conquistadors. And this fellow? Well, he's simply a throwback."

"Hold on," said Gurry. "Here's a seven-hundred-pound rabbit of a horse that I'm ridin'. And there's thirteen hundred pounds, if I ever laid eyes on a horse before. Here's a lump-headed cartoon, and there's a picture horse. Too pretty to be true. And you say they're the same stock?"

"Well," said the colonel, "there are such things as throwbacks.

There were very sizable Arabs and barbs, now and then. The strain ran big in some families. But the whole lot of 'em dwindled during a few centuries of fighting, winter famines of food and summer famines of water as they wandered around the Rockies, north and south. They dwindled. Their hips pinched in and their bellies puffed out. Their heads got heavy and their necks got thin.

"But look at their sloping shoulders. That's the real line, and the short backs. They stand over plenty of ground, also, and their legs are pictures. Now, then, given the chance of one in ten million, you'll get a throwback out of this pure blood to a type that existed several hundred years ago. And there you have it. That black is one of 'em. Perhaps there's nearly thirteen hundred pounds of him. But at any rate, there's enough, and it's all horse. You could breed that fellow straight back on a barb, I'll lay my money, and get a pure-blooded colt."

Gurry listened with only a partial comprehension, for he was feasting his eyes on the picture of the black stallion, and so, for that matter, were the other two.

They were full of questions, and Gurry, the readiest talker of the lot, did the asking for all three.

Larribee merely smiled at them. "Oh, I just found a stray horse wandering around asking for an owner, and I thought I'd take him in. So here he is. He doesn't eat out of my hand just yet, but he'll learn to. Keep away, Gurry. He'll jump a mile if you get an inch nearer. He doesn't recognize the language you speak."

"How in thunder," asked Gurry, "did you beat him up like that? Those cuts don't look like spurs, and those lumps don't look like thumps from the handle of your quirt, loaded or unloaded. What have you done to him?"

"Not a lot," said Larribee indifferently. He pointed back toward the mesa, already half a dozen miles behind them toward the south. "I thought that was the meeting place," he said.

Colonel Pratt looked him straight in the eye. "We waited an hour and a half," he said, "and then we came on slowly. There's a dust cloud yonder. You can still see the tail of it, if you look hard enough."

"I see it," drawled Larribee. He was willing to have the subject changed, but at the same time he had understood perfectly what was in the mind of the three who had waited. To him, too, came a full understanding of the spirit of this horse hunt. And he was less ashamed of the savage emotions that had run through his breast when he crouched behind the rocks and looked at Sky Blue.

"We should have started before to take a look into that dust," explained the colonel. "But we didn't. We waited for you. But finally we had to start on. The trail of three horses ought to be pretty easy to follow."

"Suppose that my horse had been dead beat," said Larribee, looking coldly back at the colonel. "But it's all right, fellows. I understand it. We know where we stand. All for all, and all for none. All for Sky Blue . . . and so you ought to be glad that I've picked up this little fellow to give the roan a harder run."

Gurry looked closely over the limbs of the black. "He'll run all day," he said, "but he'll never burn up a track. He'll carry weight, too. He'll keep you up with us lightweights, Larribee. That's all that he'll manage to do."

Larribee could sense the jealousy, but he merely laughed softly. "Shall we get on?" he said.

They turned the heads of their horses.

"One of us ought to go ahead of the rest," said Shouting Thunder. "If that dust is made by a war party, it's almost sure to be Crows or Blackfeet, and both nations are enemies of the Cheyennes. Therefore, one man should scout far ahead of the rest of us."

"The scouting's been done," said Larribee calmly.

"By whom? By you?" snapped the colonel, almost angrily, as he turned toward Larribee.

"By me," answered the latter, and yawned.

"Well, man, well?" called Gurry. "Who are those red demons yonder?"

"There's only one demon yonder," said Larribee, "and that one is blue."

"Blue . . ." cried the colonel, "blue?"

"Sky Blue," explained Larribee at last. "Sky Blue and his hangers-on, his mares and colts. That's all."

They looked silently at him, and then, turning their glances ahead, they put their horses to a steady dog-trot.

Speed would never win their race for them, only patience and the cunning of a fox. Every one of the four were devising schemes, as they struggled forward.

CHAPTER TWENTY-THREE

They caught the herd the next day, but they did not catch Sky Blue. The herd was traveling slowly and entered a wide valley, some half dozen miles across toward the mouth and narrowing toward the head.

The black stallion carried Larribee around the horses and to the top of the valley. There he turned them. He did not have to show himself, even. The smell of a human being blown down the wind was enough to catch the sensitive nostrils of the mares. They wheeled about and went kiting, for it was not the first time that they had been coursed by men and not the first time that they had lost foals from their sides, sisters and brothers.

They ran down the valley at a good clip and toward the mouth of it. Gurry rushed his horse out from a clump of brushes, shelved that flying mass off to the right, and hounded them back, swerving up the valley.

Far away, at the head of the valley, was big Larribee, ready to head off the mass of thundering horses if they came up that way. From the distance, he could look down on the wide panorama. He could see every feature of it, so crystal was the mountain air, and he gloried in the sweep of the picture, in the size of the canvas, in the big, wide-shouldered mountains that squatted contentedly all about, lolling at their ease, watching, making no comment, but not indifferent. He felt that their hearts were with the fugitives. Man was an intruder on such a scene.

He saw the horse herd reach the shallow little creek that wandered through the valley. He saw the water dashed to white by the plunging hoofs. He saw the herd speeding up the valley again, and marveled that the little foals were able to keep pace, with such apparent ease, with their larger elders. They seemed to be born with their speed in their feet, fully equipped for the mountain life and the perils of the wild plains.

Gurry gave them a good, hard run, for a couple of miles or more, and then dropped out of sight behind a hummock. There he found the colonel, who dashed out like a jockey after the herd.

In the meantime, Sky Blue seemed to know all about the duties that were imposed upon him as the monarch of the horses. He kept to the rear, since from the rear came danger, weaving from side to side, snorting a warning that made the lagging youngsters scurry, and once or twice running up beside a fat, laboring mare and nipping her shrewdly.

Up the valley they shot, with the colonel perched on the back of a good little mustang mare. He ran that herd to the head of the valley and there the black stallion carried Larribee down on them, shouting, whooping, and madly waving his arms.

Off sheered the leading horses and dashed back down the valley. He hunted them across the shallow creek and saw the water churned white and dashed thirty feet, flying into the air as they passed through it.

Over they went and left, struggling helplessly in the swift current, a two-year-old with a broken leg. It was vicious work, bitter work. But it had to be done. When men were ready to break their own limbs, they would care little about the necks of inferior beasts. Larribee simply turned himself in the saddle, snarled like an angry wolf, and smashed a big caliber bullet through the brain of that poor little mustang. Later, it would wash ashore on a sand bank. The coyotes and the buzzards would come down and eat it, and from a bright-eyed, gay, lovely colt it would have become a mere item on Nature's extensive menu.

Larribee thought of these things. But he thought still more of the herd before him. He put up the revolver and rode on, harder than before. For victory was in sight.

There was the blue roan, weaving from side to side, glancing back at the pursuer, snorting his rage and defiance, and driving on the breathless horses before him. They feared him, it seemed, even more than they feared man. They would run harder at his urging than they would from the nameless fear of the riders behind.

As Larribee sat the black, he compared his mount with the roan, and he saw the vastness of the difference. The black was a good horse, beautiful, true-running, glorious. He had the wind, the courage, the spirit, the stamina of heart and soul. He had the gentleness of spirit, also, rapidly developing under the tutelage of Larribee. He was beginning to rejoice, as it seemed, over pouring out himself for the sake of his rider.

But he was not Sky Blue. There were light years of difference between them. He had not that long stroke, that bounding ease, that machine-made perfection of stride that devoured distance and made nothing of it. A good horse, a grand horse, even, but not a Sky Blue!

Well, good as the stallion was, he could not stand forever against the pace that was being set for him.

But, first of all, the mares began to stagger and stumble, knocking up the dust with their scuffling feet. The youngsters and the young colts still seemed to have plenty of strength but theirs was not the stallion's endurance. They were running with the lead of weariness in their feet, and Larribee, noting them, grinned savagely and nodded in his content. *They ought to go to pieces soon,* he thought.

After they were gone, how long would even the peerless might of the roan stand up under their punishment? They had them well boxed. Although the trap was fairly open at the farther end, yet the appearance of one rider there seemed enough to turn the herd.

So Larribee gave the hunted horses a tremendous shove down the valley and brought them nearer to exhaustion. When he pulled up, he could see that the colonel had taken his place at the head of the valley in the narrows. He was now on a second-string mount and would be fresh for the next shove, when the runners had come around to his side of the valley again. All went very well, indeed.

As Larribee stopped, he saw the herd lose its momentum. They spread out, scattering toward the mouth of the valley like a volley of shot from a riot gun, but they were dead tired, their heads bobbing. A good man on a good fast horse could have got in among them in no time and had his rope on the pick, well-nigh. Only the roan seemed to have a great reserve left.

Was the beast tireless? Weaving in his course from time to time, he seemed to have covered twice the distance that his confederates had covered and to have done three times the work. He shone like a jewel with his sweat. But he was not flagging.

Then, on the right of the leaders, out dashed Gurry, having worked back to his former post. He was on a good fresh mustang, an iron gray, hard as steel, and ready for the cruelest work. He was one of Shouting Thunder's best buffalo ponies, and now he showed his mettle, for he went for those wild mustangs with his ears flattened, as though he wanted to get his teeth in one of them. Gurry, flinging up his arms, screeched like any Indian.

It was a thrilling thing to see that mob of tired horses veer off to the left, turning back into the heart of the trap.

They're in again, said Larribee to himself with savage satisfaction. *And this time the mill will grind them to pieces.*

No, they were ground to pieces already. At the new thrust that Gurry made at them, they fell apart, so to speak, and the tired mares simply chucked the contest. They swung to the right and to the left. They seemed contented merely to get out of the immediate path of the horsemen, and would not strain their burning lungs and their aching legs to a full gallop again. They broke apart, and the younger colts, the young stallions, were the only ones, together with a few seasoned mares that had not been in foal this season, who kept together in a pack and went back up the valley.

Then Sky Blue played his hand. It was a good hand, and a most amazing one. His neigh came out like the blast of a horn. He went through the running pack as a stake horse might run through a plow team. He came through on the farther side, fairly dissolved in speed as he dashed not for liberty, but straight at the rider who blocked his way to it.

For a moment, Larribee could not understand it. He thought that the stallion was acting as horses often do in a corral, plunging straight at those who hem them in, only to swerve at the last instant and dodge past.

But suddenly Larribee realized that the stallion did not have this maneuver in mind. Instead, there was a gathering speed as he went on, with his ears flattened and his snaky head thrust out. Gurry, who had started waving his arms and shouting, seemed to realize, also, that this was deadly earnest, and, abandoning his futile efforts to scare the roan back, he pulled out a revolver and fired.

The heart of Larribee jumped into his throat. He had not thought of the possibility of the horse chase ending in this manner. But what if that bullet went home to its mark?

At least the shot did not stop the career of Sky Blue for the moment. He leaped straight in on Gurry and with the shock of his powerful body cast horse and man head over heels.

There on the grass Gurry lay, sprawling. His mustang was struggling to get to its feet. And through the wide mouth of the valley the herd was pouring out toward liberty.

Larribee did not ride in pursuit. There was no purpose in merely running down the tired mares and colts. Instead, he galloped the black to where Gurry lay, and dismounted.

It seemed to him that Gurry was driven into the grass, flattened out, but the man's eyes were open, and his lips stirred. Larribee leaned over him.

"Don't touch me, Larribee," said Gurry. "I'm gonna die. I'm smashed to pieces." He was whispering. The shadow was already in his eyes.

Larribee leaned closer.

"I'm the first, but I ain't the last," whispered Gurry. "I give you my share in him. Nobody but you will ever have him. Like goes to like." He caught his breath and a ripple went through his broken body. Then he looked placidly up at the sky, and Larribee saw that he was dead.

CHAPTER TWENTY-FOUR

They buried Gurry on a small slope facing to the east, covered by a litter of great stones. There in a cranny among the boulders, they placed the body of the dead man and composed his limbs decently and closed his eyes. Then the three of them pried up some of the boulders above and started a noble landslide that rolled over the spot where Gurry lay and covered him with a thousand tons of stone and débris. A thunder like heavy guns told of the passing of Gurry, the horseman.

He had no written inscription. The colonel merely said, as they stood about the spot for an instant: "Well, he's looking toward the East and the racetracks that he was so hungry to get the stallion onto, poor Gurry. His heart was a few sizes larger than his brain, but he was a man."

The other two said nothing at all,

Larribee and Shouting Thunder were already busily changing their saddles to new mounts, and in two minutes the trio was riding out upon the trail of the wild band and Sky Blue.

But Larribee, as they found the myriad of hoof marks and followed them toward the northwest, knew that the minds of the others were heavy. It was Gurry who had brought the stallion to Fort Ransome. He had attempted to break Sky Blue and this had led to his escape and endless pursuit. Now the man who had started it all was gone, and they struggled forward on the trail of Sky Blue alone. The heart of Larribee was cold, indeed, with many forebodings.

Then he forgot all that he had himself endured, and the death of poor Gurry, in remembering how the blue roan had ripped through the tired herd of mustangs and gone out to fight and die or conquer. He had not been hurt by the revolver shot. At least they could see no blood upon the trail.

Larribee was roused from a daydream by the aching of his wounds, where the arrow and the knife thrusts of the Cheyenne had told upon him. To the end of his life, he would never be totally unconscious of that writhing upon his flesh.

They were climbing, now, almost every day, the weather growing cooler, until they broke through a high pass and came to the outer edge of that great plateau that in those days was marked upon maps of the United States as a vast unexplored region and named the Great American Desert. They struck Wilson's Creek at the same time.

No one could tell why it was called a creek, since it was big enough to have drilled its way through the solid rocks of the Continental Divide and hew for itself a great cañon. The story was that Wilson had seen its headwaters, and the name he gave it had been extended to the lower cañons as well. When they came to the verge of the gorge, Larribee was dumb with admiration.

For the valley fell away in great steps down to the central cañon, where the waters were mostly hidden by the precipitous walls. Only far up and far down the ravine they saw the glint of the current, rounding turns. On their side, the mountains rolled slowly up to great peaks, the heads and shoulders of which were blanketed with snow. Beyond, they could look across a withering expanse of desert, and in the valley itself there appeared the ledges and the cliffs of many colors, according to the nature of the strata through which the water had chiseled its way.

The stallion was leading the herd along the eastern margin of this valley, and Shouting Thunder declared that he was almost sure to stay on the verge of the ravine until he reached the gentler slopes of the headwater valley.

But that very day the trail dipped over the rimrock. Far below, they could see the reason for the variation. Down in the shadows of the hollow, there was a broad expanse that was green with grass, perhaps supported by some sort of sub-irrigation. The three riders, from the height, could see the herd trooping down a natural trail in single file, with the gleam of Sky Blue in the van.

Shouting Thunder saw the coming danger. He seized upon the shoulder of the colonel and nearly crushed the flesh and bones of that little man. Then Colonel Pratt and Larribee, staring, saw riders moving in a small dell of rocks beyond the horses. The colonel's glass was fixed upon them, instantly, but the unaided eyes of the Cheyenne identified them.

"Pawnee wolves. Pawnee horse thieves," he said.

It was an ideal spot to trap the herd—to trap the great leader, at least. For the trail was narrow, and the animals had to maintain their single file and proceed with caution. Some of the younger ones were continually slipping and nudging those immediately in front, and those thus nudged dared not lash out with their heels to keep a proper distance behind them.

Suddenly the Cheyenne began to laugh. "The Crows!" he cried.

The white men, despite their slower eyes, picked them out at once. They seemed a smaller party than the Pawnees, and they were gathered at a point a little lower down in the valley. Even at this distance, they were easily distinguishable on account of the length of their hair, worn longer by this tribe than by any others in North America.

"It is good," said Shouting Thunder. "They must fight . . . the Crows and the Pawnees . . . and the vultures will eat them.

Now a Cheyenne child of five could begin to sharpen his knife, for he would soon be able to take plenty of cheap scalps and count some coups, too." He laughed again.

"If bullets begin to rattle around down there, there's no telling what will happen to Sky Blue," said the colonel. "We ought to be nearer. We ought to do something, Shouting Thunder."

"The Sky People have this in their hands," said the Cheyenne. "They know who is finally going to ride Sky Blue, if men are to ride him, or, if he dies, they know what spirit will claim him in the blue fields above us." He dismounted calmly, took out his pipe, filled it, and sitting, cross-legged, in a gap between two boulders, he began to smoke with the greatest content.

The white men followed to the same point of vantage, but they did not smoke. They saw the Pawnee riders now dismounting, now crawling forward among the rocks. They could see the coiled rawhide lariats in their hands, ready to be cast.

And straight into that nest of danger went Sky Blue, leading the way.

The Crows were clambering up through the rocks to meet the stallion at the same point. If the great horse did not scent any coming danger, it was because of the wind that came down the valley, straight against him.

"There is the white chief of the Crows," said the Cheyenne quietly. "He goes ahead of the others. He is a young man. Also, his hair is not long. You see how pale his face is, even from here. He is a great chief."

"Why?" asked Larribee. "Why do you call him a great chief? Simply because he is going first toward the danger?"

"No, but because he keeps his men like a wise chief, all ready for trouble. He knows that the Pawnees are above, there, on the rocks, though the Pawnees do not know that he is coming. So the Crows have put up their lariats. They have only rifles in their hands. He goes first and finds the way that is easiest. He keeps all his men together a little behind him. He makes them go slowly, so that the haste of the climbing will not make their hands shake when they are holding the rifles.

"There, you see, he has halted them. He makes them wait until they are breathing easily. And now he goes ahead once more. Such a chief as that is worth more than a hundred rifles when a battle is to be fought. You may be sure that the Crows will wear Pawnee scalps in their belts, though they are smaller in number. They will have Pawnee scalps before the battle is over." He adjusted his back more comfortably to the side of the boulder. "This is a pleasant day," said Shouting Thunder. "I wish that all my tribe were here to watch the Crows and the Pawnees strike one another."

Sky Blue, in the meantime, had come to a narrow defile between great rocks, and there the Pawnees and their lariats waited for him on the one side. And there, on the other, the Crows were crawling higher and higher, coming to the verge of the same meeting point.

Larribee felt his heart beating wildly. He saw Sky Blue stepping proudly into the narrow way among the boulders and then, like a startled fox, stop with one forehoof raised. He could not have paused at a less advantageous moment.

Out of the rocks three or four lariats were suddenly hurled at him, and in the path before him sprang up a pair of Pawnees to bar the way. Larribee could see their close-cropped heads, their scalp locks sticking up like stiff, horsehair plumes. They themselves glimmered in the sun like coppery athletes, ready for a contest.

Sky Blue whirled about. Behind him, he saw still more Pawnees, scrambling out, and the horses of the herd were making desperate efforts to turn back and escape up the trail.

Most of them succeeded, for the good reason that the Pawnees were not paying any heed to the movements of the lesser animals. There was only one horse in the world for them at that moment, and this was Sky Blue.

The herd, twisting about, climbed like goats to get to safety, but in the confusion a big animal was shouldered from his footing and thrust off the ledge. He fell into the sheer air, turned twice over, kicking frantically, tail and mane fluttering like cut paper. He struck the lower slope, glanced off from it like a stone from a rock wall, and shot over the rim of the precipice out of sight.

Then the scream of the horse came up through the wind to the ears of Larribee, and he turned a little sick.

But its fate was a small thing. It was Sky Blue that mattered, and the stallion, as he wheeled about, had been met with a fresh shower of ropes that tangled about his neck, about his legs. Down he went, helpless, entangled by a dozen iron-hard strands.

CHAPTER TWENTY-FIVE

Sky Blue was down. Sky Blue was gone, then, and into the hands of the Pawnees.

Sweat poured from the body of Larribee. He looked at the colonel and saw that he was white. He looked at the Cheyenne chief and saw that he laughed silently to himself, and found all the more relish in the next drag upon his long-stemmed pipe.

Into the narrows among the boulders rushed the Pawnees. Ah, what a tingle the thrill of their triumphant shouting carried through the blood and bones of Larribee, there on the height. But still the Cheyenne chief was laughing.

Then, as those half-naked warriors swarmed toward the helpless, struggling horse, a flower of white bloomed among the opposite rocks, unfolded its petals, as it were, rose, grew blue with thinness of air. The dull clang of a rifle drifted upward to the ears of Larribee. Other puffs of white were curling upward from the boulders, and now the screeching Pawnees fled for shelter, their cries mingling with the furiously triumphant shouts of the Crows, who emptied their rifles and left the trail littered with the bodies of the twisting, dying Pawnees. Before the latter could find secure shelter, prepare their weapons, and fight back, the Crows were swarming after them.

The whole advantage of utter surprise was fighting on their side, routing the Pawnees before them, and well they needed this advantage, for there were not more than eight of them, and a full score of Pawnees had been riding on the trail of the great stallion. Five of those Pawnees were down on the trail, at the first discharge of the well-aimed rifles. As many more were beaten down as they scurried away among the rocks. Hardly half of the original number got back to the little rocky hollow where the horses had been left, and down into that hollow the victorious Crows followed.

There were seven of them, now. No one had fallen yet. But one man, the chief, had dropped back and was rushing on the stallion, as he lay prostrate among the rocks.

Even the fate of Sky Blue could not distract the eye of Larribee from the human tragedy. After all, was it not in the name of Sky Blue that the battle was fought? Had not his trail brought the war parties together? Was it not for his sake that they had marched and that they fought now? He was the prize, greater than scalps and the count of coups.

Larribee saw the Pawnees gain their ponies, saw the Crows rush after them. He saw a long-haired Crow brave leap up on the croup of a pony, a mighty spring, and then the flash of his knife as it was buried in the back of the rider.

That Pawnee, casting his arms wide as though to receive and fall into the embrace of a friend, swayed slowly and toppled from the saddle, but a valiant friend, turning his wild-eyed little charger in a demivolt, brought down his war club on the skull of the Crow and brained him with the stroke.

That blow rallied the spirits of the beaten Pawnees. In a moment there was a swirl of horses and riders and men on foot, fighting in the roaring hollow of the rocks. Like an open mouth, the place gave out a roar of death screams, and whoops of triumph.

The Pawnees fought back, but the whole impetus of victory was on the side of the Crows. Presently half a dozen of the crop-headed plainsmen shot away among the boulders in retreat, and behind them four Crows remained standing and raised the pæan of victory. It seemed to Larribee like the screeching of a single huge vulture.

At the feet of the victors lay dead men.

"All this is very good," said the Cheyenne, still silently laughing. "And now they will kill the wounded and take the scalps. The fools have forgotten Sky Blue! He is worth all the men that were living and dead, down there, but they have forgotten him. Only their chief remembered."

The prophecy of the Cheyenne was true enough. Larribee saw one crawling Pawnee vainly raise the stock of a broken rifle to protect himself, saw a Crow warrior easily avoid the blow and drag the victim by the hair of the head, before he drove his knife into the poor fellow's throat. Other things similar to this were happening, but Larribee could not look at them. He had glanced back, called by the Cheyenne, toward the spot where Sky Blue lay, as the white chief of the Crows rushed upon it.

The thin strands of the rawhide that held the horse were scarcely visible; they were like the threads of a spider's web, unseen except against the light or when beaded with dew. And Sky Blue had begun to kick and thrash about and roll in an effort to cast the bonds off.

The aim of the white leader was simply to catch the ends of one or two of the ropes so that he could control the limbs of the giant, but it was a great task for one man, and the struggles of Sky Blue did not make it simpler. He threw the ropes into a whirling maze.

The white man was shouting for help. It was easy to distinguish his voice in the tumult, so much more deep was the tone. It reminded Larribee of the barking of a huge watchdog, a mournful and a hopeless note welling up through the thin distance. But the frantic jubilation of the four victorious warriors seemed to drown the cries of their chief.

"There, you see," said the Cheyenne, who sat on the ledge of rock and looked down like a demigod on this mortal struggle below, "there you see that the fables of the old women are true, and that the wise man will be left to fight alone, but the fool has always the entire tribe at his right hand. It is wrong to be too right. It is foolish to be too wise. Such men die young, even though they die famous."

Larribee, listening to those words, printed them somewhere in his heart, to be remembered on another day. Yet, all the time that the Cheyenne was speaking, the very soul of Larribee was absorbed in watching the struggle between man and beast.

Twice and yet again, he saw the Crow white chief succeed in grasping the ropes. The third time, it appeared that nearly all the entangling cords had been kicked away by the stallion, and now he was half up, his head high, his forelegs braced wide, ready to lurch to all fours, when the tug of the white man jerked the front legs of the big fellow together and sent him rolling once more. But he rolled straight at the man, and the latter sprang back to avoid a stroke of those four furious hoofs.

As the chief sprang back, Sky Blue sprang to his feet, with only one lariat streaming back from him.

What could the white chief do now, in spite of his strength and the courage that he had shown? He did what any desperate and skillful rider would have attempted. He leaped upon the back of Sky Blue.

"So," said the Cheyenne, "another brave man goes to find the Sky People." He laughed, and his white teeth flashed.

Larribee, also, was shaking his head. For the Crow leader had fought bravely and well. Now, too late, his tardy warriors came running out from the rocks on the right to help him. Ten seconds before, they would have been in time to master Sky Blue. But now they were only at hand to see the rider flung high into the air, while the stallion galloped off recklessly down the steep pitch of the slope.

"Dead," said Larribee as they saw the angle of the rider's fall.

But he was not dead. He managed to clutch with both hands a pinnacle of rock and swung there an instant, dangling over the abyss that had almost swallowed him. His four remaining braves helped him back to a firm footing.

Then the madness of victory came over them. They began a scalp dance. Every one of them had more than a single trophy in his grasp. The bloody scalp locks gleamed horribly to the eye of Larribee. The whooping, the chanting voices of the victors rang in his ears like a wild cry that celebrated not their triumph in battle, but the victory of the stallion, which had again conquered.

It seemed to Larribee that those little figures were like roosters, prancing and crowing in a yard, regardless of the fact that the farmer was approaching with his axe to slice off all their heads for dinner. He looked at the colonel, and saw that the little man was mopping his forehead.

Catching the eye of Larribee, the colonel muttered: "It's a horrible thing, Larribee. There's a curse on that blue roan, I feel, and more trouble than this will come to still other men before it's finished. By heaven, Larribee, I'd vote to give up the fight and go back home, except that there's an imp of the perverse in all of us that keeps us on the trail, once we've started. There's a demon in that stallion, Larribee."

"Young Ransome put it there," said Larribee, "and what he put in, some other man can take out again. I took it out once before. You saw that."

The colonel sighed, and shook his head.

The Indian chief pointed his brawny arm.

"Look," he said. "And listen. That is the one who conquered. That is the one who truly laughs."

Far, far beneath, on that stretch of emerald green grass, they could see Sky Blue again, with mane blowing and tail arched, and the summons of his neigh rang far up the side of the rocks.

His herd came down to him. They had left the first trail and worked across to another toward the right. Now they streamed down the rocky slope and came out on the green plateau beneath with much joyous whinnying.

"The white chief," said the Cheyenne, "he is not yet happy, and yet he is not worrying about all the good warriors who have died today. The Pawnees who have fallen, the coups that his tribe counted, and the victory that will make the Crow women sing and laugh, do not make him happy, for he is thinking of only one thing, listening to one thing only, and that is Sky Blue, neighing in the valley."

Larribee stared down at the white chief and saw he was leaning against a vast boulder, with a hanging head, like a man lost in daydreams.

CHAPTER TWENTY-SIX

The colonel was for going on. He pointed out that the herd was gaining on them constantly, and, if they approached with any care whatever, the three of them ought to be able to handle the four Crows and their white leader, especially while the braves were celebrating their victory, but Shouting Thunder, who maintained his air of amusement and detached assurance, like a prophet or a demigod, shook his head and insisted that it was better to wait.

In the first place, he said, the white leader was an exceptional fellow and might do all sorts of surprising things if he were attacked, at that moment. But, he also said, if a little patience were used, they would soon see that party of Crows diminished.

Larribee and the colonel did not see how this could be, but they had to admit that Shouting Thunder was more likely than they to have knowledge of Indian ways.

So they remained at their look-out, and very soon they saw the Crows climbing up the side of the steepest of the nearby pinnacles of rock and bearing the bodies of the dead, having first plundered the fallen and gathered up as spoils the horses and weapons of the vanquished Pawnees. At the top, the three dead Crows were stretched side-by-side, wrapped in their accouterments, and the big buffalo robes securely lashed around them. They could see the gleam and trembling of the painted features in the headdress of one of the dead. Shouting Thunder said this must be some great warrior. Otherwise, so many stained feathers could not have appeared in the air. Once the bodies were laid out, one of the Crows remained standing on top of the rock. The others climbed down and three shots in rapid succession echoed dimly to the watchers on the rimrock.

"They are killing three horses," suggested Shouting Thunder. "So, you see, the souls of the dead men will be able to ride over the thin blue prairies above our heads. That is what we believe," he added, "though I know that you white men believe nothing except the flesh in the meat pot and the fire that boils it."

Presently they could see the solitary man on the rock top extending his arms, apparently lifting his head to the sky.

"He is singing to the spirits of the dead," said Shouting Thunder. "Now those ghosts are going upward happily. Why should they not be happy? They have been killed in the midst of a good battle that their side won. Their scalps are on their heads. Their medicine bags have not been stolen. Their squaws will remember them as heroes and so will their sons. You know that a brave man after death always leaves a shadow inside his lodge after the fire is lighted at night.

"Now those three ghosts of the Crows are riding on the spirits of the dead horses. We cannot see them, but the hoofs of the horses are striking the air, you may be sure, and they are rising like eagles. Well, they will circle low for a time to listen to the song of the singer. He is saying good bye to them, telling them that the Crows will mourn because of their going. It is a good thing to be mourned, I think."

Thin as fading memory, the chant of the singer wavered across the air to the ear of Larribee. Then he saw the mourner drop his arms and begin the descent from the rock.

"Now the three ghosts are rising," said Shouting Thunder earnestly. "Look upward carefully, you who doubt. The spirits have been seen entering the sky. They go very fast, and the sun must be just right. There! There! Do you see? Wasn't that a streak passing across that white cloud? There! Another! That is the path they have ridden in. Now they are gone into the blue, where horses never are tired and snow never falls, and arrows cannot help but reach the mark."

So he ended, but his white companions did not smile. Instead, they looked seriously at one another, moved by the perfect faith of the Cheyenne.

"What happens," said the colonel to Shouting Thunder, "when the ghosts of the Crows meet the ghosts of their enemies up there in the blue prairies?"

Shouting Thunder replied: "There are battles, of course. But the Cheyennes are the rulers over the braves who fight up there. There are more Sioux, but the Cheyennes ride stronger horses and strike harder blows."

"Do they kill and take scalps?" asked the colonel.

"They count coups," said Shouting Thunder, "and that is the really glorious part of war. Afterward they sit with the Sky People and chant about their fighting. I know a medicine man who is very holy. He says that one evening in the autumn of the year, when the prairie was brown, he heard the chanting come down on a small, soft wind out of the sky. The ghosts he heard must have died a long time ago, because he heard the words, but he could not recognize the language."

"Well," said the colonel, "there's another sort of powwow going on down there in the trail. What are they arguing about? They're pointing up here to us, by thunder. They've spotted us, my friends."

Shouting Thunder shook his head. "They have not seen us," he explained. "You see how the four Crows are pointing? Well, they are only pointing at the back trail. I suppose they are saying that the stallion the color of the horizon is really a demon, leading them on to trouble, and bringing it about that men should kill one another. They want to take the trail back home.

They have plenty of horses now, and they have plenty of plunder. They want to go back and sing their war songs and dance the scalp dance around the fires. They could feast for a month, after such a battle as this, and still they would have new things to say.

"But the white chief, as you see, is pointing on down the trail. For he has a heart that is stronger and stronger, the more he sees the danger before him. He is telling them that there will be a greater glory, I suppose, if they will follow him on the trail of the blue roan. He is telling them, if there is a spirit in the horse, there is all the more glory in capturing it and making it a servant. But the others will not be persuaded. They are far away from their homes. Even the heart of a brave man grows a little sick when he is a long distance from home . . . while cowards will become heroes within sight of their own lodges.

"Look . . . now the chief has taken two horses. Do you see? Each of them is white on the side, as if it were painted. Pintos are very tough, and the white chief is wise to choose them, now that he is riding on the trail of Sky Blue. They say good bye to him. Do you see? He takes with him no scalps. He takes with him none of the plunder. He travels light, and he will travel far. Ha!" broke out the Cheyenne with fire in his eye, "the scalp of one such man would make a whole tribe rich for a generation. The scalp of one such man, hanging in the lodge of a lucky chief, would make all his children grow up to be heroes." And his nostrils quivered.

The colonel looked away in a sudden disgust, but Larribee merely rubbed his chin and smiled downward at the scene of the parting.

For Shouting Thunder proved to be right, and now the four victors herded their horses laboriously up the trail and their white leader went on down the same trail toward the green field on which Sky Blue and his distant companions were grazing.

"What shall we do?" asked Shouting Thunder. "There are four men loaded with glory and with fresh scalps. Here are three of us with rifles that do not miss easily. Shall we waylay them and make everything that they have ours?"

"Why should we load ourselves down?" asked the colonel.

"Scalps and glory," said the Cheyenne seriously, "are weights that even small men can carry easily." He looked steadily at Larribee, but the latter shook his head.

"Your Sky People, Shouting Thunder," he said, "if they are watching us all the time, as you say, don't want to see us fritter away our time. If our medicine is strong enough to take Sky Blue, very well. Don't ask it for anything else."

Shouting Thunder stared at the slowly approaching warriors and sighed. But he said at last: "Very well. My brother has spoken. All the words of my brother are wise."

Since they were not to fight the Crows, it was best to withdraw from their back trail as far as possible, so the horses were picked up at once and they made a detour to the right. Then, finding a good and easy way into the valley, they rode down into it.

The evening settled like a fine blue dust as they journeyed down among the rocks, and, when they found a grassy cove beside the waters at the bottom, they camped there and made a small fire among the rocks. With good water and plenty of it, with hot food to eat, they made an excellent camp. In the morning, they were astir with the first light, as usual, and journeyed straight up the valley. Even the hardest stretches of rock were so beaten by many hoofs that it was not hard to keep on the trail of Sky Blue's herd, behind which the white chief must still be traveling.

The three of them and their horses seemed pitifully small and weak in that gigantic ravine. But Sky Blue seemed, to their imaginations, to be fitted for the grandeur of the scene. It was his wildness that made him a part of Nature, and it was civilization that made the white man small. All the three thought of this, but not one of them mentioned it. So their journey that day was clouded by a grimmer silence than ever.

They remained in the windings of the cañon until the middle of the afternoon, when the heat was like an oven, reflected from the rock faces. Then the trail led them across a wide, shallow ford and up the smaller gorge of a tributary stream that here tumbled into the creek. It was a very narrow ravine, and the small stream of water filled it with a confusion of shouting voices. Crowds of men seemed to be laughing and shouting. They appeared to be riding deeper and deeper into a trap. But toward sunset they climbed from the gorge, as up a rude flight of steps, to the level beyond, and when they halted in the darkness the flat hand of the desert had gathered them. Only, well to the east, they could see the mountains blocking out the lower stars.

The colonel, as they finished their dry, unpleasant meal of parched corn, pointed ahead of them toward the sands. "He's out there, the chief," he said. "And he's out there alone."

Neither Larribee nor Shouting Thunder answered, but they were thinking, like the colonel, of what mighty nerves, what a heart of adamant must be in the solitary leader of the Crows, struggling yonder in the sands, resolute and patient on the hopeless trail.

Chapter Twenty-Seven

For the first time since the search began, they kept no watch, since the Crows and the Pawnees were both off their trail, and the solitary man who struggled after the stallion was not likely to attack the camp of three armed fighters. Besides, the number of their horses was a reasonably sure guard against molestation, except by cunning Indian thieves.

Larribee, resting for a moment on his elbow before he lay back to sleep, regarded with pleasure the black silhouettes that stalked about to crop the sweet grass that grew in little sun-cured patches, here and there, a sparse collection of morsels, but the finest horse food in the world.

Since the fear of Indian surprise was practically nothing in this naked back yard of the world, they did not need to hobble the animals. Some of them might graze far, but hardly out of sight.

Larribee lay down, looked for a moment into the stars, rather small and withdrawn behind the desert haze, and then slept. Into his dream came a soft thunder, like the noise of distant, rising waters, flooding nearer and nearer, and then he was awakened by the sharp voice of the Cheyenne, shouting: "The horses! The horses!"

The call got Larribee up with a leap. The noise of the thunder was not in his dream only. It was there upon them, flooding out of the desert, softly and swiftly, and then to the left he saw many tossing heads against the rim of the sky. And one great form, that seemed dimly illumined by its own light from within, ran before the rest. Sky Blue!

He saw the colonel and Shouting Thunder rushing out toward their own scattered herd, and then, before he himself could stir, the avalanche poured around him. Flying sand blinded him. He was only aware of Sky Blue galloping straight past him, so close he could hear the pounding of the great hoofs. The sand-muffled roar of many hoofs poured past—sand filled his hair, his eyes— sand drifted down his neck and grated on his skin. Then the phantoms had passed.

He saw, in the paleness of the early dawn, the colonel and the Cheyenne, each bringing in one horse. Then he realized what had happened. They had been safe enough from human tormentors, but they had not been safe from the attack of the stallion. Now their overflowing wealth of livestock was stripped away. While the colonel and the Cheyenne each had a set of four hoofs to carry him along the trail, Larribee was without help.

Neither Shouting Thunder nor the colonel spoke as the small fire was lighted to cook the morning meal. It was not until they had eaten that Shouting Thunder, his face still only half seen in the dawn light, said: "Brother, I know the way from here to my people very well. It may well be, also, that I shall be able to find a horse on the way, and so I can turn back, find the trail, and overtake you. But you are not familiar with the desert. You do not know the mountains and the passes. You do not shoot very well with a rifle, and the game a man must kill here is always running, half lost in the rim of the sky. So you must take my horse and go on. I shall turn back. That is the wisest."

There was very little sentimentality in the heart of Larribee, as has been pointed out. But at this speech of the Cheyenne's, he choked a little. He reached out a hand and gripped his red brother's. At last he was able to speak, and in the idiom of Shouting Thunder's own manner of thought. "I can find my way back," he said. "After all, the sun rises in the east and sets in the west. I can find my way . . . and I can snare rabbits, if I can't shoot 'em. As for whoever finds Sky Blue and rides him, why, your blood runs in me, now, brother, and my blood runs in you. It makes no difference which of us rides the stallion."

Shouting Thunder would have spoken again. His lips were parted, and he was shaking his head to argue, when the colonel said dryly: "That settles it. You can't expect the Larribee to make his bad luck your bad luck, Shouting Thunder. Besides, I yelled to him in plenty of time. He had to take ten seconds to get the sleep out of his wits, and so it's his own fault that he's without a horse. He could have caught one as well as you or I. He's as fast on his feet and as sure with his hands to pick up a trailing lariat."

With that, he set about saddling and packing for the day's journey, and in the rose of the morning he and Shouting Thunder mounted. The Indian was very much troubled. When he said good bye to Larribee, he laid both hands on the shoulders of the white man.

"Half of me stays here with you, brother," he said. "So take good care of yourself. Half of my spirit is your spirit."

"Well," Larribee said bluntly, "I suppose half of my scalp is yours, too, and you can be mighty sure that I'll take care of that. Good bye, Shouting Thunder. Good bye, Colonel. Get on. You're losing the cool of the day."

Yet, he could hardly believe that he was being deserted, even when he saw them riding away from him. He could hardly believe it, and he asked himself if he would have done the same thing under the same circumstances. He could not answer his own question.

The flashing rim of the sun, looking over the edge of the world, struck through the midst of these speculations. It was high time for him to march, if he were to reach the water in the valley behind him, before the middle heat of the day had parched his throat. He turned fairly toward it, and now the sun, half risen, blinded him with its golden semicircle. But Larribee shook his head. He knew that it was utter folly, but it seemed to him that between him and the flare of the rising sun was the ghost of Sky Blue, roving across the world.

Straightway, he made his pack, and made it light. He looked, with a grim smile, at the saddle that lay on the ground. That would have to be abandoned, of course. But he could not leave the bridle. Someday, he could not guess how it might come about, this bit, tooth-dented, a wisp of dry grass clinging to it, might be fitted into the iron jaws of Sky Blue. That day, if it came, he would conquer or die. So he shouldered his pack, turned his back on the sun, and started at a plodding step over the sand.

The desert made bad footing. He slipped inches back for every stride he made forward, until he learned the short, choppy stride that is best for such travel. After that, he made good time, perhaps, but it seemed to Larribee less than the movement of an hour hand across the dial of a clock, when he measured the limitless face of the sky, in which the sun was moving.

That sun went rapidly to the zenith; the throat of Larribee was hot and half dry, for he only dared to moisten it, from time to time, from his water flask. The water was warmer than tepid and it was discolored and tasted as if foul with rust.

Twice and again, Larribee turned about and looked earnestly toward the east. He could make the return march, still, to the life-giving water of the stream. There he could take his time, following down the valley until it split the mountains apart and led him on an easy journey toward the plains. Water, at least, would be sure for him. But if he faced forward. . . .

The Cheyenne had some knowledge of this waste over which he was traveling. Once, on a far-striking war party, in the days of his boyhood, he had traversed the region, so that he and the colonel would be reasonably sure in their march of finding water from time to time. But, as for Larribee, he had only the trail of the horses to follow and wild horses might drink only once in three days or four, and still flourish. Besides, they had what seemed to Larribee wings to transport them.

But after each halt he turned his face to the west again. A strange feeling rose in him, not for the first time, that fate had written down the name of the man who was to ride Sky Blue, if ever the great horse were ridden. Perhaps it was the urge of fate that drew him, with an invisible, but resistless might.

The sun now scalded his shoulders. The sweat ran down his face and dried before the trickle had reached his chin. He was no longer the seal-sleek fellow who had left the Cheyenne camp. The lines of his face were squarer and the arch of his ribs was striking through the surface layer of fat. Well, he would be thinner still, he told himself, before he died in the desert or under the hoofs of Sky Blue.

It seemed to him, after a time, when the sun was standing to the west before him, that he saw the blue glimmer of water before him, first to the right, then to the left, far ahead. He turned his steps toward the blue, but then he remembered the desert mirage and smiled bitterly, forcing himself ahead along the beaten track of the herd.

Once and then again, he thought that he saw cool groves of green trees looming. Finally it appeared to him that a horse was in the distance, wavering up and down, as though at a long-striding gallop, in the heat waves that struck upward from the surface of the sands. The last image irritated Larribee so much that he cursed through his set teeth, for it seemed as though Nature were mocking him, taunting him with all that might be, and was not.

He thought, now, for the first time in many days, not of the blue roan, but of the life he had left so far behind him—the cool, aromatic air of the saloons, the whisper of cards in the gaming rooms, the clicking of golden coins and their yellow shimmering under the lights. He thought of the familiar soft green felt under the tips of his sensitive fingers.

He would have to spend weeks getting the callous places on his fingertips off, before ever his touch was as light and accurate as it had been in the old days. He wondered how he could go about assisting time in that denuding process. Lye, perhaps, would eat the surface away and let the epidermis grow again, as soft and delicate as a baby's skin, the only skin for a gambler's hands.

That was the good life, the easy life, flavored with wine and good food, drenched with tobacco smoke. He bit his lips, thinking of the feel of a Havana between his teeth.

He roused himself from this haze of regret, and, glancing to the side, he started and then stopped dead. For it seemed to him that the horse of his imagining had grown larger and that it was a black.

Chapter Twenty-Eight

He examined the vision carefully. He wiped his forehead, shaded his eyes, and stared again. Then he knew that it was no mirage. It was a black horse, a big fellow, jogging steadily across the desert! The black stallion, then? What other could it be? And it had left the herd of Sky Blue, because it could not endure the roan's mastery, and it had started drifting toward the east, where its own range had been of old. So Larribee told himself, and suddenly he began to run forward, stumbling a little in the sand.

The horse saw him coming and broke into a flowing gallop. Larribee stood still, groaning. At once, the stallion dropped from gallop to trot, still steadily toward the east. And Larribee, pitching his voice high, shouted with all his might, then shouted again. The black horse stopped, turned, and, with forelegs braced, as if ready to spring to either side, it faced toward Larribee.

He went toward it now, though it was still at a distance, with his right hand extended, palm up, the age-old sign of friendship. As he went, he was talking long before the horse could hear him. He had no saddle, to be sure. Well, he would not mind being soaked with sweat and his legs chafed raw, if once he had the might of the black beneath him.

It was the black, to be sure. It was the same glorious stallion, hard as iron, strong as iron, with short ears pricked and keen eyes blazing. Suddenly it jumped back, whirled, and galloped furiously away. Larribee stopped short. It was folly to follow that stride, matchless except for the gallop of Sky Blue. He could only stand there, with his heart trembling, and see the beauty disappear.

He thought of the many hours he had spent on the back of the stallion—the many wasted hours, when with gentler words and more soothing touches he could have made the wild horse more completely his own. It had been easy enough to tame the big fellow. He had responded like a yearling, a corral-bred thing. But he had taken his conquest too easily, too much as a matter of course. Well, now he paid the penalty, watching the black disappear.

But it did not run to the east steadily. It swung to the south, to the west again. It turned in a vast circle, and presently it was galloping straight back at Larribee.

He could not believe his eyes. He closed them and found, somewhere in his heart, a spring of faith that welled up like a clear fountain. When he opened them, the stallion was ten yards away, halted, and with a high head facing him. Suddenly Larribee laughed, a broken laugh of relief and joy. For he knew his power, and that it was not the power of hand or foot. He walked straight up to the great horse, confidently, and the stallion came one step to meet him and sniffed his hand. That was all.

Actually it parted its teeth to take the bit, and whinnied once, as though rejoicing, when Larribee sprang upon its back. He had improvised not a saddle, but at least some protection from the sweating hide of the horse. It was his blanket, with two frail straps bound under the stallion by way of cinches. His legs dangled, and, before an hour was over, he was to learn how the groin can ache and the legs become leaden without the support of stirrups. But what was that, compared with the misery of trudging across the desert with blistered feet?

He laughed, now and again, out of the fullness of a grateful heart, and the stallion, hearing him, never failed to turn its head and throw its ears forward, as though equally pleased and approving of its master.

Affection had mastered the black. Affection or destiny or some other mystery had brought it back to Larribee at the moment when he was ready to despair. He told himself that he knew, or almost knew, things of which he could not talk to any man.

In the meantime, the sign of the horse herd was drifting beneath him, and his legs ached more and more until he thought they would surely fall off. Then he remembered that the Indians had ridden without stirrups for generations. Well, he would grow accustomed to it, also.

So that day passed into the red sunset, and through that he saw the shining face of water, like a mirror thrown down on the face of the sands, and near the water forms that seemed made of smoke.

They were the colonel and Shouting Thunder. When he came up, the colonel merely smiled, but the Cheyenne leaped up with a great shout and fairly lifted him from the back of the horse.

Well, it was good to be back with them, but the sufferings of that day did not depart into the distance and become as a dream. They remained clear and strong in his mind. They were not a barrier between him and the others. Rather, this day was the crystal through which he was enabled to look into the souls of other men, these two, above all.

When he had finished his meal and lay in his blanket, ready for sleep, he asked himself again what he would have done, had he been in the place of the others, and again he could not find an answer.

Five days they rode through the desert.

They saw the mountains to the east disappear. They saw blue

ranges reach out their horns from the south and the north, and they went past these. Though it was always sun-burned desert, they found, in the trail of the wild herd, muddy pools of water and patches of grass that made grazing good enough to support the horses.

At least there was still strength in their mounts, but they began to grow thin, except the black. Perhaps there were two good reasons for this. One was that the stallion had matured in the wild life. The other was that Larribee constantly spared him.

The cramping effect of riding without stirrups got him in the habit of jogging or walking a good many miles on foot every day. When he saw how this relief freshened his horse, he continued the practice, although he no longer felt the need of the stirrups to any great extent. Afterward, the colonel adopted the same practice. Only Shouting Thunder scorned to set foot on ground.

"When my horse dies," he said, "then I shall run . . . and see whether or not you leave me far behind." He laughed a little as he said this, full of a grim confidence, and continued to goad his mustang ahead, cruelly.

But it was not an easy trail. Every day the colonel was more and more worried.

"When we had spare mounts," he confided to Larribee, "we had some ghost of a chance. But now the herd travels without anything on its back except a little worry because we're behind. But our horses are being ground down, except that black, and he's iron."

They had further bad luck, in that the wind hung steadily in the east, so that the human scent always preceded them and prevented them from getting close to the fugitive horses. Otherwise, they might have captured some of their own horses again.

It was a mystery to Larribee how the stallion could find his way so surely from water hole to water hole, but that was explained by Shouting Thunder.

"Sky Blue is the leader," he said, "when it comes to the pinch of trouble. But on the march, I'll tell you what you'd find . . . one or two old mares with their heads down and their eyes half closed. They've been across this march a dozen times, and they can smell water forty miles away, men say that know. When my father gave me as a hostage to the whites when I was a boy, the soldiers took me away across the prairies. It was a time of great drought. The river dried up to muddy trickles, the water holes were dead and covered with dry green scum. The soldiers were dying, and some of the horses were already dead. Then my uncle, who was with me, told the white chief that he should let the horses find their own way. So this was done. And it was an old mare, nearly white with age, her ribs sticking out, who led us from water to water. So we lived, and I reached the towns of the white man and there I learned the tongue of my brother." He smiled suddenly at Larribee. "Except for that," said Shouting Thunder, "I should be dead, and you would be dead, my friend. But the Sky People watch over us. They have joined our blood together. They have made us brothers more surely than one mother could have done."

It was quite a sentimental outbreak, on the part of the Cheyenne, and Larribee replied to it with a nod and a smile. But he could not help remembering that the Indian had been persuaded to leave him behind, on foot, in the desert. Again he asked himself, if the same problem were put to him, what would he do? And again he could find no answer. He remembered only that the black horse had come back, as if purposely to find him.

It was a time of the dissolving of old thoughts and the destruction of old certainties. There had been a day when he knew what he wanted from life—money, leisure, and a little dash of excitement from gambling or fighting—but now the old standards grew as thin as ghosts, and new ideas sprang up in his mind. He looked every day at the Cheyenne and at the grim face of the colonel, and told himself that he did not know them really. He knew no more than their courage and the color of their skins.

It was on the evening of the fifth day of that march that trouble came upon them again. That night the sun sank in dusky crimson that swallowed it and reduced it to a blur long before it reached the horizon. The air was still and hot and heavy about them.

"The wind will blow," said Shouting Thunder, "and the sand will blow with it."

CHAPTER TWENTY-NINE

It did not blow that night, however, nor in the morning, when the sun rose, dull and crimson, as it had set the night before. Shortly thereafter, there was a wall of purplish haze that stood well up from the horizon, and all the sky, as it seemed to the eye of Larribee, was thinly veiled with purple, also, like the evening sky on an autumn day, except that this, of course, was far more luminous. It looked like a sky painted on canvas.

"The wind will blow," said Shouting Thunder several times.

They believed him. There was something so strange about the atmosphere, it seemed as though anything might be likely to happen, but, when the stroke of the storm came, it was so sudden that they were greatly surprised by it.

The colonel, at the time, was some hundred yards or more behind them. They had noticed nothing unusual for an hour or more, except that the wall of purple haze rose in the sky as the sun rose, fencing in a smaller and smaller circle of the heavens, and the air, though there was not a breath of wind stirring, was now filled with an impalpable dust.

It filmed over the skin with the thinnest red, and it gave them the look of having been rubbed over with finely powdered dry blood. This dust was not a thing to be noticed in the air. But it dried their throats and gradually began to sting the eyes, which continually ran. The nose and throat, as well, were now irritated, so that they were continually coughing. As they were marching,

176

they saw before them the dull silhouettes of the herd of Sky Blue.

Suddenly Shouting Thunder pointed straight ahead. "There," he said.

"What?" asked Larribee.

"Look, and you will see."

"I don't see a thing, except that purple rim along the skyline," said Larribee.

"See the shadow moving toward us," said the Indian. "Dismount, dismount, now, Larribee. Make your horse lie down and you lie to the lee of it. The wind is going to come out of the west, and a great deal of trouble with it. Tie a handkerchief over your nose and mouth, if you have one. Breathe small breaths. Be patient, and you will live."

Now Larribee thought that he could see the thing. It was like the shadow of a walking man, which lantern light sometimes throws on a distant wall, a very obscure and grotesque thing. It strode out of the purple of the west, and at the same time he heard a dull humming and moaning, like that which telegraph wires make when a strong wind is blowing through them.

Larribee turned back and saw that the colonel, having arranged his cinches to his satisfaction, was in the act of remounting his horse. He shouted at the top of his voice and waved frantically, but the colonel did not hear. Every second, the air was thicker and that electrical humming louder. Larribee was possessed by an odd delusion that the sound was moaning upward from the ground about their feet. He gave another glance at the colonel, who was settling himself calmly, methodically in his saddle, as though he noticed nothing wrong, and then Larribee, having shouted again, vainly, as he guessed, started to make the black stallion lie down.

It was not easy. The big horse was not irritated by the pulling and hauling of his master, but he could not understand what it was all about. Shouting Thunder already had his mustang down, before Larribee managed to get both the forelegs of the stallion off the ground and to his knees. Then a powerful thrust of his shoulder bowled the big fellow over. There was something pathetic in his puzzled submission to the movements of his rider. As the black struck the ground, Larribee felt the first stroke of the wind, like the blow of a thousand small, powerful hands against his face and body.

Shouting Thunder was not five steps away, but already he was obscured in a blanket of dense mist, and, when Larribee looked back, the colonel was not to be seen.

He shouted, foolishly, knowing that he could not be heard, for now there was such a mournful rising of the wind that a scream from a human throat could hardly have been heard ten feet away. The air was thick with dust. It seemed unlike any other dust. There were no interstices between particles. There was simply a solid flow of grains, incredibly light, but incredibly close together.

He remembered the handkerchief warning. But there was the stallion to think of as well. He had two big bandannas of a thin silk. One he fastened into the cheek piece of the stallion's bridle and across his muzzle. Twice, during that process, the black strove to rise. But the soothing, stroking hand of Larribee made it lie down again.

He finished preparing the black for the storm in complete darkness, for the sand had worked into his eyes so that he was blinded. And now the first dust was blowing over and the purple haze that shrieked about them carried with it grains large enough to whip and excoriate the skin. He lay down in the lee of the horse and tied his second bandanna over mouth and nose. Then he composed himself, as the Indian had advised, and waited. But it was not easy to be patient. The harrying blows of the wind sometimes seemed like the trampling of a giant, jumping up and down upon him. As the hurricane reached its full force, he was certain, once or twice, that the whole bulk of the stallion, lying flat as it was, had actually been shifted a little toward him.

In the meantime, his clothes were hardly a protection. They were simply acting as a sieve. Perhaps they kept out the largest grains of sand, but the finer were working down his neck, up his wrist bands, and through the very fabric of the cloth, like a blast under high pressure. His trousers ballooned. Sometimes the vast weight of the wind scooped at him, and he felt half of his weight taken from the ground. Then a solid stream of sand poured over him. He dared not look, but, by feeling, he found out that the sand had banked high behind the horse and now it was washing over.

He got to the head of the stallion, still feeling his way. With his arms he made a shelter to keep the sand waves from immersing the nostrils of the great horse. Perhaps the stallion could rise and live through the storm, but without the shelter of his body as a windbreak, what would become of Larribee himself?

Time had been magnified. It seemed to race away. He told himself that the long hours had run away to darkness, and still they must lie there. Then the friction of the sand against his skin became the most intolerable torture. The itching was beyond credence and there followed this, in places, the burn of the raw flesh as the skin was chafed away. Yet, he remembered the words of the Cheyenne. Patience would conquer in the end, and anything was better than to rise and be harried away across the desert by the terrible force of that blast.

He kept his eyes closed so long that gradually the tears washed the balls clean. He could see again. Through the shelter of the lashes, the burning hot pupils could look out and see the gleam of purple-red daylight. Still, the weight of the wind was a thing not less solid but more, as it seemed.

Suddenly it stopped. As the first stroke of it had come in an instant, so in an instant it ended. There was not even the haze of fine dust following that had preceded it. Looking toward the east, he saw a vast purple wall receding toward the horizon, covering more than half of the wide arch of the sky, in the beginning, and then walking back and back. There appeared to be ten thousand striding giants, long-robed, retreating in that wall of mist.

Larribee stood up. The stallion, at a word, sprang to its feet, and, nearby, the Cheyenne arose with his mount. Then Larribee turned and looked anxiously back toward the spot where he had seen the colonel before the purple ink of the storm had blotted him out. But there was no sign of the colonel. Hastily, eagerly, with a great fear, Larribee stared about, looking for some telltale mound.

But everywhere the fierce hands of the wind had scourged the desert to a dead level, with only long streaks, here and there, that looked as though ten million whips had been lashed over the ground. But there was no sight of the colonel.

Larribee pointed, and Shouting Thunder came up to him. He looked at Larribee, and laughed a little.

"That was only a small blow," he said, "but it has made you a red man, my brother."

Larribee was too worried to be amused. "Back there," he said. "Where's our friend? Where's the colonel?"

"The wind has driven him a little," said Shouting Thunder, still smiling at the red face of Larribee, streaked with white where the tears had washed the surface silt away.

As the storm went farther away, sweeping the vast purple curtain along, the sun came out and shone, dazzling bright, with a fair, new-washed face. But still there was no sight of the colonel.

When the wall was an obscure thing, stretched across the eastern horizon, still they had no view of Colonel Pratt.

"So," said Shouting Thunder. "Sometimes I thought that it would be the colonel. He was quiet, but he had a great heart and seemed to live for the sake of the horse, only. But now you see that even a puff of wind was enough to blow him away."

"We must turn back and hunt for him," said Larribee.

"He may be as far as a horse can run in these hours," said the Indian. "Besides, we cannot turn back. You cannot turn back for my sake, and I cannot turn back for yours. If he is dead, we cannot help him again, and, if he is living, he will find our trail again."

Larribee took a great breath. He shook his head. He felt that it was the blackest treason, but he knew that the reasoning of the red man was stronger than his conscience. He turned his back upon the thought of the colonel, saying gloomily: "If we wait, the horses will get out of range of us. Their trail is out. The sand has been swept clean. We have to find them again, Shouting Thunder, and we can't wait for live men or dead."

CHAPTER THIRTY

They found the herd, not that day, but the next, picking up the trail about noon, and that night sighting the horses themselves. Whether it was due to the intelligence of the stallion, the effect of the storm, or the instinct of one of the leaders, if there were such, Sky Blue and his crowd had gone off at almost right angles to the original line of the march.

It was only the shrewdness of Shouting Thunder, wise in the ways of the desert, that enabled them to get to the herd once more, for he cast straight ahead into the void for half a day's ride, and then cast out in a vast semicircle to cut for sign.

But, having found the herd's trail once more, and having identified it surely through a distant glimpse of Sky Blue himself, Larribee felt a greater uneasiness than he ever had felt before. The pace at which they were riding was telling even on the black now, no matter how much he favored and pampered him, and the mustang on which Shouting Thunder rode was merely a shambling skeleton.

There is a tale abroad to the effect that once, in the old days, a white man abandoned a horse as exhausted and useless . . . that a Mexican found the poor beast and made it carry him for three more days before he forsook it as worthless . . . and then came the noble Indian and extracted a full week of travel from the nag before it fell dead beneath him.

While Shouting Thunder's methods were not quite as cruel as the tale suggests, more than once the flesh of Larribee crawled. When first they sighted the horses, there were three of them off to the south.

"Now," said Shouting Thunder, "we catch remounts. Those fellows down there are tired of following Sky Blue's pace. They want to drift to the side and take a more leisurely pace. You'll find his teeth marks on them, I bet. We'll have a look at them, my friend."

They turned to the south, and in an hour they had hold of the trailing lariats, worn short and thin, to be sure, of two of their own horses. The horses had lost weight, but nothing compared to the mustang that Shouting Thunder abandoned on the spot. Now they went forward at a quicker pace, the Indian riding the two mustangs a half day each, and Larribee's great weight borne by the black stallion alone. Even so, he more than matched the work of the mustangs, and kept in better flesh, as well.

They were passing now into a different and a better country. The sheer desert flat gave way to long swales and hollows, and the ground was a drab green, from a distance, with the growth of cactus, smoke trees, and mesquite. They had plenty of fuel for fires now, and their food was better, also, for they bagged plenty of rabbits and got a young deer on the second day in this more cheerful region.

Their close pursuit had begun to tell by the fourth day of this swifter riding. They picked up two more of their saddle string, catching them with ease, and now they went ahead with renewed vigor, with spare mounts for each.

Sky Blue's herd was melting away. The wild old mares and their foals were the first to stop and turn south or north from the line of the pursuit. There still remained a hardy group of seven or eight animals with Sky Blue. When the pursuers caught sight of them, however, the stallion was nearly always in the rear, urging on the band before him.

"Think," said Larribee, "where he would be now if he were not loaded down with all that baggage. Why, a thousand miles away from us."

"Well," said Shouting Thunder, "what man would be happy to win a race if there were no one to see his victory?"

He had a way of stopping the speeches of Larribee in this fashion with a terse statement. Larribee had grown used to it, and now he merely smiled, for they knew one another very well after the long trek. Two companions were behind them, one dead, the other perhaps now dying, and they were left alone to pursue their common goal.

In spite of extra saddle horses, they could not close in on Sky Blue. They could whittle down his herd, so that finally there were in his company only two young mares, as fleet as gazelles and as tough as coyotes. These clung to him, and their speed of foot was sufficient to keep the riders in the distance.

But it was never a great distance. Every day they had a glimpse of the trio, not so very far away, and each of these sights gave them fresh energy to push ahead. They were like hounds when they lift their heads from the scent and run with a clear view.

Then Shouting Thunder began to give way. It was a strange and awful thing to see him crumble under the long physical and nervous strain. The physical alteration was great enough, for all the spare flesh was burned away from his great frame. His cheeks were hollow. His eyes stared from the shadow of over-arching, massive brows. His lips were compressed. His nostrils flared. The breath of his greater determination seemed to be constantly passing in them. The unfleshed cords of his neck stood out, and at the base of it was a deep hollow.

But his spirit had altered more than his body. He began to be silent. Sometimes when Larribee spoke to him, he could see the Indian make an effort to control himself and then bring forth a gentle, quiet answer. By degrees Larribee in turn became silent, and spent much time anxiously watching his companion. A crisis was clearly at hand. Sometimes when he wakened in the night he would see that the Cheyenne had finished his sleep long ago, and was sitting hooded in a blanket, or striding restlessly up and down, waiting for the white man to waken.

At such time it was always the desire of the Cheyenne to press on, and, when he saw that Larribee was awake, he would indicate that desire by extending his long, sinewy arm in the direction of Sky Blue.

Larribee might argue that the horses already were worn out by the miles they had covered on that day, but arguments were of no use. The chief could only be silenced by an absolute "No."

Then one morning Larribee wakened to find that he had been deserted. He went on, greatly depressed, and in the middle of the morning he came upon Shouting Thunder stripping a saddle from a dead horse and changing it to the last strong mount in his string. He said nothing. The Cheyenne said nothing. Neither of them exchanged a word all during that day.

They camped that night in a mesquite break. A cold wind blew over them. The grit of sand was ever in their eyes, the moan of the wind in their ears, and their throats were doubly parched by the cold fire of alkali water. The ponies of Shouting Thunder's string were too tired to search for the scattered blades and bunches of grass. Only the wild-raised stallion busily hunted here and there. But he himself was far spent. His ribs stood out. The hollows could be seen even in the starlight, and his temples were sinking above his eyes, like those of an ancient horse.

Then Larribee broke the day's silence, saying: "Shouting Thunder, it seems to me that something is troubling you. Tell me what it is."

Shouting Thunder looked sullenly at him and answered:

"Well, brother, what is in my mind should not trouble you. Lie down and sleep. You still have fat to cover your bones and keep you warm."

Larribee did not attempt to answer this petulant speech, but he slept a troubled sleep all the night, remembering what the Indian had said, and feeling that the end of their long partnership was at hand.

When he awoke in the morning, however, Shouting Thunder was still there. They ate a wretched breakfast of venison that had been jerked by hanging it on a rope strung between their two horses as they rode along under the withering sun. It was as hard and black as a stone, with sand deeply embedded in it. It had no taste. It was like chewing wood. But they worried down a few mouthfuls apiece, and then they went on with the day's march. Twice in the course of the morning the Cheyenne changed his saddle from one stumbling pony to another. Larribee rode a length or so in the lead so that he would not have to watch Indian methods of encouraging a half-dead horse along a trail.

The wind died out in the midmorning, and the air turned sultry and dead. Breathing was difficult, and the ponies of Shouting Thunder stumbled more and more. But they kept on, for Sky Blue and his two skinny mares were hardly a quarter of a mile away. Even the head of Sky Blue was not carried high.

Something may happen now, Larribee thought to himself.

It was about noonday when they dropped suddenly into one of those narrow, steep-sided valleys that occasionally crossed the country. At most times the beds were dry or contained only a trickle of muddy water. Only when heavy rains fell in the hills of the headwaters did the courses fill with raging currents.

It was a desolate valley. It looked like a number of half sections of troughs, the largest on top, and at the bottom the least in size. It was a dry, white bed of pebbles and stones that this lowest trough showed.

As they dipped over the rim of the upper level there was the sound of thunder coming from upstream, distant but approaching. In that direction he could see the hills, their heads obscured with the inky dark of rain clouds.

He glanced toward the Indian, but Shouting Thunder, a fixed sneer upon his wasted lips, said not a word, and gouged the sides of his mustang to force it forward.

When they were well committed to the valley, the noise that approached them grew louder every instant. Well below them, Sky Blue had bounded up the steep bank of the bottom channel, but the place that had been possible for him was too difficult for the two mares, and they ran up and down, hunting for an easier place of ascent, while their master waited impatiently above.

Larribee hurried the black stallion forward. All the spurring and whipping of Shouting Thunder could not avail to keep him alongside, and so Larribee and the black slid down ahead to the stones and pebbles of the lowest bottom. As they reached it, Larribee looked to the right, and he saw the danger coming upon him like a stampede of buffalo.

CHAPTER THIRTY-ONE

It was what he had expected, but it was nonetheless fearful. Those black clouds over the hills must have split apart and emptied all their contents suddenly into the five hundred little ravines and smaller valleys that wound among them. And the thousand little heads of water, rushing down, had met and gathered in the central gorge. Now it came roaring, the forefront of it twenty feet high.

It crowded the lowest gorge. It spread a white arm of foam and thunder over the wider plateaus on either side of this bottom trough. It carried lightly in its tumult, stones, and even boulders, which Larribee saw bounding in the muddy froth like substances without weight. That moving wall had ripped trees of old growth from the sides of the ravine. It flourished the stripped poles in some of its million hands, hurling them straight ahead, or tossing forty-foot shafts into the air and catching them again.

The face of that charging water was terrible enough, but the sound of it was far worse, for it came with a roar and with a scream, as though thousands of buffalo were rushing there and dying as they ran.

Larribee looked at the bank before him. It was a full twenty feet high, and almost perpendicular. He looked behind him. The way there was still loftier, though a little less steep, and on the upper bank was Shouting Thunder, with a lariat coiled, ready to cast it to his blood brother in case of need. Naturally he remained where he was.

Larribee dismounted. Plainly the black could not make the ascent with the weight of a man on his back.

One of the mares had now managed to clamber up the bank to the side of Sky Blue; the other was now attempting it, but, failing near the crest, she slipped down and rolled on the pebbles below.

To that same place—it seemed the easiest in sight—Larribee ran with the black on a long lead. Above him he saw Sky Blue rearing back and retreating reluctantly, as though he wanted to stay close to the second member of his dwindling herd. Down the bank he galloped, and at a lower point he neighed loudly, to call the mare from below. The sound came to the ear of Larribee like a voice in a dream, or the blowing of a far distant horn that the roar of the city all but drowns.

The second mare, in the meantime, a young gray with black points, thin as a greyhound, but lovely in spite of her leanness, had scrambled to her feet and cantered down the rocky bottom to the point where big Sky Blue was calling her. He had wisely chosen an almost practicable slope for her to mount.

Now Larribee, driving in the toes of his moccasins and clinging with his hands, got to the top of the bank. He tightened the lariat that fastened to the throat of the black and shouted and waved as he pulled. The stallion rushed the bank. The impetus of his charge carried him halfway to the top, but there the force failed him. He struck vainly at the surface, and loosened an avalanche of earth and stones that washed him down to the bottom again.

Larribee dared not glance to the side, where the front of the water heads were pouring. But the black stallion glanced and, with a human scream of fear, wheeled and started down the bed of the river. The rope burned through the hands of Larribee. He shouted. He felt that his voice was lost in the uproar, but some electric message passing down the rope stopped the black.

Flight for him straight ahead was certainly vain. He might as well have tried to escape from a railroad train running away on a downgrade as from the speed of the currents that poured through that flume.

Just before them, as Larribee ran down the upper bank, he saw the gray mare gain the upper edge of the bank, topple there, then regain her hold with desperately clawing and striking fore-hoofs. Off she went, staggering over the level, with Sky Blue at her side, as though to encourage her and congratulate her on her escape.

Larribee was not thirty feet away. He could turn and hurl his second rope over the head of the stallion. It was an easy cast, with Sky Blue defying mankind and giving himself to the rescue of his mare. Yet the thought entered Larribee's head only to be cast out again. For the black was there below him.

On the opposite shore he was aware that Shouting Thunder was wildly gesturing, striving to point out the priceless opportunity that was being missed, but Larribee gave him no heed. He gritted his teeth. He leaned back with all his might against the lariat, and felt the rush of the black attempting to climb the slope. That rush would fail midway to the top. From then on it would be a matter of sheer force of hoofs and whatever power Larribee himself could lend.

The rush came. The rush stopped. Larribee laid back with all his might upon the rope. He saw the white heads of the water to his left, but he gave them no regard. He felt the upward course of the horse stopped. There was merely a succession of heavy jerks at the rope as the stallion struck out with all fours, and succeeded only in dislodging the rocks and soil beneath him.

Larribee dropped his head back between his shoulders and

looked up to the face of the sky, streaked with moving clouds and patched with brilliant blue. At that moment he felt the ascent of the stallion begin again, moving little by little, and then finally a sudden lurch that carried him straight over the upper rim. So sudden was that lurch that Larribee lost his footing and rolled headlong. He still had his clutch on the lariat, and, twisting over, he saw a mighty, scarred log driven from the water and shooting over the back of the black, missing it by inches.

The inner edge of the torrent ripped the wall of the ravine away; it struck the hind legs of the stallion. He was sinking. No, he had gathered himself again and sprung well in on the firm terrace, just as the lateral rush of the water, spreading more thinly over this ground, reached him, staggered him, and dashed white spray over him.

That small wave struck Larribee, also, before he could flounder to his feet, and it sent him rolling like a stone. It was the end, he told himself. Five hundred hands had hold upon him. They tore at him. Fingers closed upon his throat and nose to stifle him. Then all his weight came hard against the lariat, almost snatching it through his wet hands. He pulled himself in, an arm's length at a time, upon that anchorage. Regaining his feet, he caught one life-giving breath of air, one glimpse of what seemed to him a white world filled with dashing spray, and yonder his rock of hope, the black horse, almost overwhelmed, but steadfast in his place, as though he recognized the pull of his master's hands and well knew that it was life or death for him to keep his footing.

So Larribee won back to the horse, got on his back, and rode him through the swirling shallows to the dry safety of the third level of that ravine. He dismounted there, supporting his exhausted body by casting one arm over the streaming neck of the horse, and, looking back across the white, wide dashing of the water, he saw Shouting Thunder far away upon the farther bank.

When the Indian was certain that he had the eye of Larribee, he waved him on several times and pointed forward. Plainly he intended those signals to encourage him on the trail of Sky Blue. *And the Cheyenne himself?*—thought Larribee. *Leave him behind, after these weeks of brotherhood?* Shouting Thunder answered that mute question. He touched his breast and shook his head, as though to indicate that he was now of very little worth. He pointed to the mustangs, thin as knives, downheaded, thoroughly beaten by the terrible labor they had performed. Again he shook his head and waved to Larribee to continue. He pointed to the water that flooded down the banks higher and higher. Then, with a stiff arm that indicated the sun, he made a number of circles, as though to indicate that it would probably be many days before that water fell to a fordable level.

Perhaps it was the uproar of the dashing waters. Perhaps it was the sudden division of Shouting Thunder from his side, but it seemed to Larribee that he had come to the end of the world. On the farther side of the water it was cheerful, pleasant, filled with comforts, but upon this side it was dreary past speech, wretched. So he waved his hand to Shouting Thunder and turned. He was too weary to mount the stallion, and, with a hand entangled in the wet, black mane to help him forward, Larribee stumbled out across the plain beyond.

He did not look back again. He knew that the Cheyenne would be standing there at watch, and the sight of him, lonely and beaten, he feared, would be too much for his strength of will. He would weakly turn and go back. But there must be no turning back now. He lifted his head. Scarcely a hundred yards before him marched Sky Blue and the two exhausted mares. Their heads were down and their feet were trailing, but the head of the stallion was high, his neck was arched, his tail was carried proudly.

Larribee shook his head with despair. If it had been clear common sense that ruled him, then he would have turned back without further thought. But he was really far beyond the realm of reason. He was in that dreamy realm of the mystic to which Shouting Thunder had introduced him. Remembering the words of the Indian, he told himself that whatever fate ruled this world, it had determined beforehand what man, if any, should ride Sky Blue.

His own will was not enlisted. It was an extraneous force that pushed him onward relentlessly over rough and smooth. He continued until they came to a hollow. In the bottom of this he was shut off from any possible view of Shouting Thunder in the vanishing distance, and here he threw himself on the ground, sick with exhaustion, his face turned to the sky, but his eyes fast closed.

CHAPTER THIRTY-TWO

He made a short march that day, for the good reason that a long march was not necessary. The mares could not make one, and Sky Blue resolutely stuck by them. Larribee, as he stared at the thin hips of the mares and the loftier form of the stallion, had many thoughts that never had drifted over the portals of his mind before.

Life, it seemed to him, was not what he had dreamed it to be, not what he had lived of it. Pleasure could not be stolen, as he had striven to steal it, with crooked dice and card tricks. The cheat could win money, not happiness. Happiness was what those bloodthirsty Crows had tasted when they routed the outnumbering Pawnees. Happiness, again, was what the white leader of the Crows knew when he left his warriors, gave up his share of the great celebration of the nation, and faced forward alone upon the trail of the stallion. Happiness, once more, was that long struggle that he had shared with Shouting Thunder until this day. And now it was happiness, also, to struggle forward alone, just as the white chief had done.

His heart swelled, you may be sure, when he thought of that solitary man. If ever they met, for the sake of Sky Blue, there would be a battle worthy of the giants.

When he tried to analyze the emotion that forced him on, he could not say that it was merely for the possession of the stallion that he marched and endured. It was merely that by a long list of disasters, Sky Blue was fenced away from the hands of man and pronounced an impossible achievement. The lure of the unattainable was what urged Larribee, then, with an irresistible spur.

As for a horse to ride, was not the black enough? For gentleness and strong-hearted devotion, was not the black perfect? He was all that, and yet he was not a feather in the scale weighing against Sky Blue.

That sense of fate that now possessed Larribee told him, with a still and solemn voice, that one day he would again be seated on the back of the blue roan. On that day he would conquer, or on that day he would die—he or Sky Blue, or both together. He thought of it with certainty, without fear, with neither hope nor fierceness.

At the end of that march he came to a pool of water that looked black and foul, yet it was as sweet as spring water to the throat, and wonderfully cool, as though the full force of the sun had not beat on it all that day and the many scorching days before. On the eastern side of that pool he made his camp. On the western side was the stallion and the two mares.

Some brush grew here. Utterly weary, he forced himself to cut down enough to pile up a good bed. He steadied his shaking hands, and, with the rifle that he had unstrapped from the side of the black and carefully cleaned to prevent rusting, he shot a sage hen. It was tough meat, rank with the smell and the almost unendurable taste of the sage. But Larribee cooked it and ate it greedily to the last morsel. He had no salt, no bread. He had nothing but a few scraps of the wood-like jerked venison and a few grains of the parched corn. Even his ammunition was growing low.

But he cared little about that. He was willing to throw his fate on the chance of tomorrow. So that night he lay under the clean face of the stars and told himself that he was not alone. His friend, a thin black stallion, was grazing beside him, and presently it would lie down, so close that he could reach out his hand and touch it. On the other side of the still water was Sky Blue, the enemy, or, rather, not an enemy at all, but the great goal of all his effort.

He fell asleep. He had no dream, but a strange sense that life was blowing through his soul, as the cold wind blows through the naked mountains, and that the obscure vapors were being carried away, and he was being purified.

When he awoke it was at that time when night seems darkest, but the distant mountains were black and visible in the deep darkness, so he knew that light was coming up behind them in the east. Day was about to begin.

He forced himself up on his hands, and then he saw, seated beside the dying and dead coals of the fire, the figure of a man. He was wrapped in a blanket, his head was bowed; he looked like one who is asleep sitting up.

The heart of Larribee grew soft. "Shouting Thunder," he said, "I knew that you would manage to cross. I'm glad we made a short march today, though I don't know how you managed to find the trail after dark."

"I saw you camp when it was still daylight," answered a quiet voice. "And I am not the Cheyenne."

"Who the devil are you then?" exclaimed Larribee. He brought out a revolver as he spoke.

"There's no need of the gun," said the stranger. "It's foolish to pick up a gun now."

Larribee felt ashamed, for he saw the logic of this. If the other man intended harm to him, there had been plenty of chances to murder him while he was still asleep. Larribee sat up straighter and shook his head to clear his wits. "It's a strange thing," he said. "Here's a horse that ought to let me know the minute that a stranger comes in sight . . . he's better than a watchdog." For the black was standing there beside him, facing toward the stranger with eyes that glimmered in the starlight, but never a sound of warning had he made.

"Don't blame the horse," said the other. "The fact is I took a good hour and a half moving up to the camp, and I came so slowly that he didn't know whether I was a rock or a stick at first. Afterward he stood up to make sure, and I inched my way into the camp."

"What made you so cautious?" asked Larribee.

"Oh," said the other, "I know you, and I know that you have a nervous hand with a revolver."

"You know me, do you?" said Larribee.

"About as well as you know yourself," said the stranger.

"The mischief," said Larribee.

"At least, I think I know you that well," said the other. "I've been at your camps a dozen times or so."

"If you were a shade smaller . . . no, a good bit smaller, and had a different voice . . . ," said Larribee.

"No, I'm not the colonel," said the other.

"Then who are you, if you've been a dozen times at my camp?"

"No one you could call a friend," said the stranger.

"Look here," said Larribee, "I don't like mystery."

"Don't you? I think you do," said the other. "And you'd admit it, if you'd look fairly and squarely at yourself."

"*Humph*," said Larribee. "Suppose you tell me how you make that out?"

"Suppose you tell me," said the stranger, whose quiet and assured voice never varied except to hold a shade of amusement from time to time, "suppose you tell me what keeps you on the trail of the stallion, with a couple of dead men already behind you, and death scratching under your own door more than once, Larribee."

"Tell you?" said Larribee. "Why, if you'd ever seen Sky Blue

you would know why I trail him. Suppose you tell me what
has . . . ? By thunder," he broke off.

"Well?" said the form in the darkness.

"I know you now . . . ," said Larribee.

"I don't think you do," said the stranger.

"I do, though. You're the fellow who was with the Crows."

"That's a fair guess," he said. "I'm the man."

"You're the one who almost had Sky Blue in your hands."

"I almost had him," said the stranger. "That's true, also."

"Well," said Larribee, "if that's the case, here's my hand.
You're a man, stranger." He rose and made the offer, but the
other, rising in turn, stepped back a little.

"You don't want my hand, Larribee," he said. He was almost
as tall as Larribee, but, even with his robe, he looked much
slighter. The latter stared hard through the dim light.

"Why don't I want your hand?" asked Larribee. "There's
never been anything between us."

"There's been hell between us," answered the stranger calmly.

"Go on," urged Larribee. "I tell you I hate these mysteries
and this sneaking up in the dark. What is the meaning of it?"

"If I had come up during the day, you would surely have shot
me down," said the other.

"I?" cried Larribee. He paused and studied the vague form
before him. "I don't suppose that you mean this for a joke," he
said, "but my temper is getting a little short. Stranger, I respect
you. I've seen you handle those Pawnees like a lot of schoolchil-
dren. And I've seen you leave your own men and take the trail
alone. But I hate this beating about the bush."

The other stepped back a little. "I'll tell you my name," he
said. "But remember, Larribee, that I could have killed you in
the dark of the night while you lay there."

"*Tush*," said Larribee. "I'm not a murderer. Out with your
name, then."

"I'm Josiah Ransome," said the other.

The name struck the mind of Larribee as the point of the hammer strikes the cap. He leaped across the intervening space and caught Ransome by the throat. There was no resistance. It was a yielding form that he attacked.

Suddenly he remembered, and his hands dropped helplessly to his sides.

CHAPTER THIRTY-THREE

Ransome, fingering his throat for a moment where the brief touch of Larribee had bruised the flesh, did not speak first. It was Larribee who said: "I'm sorry, Ransome."

No more perturbed in manner than he had been before, Ransome answered: "You shouldn't have done that, but you're only human, I suppose. You couldn't help having it all come over you . . . that I'm the cause of your being out here and all the trouble that you've had. Gurry would be living and making money on the racetrack if it hadn't been for me, and you'd be getting rich placing your bets."

At this statement of the facts as they might have been, Larribee turned a keen eye upon the past and saw it as it had been, and he saw, above all, that he was no longer what he once had been. "If you hadn't taken Sky Blue out of my hands," he replied, "I would have sponged on him while he was young enough to win races, and then I would have slipped into the ways of a rotten gambler. I know myself now. I never would have got my hands. . . ." He stopped.

"On what?" asked Ransome.

Larribee laughed. "On something worth doing," he said tersely. "I think you know exactly what I mean, Ransome. Sit down here. There's enough light to start breakfast."

"Get the fire going," answered Ransome. "I have some deer meat that was killed no longer back than yesterday evening. I'll bring it up with the horses."

When he came back, the firewood for the breakfast had been gathered, and the flame was mounting brightly through the semidarkness of the dawn. There was enough light to show the hollow sides of Ransome's two pintos and the man himself.

If Larribee had met him in the daytime, he never would have recognized that pampered son of the major. It was a bronze-faced wraith that he saw, a hollow-eyed, sunken-cheeked, lean fellow whose eyes were bright with a strange fire and whose lips were drawn back a little at the corners into a sad smile.

Larribee did the cooking and busied himself over it with his head down, for the good reason that he did not care to look too closely at his new companion. Ransome sat down, cross-legged, like an Indian, and smoked an Indian pipe with a red clay bowl.

"You've turned Crow," observed Larribee.

"Have I?" asked Ransome. "Yes, in a way, I suppose. They're a good lot, mind you, the Crows."

Larribee grunted. "The Cheyennes don't like 'em," he said, "and I'm a Cheyenne. This meat is done now. Here you are."

They sat down and ate. They had the roasted, unseasoned meat and clear water to drink with it, but each thought that he never had tasted anything better.

When they had finished it was not yet sunrise, though the pink was bright in the east and a pale band of the cheerful color circled all of the horizon.

Ransome refilled his half-emptied pipe and began smoking again. "I thought that you were gone yesterday," he said.

"Were you at the ford?" asked Larribee curiously.

"I was above it. I was in the patch of rocks on the hill north of it. I'd gone over there, and I looked back and saw you beggars coming along, so I waited to see what your luck would be. I'd made up my mind, if you got across, I'd put a rifle bullet through you, Larribee."

The latter nodded, as though this were the simplest and most easily understood remark.

"Then, when you went down into the ravine," went on Ransome, "I made pretty sure that that would be the last of you. I wouldn't have laid one dollar against ten on your life. I sat still and grinned and waited for the water to swallow you. Afterward I saw that you had your chance . . . that you were as good as across. My blood boiled, I can tell you, when I saw Sky Blue in casting distance from you. I took up my rifle and drew a good bead on you. It was the time when you turned and raised your hand with the rope in it."

"I know," said Larribee, nodding. He was smoking, also, contentedly, with his eyes half closed. His attitude was that of one who hears of events that have happened in another time, long before his own day. But he was thinking to himself, without emotion: *One day I'll have to kill this Ransome.*

Ransome went on: "Then, when the white water caught you and rolled you under for two seconds, I was rather sorry, but when I saw you up again, fighting for your life, and the way that black anchored himself and held you . . . sort of turn and turn about . . . then I got up my rifle again. But somehow I couldn't shoot."

"That was decent of you," said Larribee. "I think I would have shot."

"Well, I came within an inch of it. I was closing my finger over the trigger, and then something stopped me," he explained in the most casual manner. "I think it was because I looked over the whole affair and guessed that fate intended that you should get Sky Blue. When you got out of the white water, I mean, and it was clear that you were coming off scotfree. That was the time that I did my thinking. It was a little too much luck, or whatever you want to call that."

"You sound to me," said Larribee, yawning a little, "like a praying man."

"It's a habit I've got into," said Ransome. "How about yourself?"

Then Larribee looked back at the moment when he was pulling against the lariat and his bulging, straining eyes were staring up into the face of the sky. He had prayed then, he did not know to what. He said tersely: "Well, I've done my praying, too . . . for a horse."

Ransome smiled. "It's a long way to Fort Ransome," he suggested.

"Yeah. About half a life," confessed Larribee. "What happened to you, Ransome? You've walked out from a comfortable home, and all that sort of thing."

"It was comfortable"—Ransome nodded—"but I left just when the discomfort would have begun. There wouldn't have been any peace for me after that day, with my mother despising me openly and my father despising me secretly. I got out my best horse and slipped away with a light pack and a good deal of money. I didn't even leave a note behind me, because I thought that it wouldn't be necessary.

"On the way I had an idea. About Sky Blue. I'd been the ruin of him. I'd ripped several men out of their normal lives and started them out on the chase, you see, and I promised myself that I'd catch that infernal beast and bring him back, and then everything would be nearly all right."

"Did you see us on the trail?" asked Larribee.

"Yes, I saw you. Of course, I saw you more than once. But I kept out of the way. I knew what sort of a reception I would have had from the three of you. Then, out on the plains, I had an exceedingly queer adventure."

"What was that?"

"It was like this, you see."

"Well?" urged Larribee as the other hesitated.

"I was taking a bead on an antelope, a long shot. Just as I

was getting the bead, I shifted the gun a little to make allowance for a wind that was blowing, and, as I shifted it, I saw an Indian's face looking out through the tall grass of a hummock, and the Indian had a rifle leveled at me. Mind you, I looked at that gun so hard that I made out the octagonal barrel of it . . . a real old Kentucky rifle of the most antique brand. So I shifted my aim down, and we fired at the same instant. Perhaps my bullet was a shade ahead of his. His shot clipped through my shoulder and made a fine long cut of it. Mine ripped through the middle of him, and up he jumped, a crop-headed Pawnee, with feathers and all. He gave one whoop and dropped back into the grass. I started crawling toward him to see if he were done for or just ready for more fighting."

Larribee nodded. "A dangerous business," he said.

"It's mighty dangerous. And I played the fool, too," said Ransome. "I had a fine double-barreled rifle, but I didn't stop to load the empty barrel. I just cut away through the grass, and I suppose that I made as much noise as a pig. At any rate, when I was about halfway to the right place, I thought I felt something behind me. I know I didn't see it, and I hardly heard it, either. But I turned sharp around, and there was a pair of the same crop-headed rascals sneaking after me, with their rifles at the ready.

"I took a snap shot at one of them without raising the stock of my rifle, and I got him dead center. He bowled right over on the grass, holding onto himself with both hands, and started kicking up the grass. The other Indian let drive at me, but I was so close that he must have been overconfident. At any rate, he took such bad aim that he missed, and then he chucked away his rifle and came in at me with his knife.

"Well, I didn't have time to get to my feet even . . . I only managed to rise to one knee, and then I clubbed him over his head with the butt of my rifle. He went down, too, and went down like a log." He paused and puffed slowly at his pipe. "I'm afraid that I've made myself out a hero, Larribee, disposing of three red men like that. As a matter of fact, I was scared to fits. I've heard about how you fought it out with big Shouting Thunder. That took real nerve. But I was a cornered rat, you might say. At any rate, I was watching the second fellow die in the grass and the third one come back to life by degrees, and I was wondering what I should do about him, when I looked up and saw a dozen more red men come trooping in on me. They were all around me, mind you.

"I picked up my rifle, but I'd broken it past fixing on the hard skull of the third man. Then I saw those new Indians making signs of friendship. Next I noticed that they wore their hair in a different fashion. It was very long, d'you see? In short, since I was practically disarmed, there was nothing for it but to let them come up, which they did. Then I discovered that they were enemies of the fellows I had killed. They were Crows, in fact, and the three I had put out of commission were all Pawnees. So that explains how I got in with the Crows and all the rest of it."

CHAPTER THIRTY-FOUR

"It explains a good deal. But not everything," said Larribee. "They took a knife and passed it into the Pawnees you had stunned, I suppose?"

"Yes. They did that as a matter of course. They took the scalps and the loot of all three and brought the whole pile to me, by jingo, with the three scalps lying on top of the heap, a most disgusting sight. I managed to make them understand that I didn't want any of that stuff. But one of the Pawnees had a goodish sort of a rifle, and I took that for my share and a good lot of ammunition for it. I wondered, at the time, what poor white had been murdered for the sake of the weapon."

"The Crows made a great fuss over you after that, I suppose," said Larribee.

"You've no idea, really," said Ransome. "I was the right sort of medicine, in their minds, right away. They couldn't do enough for me. They took me back to their nearest village and held their scalp dance with a lot of fuss and feathers. I had to make a speech."

"In Crow?" asked Larribee.

"They had a half-breed with them who spoke English better than I ever will. I made my little speech. It cost me about a dozen words, and I simply said, like a fool, that I was lucky and all that, but that I had a natural leaning toward Crows and away from Pawnee wolves. That interpreter took hold of my dozen words and expanded them. He was a regular improviser. Before he was going a minute, he began to get the whoops out of them. By the end of three minutes he had them swaying, pulling out knives, and making faces. I thought the scoundrel was misrepresenting me, and that the whole tribe was getting ready to cut my throat. Instead of that, it seems that he was telling them . . . I learned from the rascal himself later on . . . that I always had thought the Crows were the greatest people in the world, and that I had come out there into the plains 'specially to join them . . . that the three dead Pawnees were simply my peace offering and gift to the tribe . . . that I was ashamed of making such a modest present as three scalps, and that I hoped to do a lot better later on. Well, before he finished, they were in a stew. They all got up and made speeches. Before the evening was over, five chiefs had fetched around to me and offered me daughters in marriage, together with whole flocks of horses. But I didn't want a red wife, and there was only one horse in the world that I wanted."

"I understand," said Larribee. "And they gave you men and horses to follow the blue roan right off?"

"Well," said Ransome, "another little thing happened. But you'll think that I'm blowing my own horn a good deal."

"Tell me about it," said Larribee.

"The Pawnees were pretty hot at those Crows," went on the narrator, "and they sent out a big war party to beat up the camp. They made a feint at the camp one morning about dawn, and the whole body of warriors tumbled out, grabbed horses, and started out to fight the Pawnees, as brave as you please. As soon as they were a good distance off, a small band of Pawnees who had been left behind for the purpose came riding in and took the village from behind. That was their scheme for fighting. A scalp is a scalp in the eyes of an Indian, you know."

"I know," said Larribee.

"It happened," said Ransome, "that I was not at all ready to go galloping off with the first war party. I thought they could handle their battles for themselves, and I was very glad to hear the sound of the shooting die out in the distance. In the meantime, the old men, the children, and the squaws gave me some pretty black looks, I can tell you. In the midst of all this, while I was congratulating myself on getting out of danger, in comes the second party of the Pawnees, whooping and yelling like demons. We had about one minute to get ready, and it was a pathetic and awful thing to see the old men grab their antiquated guns and old bows and arrows, whatever had been left behind by the fighting warriors of the camp.

"There was no funking. The men got their play bows and fitted sharp arrows on the strings. The women picked up clubs and knives, anything they could lay their hands on. There were three wounded men in the camp, and they came out, with two or three of the sick, barely able to walk. They all came out and gathered together on the run . . . or the crawl, as the case might be . . . and they stood up in a line in the main avenue that ran through the camp like brave . . . well, brave fools."

"Well," said Larribee, "what else could they do?"

"You see," said Ransome, "when I heard the roar of the hoofs coming, I knew that the Pawnees would wash right through our pitiful ranks and spear and knife us as they went. So I waved to the Crows and yelled, and they got my idea and drew back to one side of the open way, and scattered out among the teepees. Do you see?"

"Not exactly," said Larribee.

"It worked like this," said Ransome, his eye kindling a little and his nostrils flaring as he spoke, remembering the action. "Those Pawnees came in a dense crowd through the gap among the Crow lodges. They were yelling like fiends, and the sound of the horses made me think there must be a thousand of them. But as they came by the armed party, we let them have it. You can see how it would turn out. There was no doubt from the first. We couldn't miss. Every bullet and every arrow was bound to hit a man or a horse, and, as the men dropped off or the horses rolled, there were those squaws, shrieking like fiends, to run in with clubs and knives and finish off the survivors.

"Well, the Pawnees ran the gantlet, all right, but those who got through rode as if a special demon was clawing the rump of each horse, and they had no intention of coming back. What the Crows did to those Pawnees was a good deal too horrible for words. I tell you that I saw a boy of thirteen the next day wearing two brand-new, fresh scalps. And he wasn't getting a crowd of attention, either. There were others doing the same thing.

"Now, when the main body of Crow warriors got back from chasing their Pawnees, they had done nothing but skirmish at a distance. One of them had keen killed, and the dead body was brought back, and there were half a dozen more or less seriously injured. But back there in the home camp they found the Pawnees laid out, and not a single scratch had been received in the defense of the village. There was no chance, of course. We stood in the dark and fired into the solid mass of the riders. Children could have done it. Children and old men did do it, as a matter of fact. So there you see how it went.

"From my particular point of view, what mattered was that they insisted on giving me the whole credit. They said that I had devised the scheme, which was fairly true, for what the scheme was worth. But what chiefly counted with them was that they said the Sky People had kept me there in the village to protect it, and that I must possess about the strongest medicine known. So that gives you an idea of why I got a high standing with the Crow nation."

"You deserved everything that you got, Ransome," said Larribee. "That was a fine thing. You're talking yourself down."

"I'm not," said Ransome. "I'm telling you the facts, but the telling makes it seem worse than it was. However, after that night I could get what I wanted out of the tribe."

"Naturally," said Larribee.

"I'm ashamed to say that I laid about and got fat at the feasts that were given in my honor. And while I was lying about, I heard the story of how the three white men had been captured by the Cheyennes, and how one of them had fought big Shouting Thunder to the finish, and become a blood brother to him in the course of the fight. Well, that was enough for me to identify the three of you, and you as the great fighter.

"I decided that I would have to get out on the trail of Sky Blue at once. Mind you, I had changed my mind since I started on that trail. I began by wanting to put myself right, and by capturing the stallion and returning it. But in the weeks that followed, when I was led on from day to day, I made up my mind that I wanted the big horse for myself."

"I know." Larribee nodded. "I've thought of murder, even . . . murder of my own camp friends, even. Go on."

"Have you?" said Ransome eagerly. "Well, Larribee, I'm glad to hear that, because it will make you understand. Sky Blue was in my blood. He's still in my blood. I told the Crows about that horse. I called him a medicine horse. And I got a picked batch of seven strong young warriors and some of the finest ponies in the camp, and I started off after Sky Blue.

"You know how we fell in with bad luck and got at Sky Blue just at the time that a pack of Pawnee thieves came onto the same trail. The mischief was in that. I can't say otherwise. The rest of the way I've gone on alone, and I found the four of you riding along, then three, then two, and finally just one man . . . yourself. That's why I came in here, Larribee."

"I still don't see," said Larribee. "Won't you tell me why you came in?"

"Tell me this," said the other. "What sort of chance do you

think you have of catching Sky Blue so long as you work by yourself?"

"A mighty skinny one," admitted Larribee.

"In fact, you've been plugging along, simply blindly hoping that something will happen. Isn't that true?"

"Yes, that's about it."

"Now, then, Larribee, don't you see that the something has happened?"

"No, I don't."

"Well, then, look here. You and I have stayed with the trail the longest. The horse ought to fall to one of us. So, then, let's throw in together . . . brains and body and horses and all. I have two tired horses and you have one good one. We both want the blue roan as badly as we could want anything. Suppose, then, that we play together. We work like fiends to get the big fellow. And if we nail him, then we'll roll dice for him."

Larribee stared at him. "Where in thunder will we get dice in this part of the world?" he asked.

"I have a pair," said Ransome, "in my saddlebag . . . I don't know why I've kept them. For luck, perhaps. Will you take this chance with me?"

Larribee sighed. "It would be a hard thing," he said, "for a man to give up Sky Blue because of what a pair of dice said to him."

"It would," said the other. "Each of us would have to trust to his honor and to fate. Here's my hand waiting for you, Larribee. Will you take it?"

And Larribee, with something of a groan, stretched out his great hand and received into it the skinny, cold fingers of Josiah Ransome.

CHAPTER THIRTY-FIVE

For a day Larribee inwardly regretted that he had admitted Ransome to that partnership. After that his regrets disappeared. Almost at once, Ransome showed the power of intelligence applied to every problem of the trail. He used his wits and picked up valuable information. Even Shouting Thunder, cunning as he had been in following the trail through the obscurities of shifting sands and over rocks where only the dimmest imprints were left, had clung rather blindly and stubbornly to the trail itself and refused to take chances by striking off ahead in the probable direction the horse would follow, so cutting corners and saving miles of distance. He stuck to the trail as to the windings of a necessary road. But Ransome was very different. He played as at a gambling table, taking long chances, and suddenly Larribee was able to understand how his companion had been able to keep to the trail with so much less effort than he and his friends had expended.

If the trail of the herd seemed directed toward some distant pass, then Ransome forgot the herd and made the pass his goal. He traveled toward it as a bird flies, and the straight line was sure to save whole leagues from the curving line along which the wild horses traveled.

He would say: "Add two to two. Our pounds in the saddle are anchors that hold back our nags. There's the stallion with nothing to hold him but the tired mares he herds along. Well, if he's fool enough to do that, let's use human brains and beat him."

"But the horses," argued Larribee, "know where water is, or can smell it out better than we can. We're apt to die of thirst, taking short cuts."

"We're apt to die anyway, sooner or later," said Ransome in his calm, sure way. "We gamble on water or we gamble on miles. We have to gamble to win. For Sky Blue really holds the best cards. He's stronger and he's faster. How else can we beat him?"

Larribee spent two days with his heart in his mouth taking those chances. After that he mildly surrendered to the superior wits and guidance of his companion. For he could see the results. They saved from thirty to fifty percent of the distance they would otherwise have traveled, as a rule. And they noticed the effect on their horses at once. The mustangs, to be sure, picked up but slowly, but the black stallion, as they got into a country of better grazing, altered almost at once, his head coming higher, his barrel filling out. The old spring came back into his step to replace the leaden and mechanical heaviness of gait that had been his for many days.

He was regaining his antelope qualities. On the other hand, the blue roan was no longer setting the pace. At the end of nearly every day he had to endure a long, hard run, which was sure to strip pounds from his flesh and draw on his reserve strength. How could he learn to imitate the men and straighten the winding courses along which he wandered during the day, pausing of necessity to crop the grass here and there?

They came in this manner into a new land. To Larribee it seemed the wildest and the most beautiful he ever had seen. It was a land of moving waters, of many trees, of noble hills, and great-shouldered mountains behind them—a wide valley, watered with more than a score of small streams that wandered down from the hills, and at the mouth of the valley formed a river. All of this was a green land, where the grass grew so luxuriantly close that the hoofs of a horse sprung upon it; in an hour or two the most famished animal could get its fill in this land of plenty.

When the blue roan entered the great valley he traveled up to its head, where it narrowed to closely crowding hills, with the mountains behind them. Then he wandered down again, crossed the streams by the many fords, and turned up the farther side of the valley again.

"He's found his domain, Larribee. He's found his chosen realm, I tell you," said Ransome. "And here he'll settle down. I've been half expecting him to find a place after his liking. And now at last he's landed where he wants to stay."

Larribee looked over the valley and nodded. "It's a place where a horse would like to camp," he agreed. "And where a man might like to stay, too. I never saw better. You could spread your elbows out in this part of the world, Ransome."

The other looked sharply at him. "It's a long cry from here to saloons and card tables and dice, Larribee," he said.

Larribee met the glance and merely smiled. "It's a long way and a long time," he said. He could not help having a very odd feeling that Ransome was disappointed in this attitude of his.

"I thought you wanted Sky Blue for the racetrack," said Ransome as sharply as before.

"I want him as you want him," said Larribee. "I want him as even an Indian would want him. But look at this place, Ransome. This is a regular hole-in-the-wall place for a horse. He can dodge us and hide up in the valleys, get fat, and laugh at us."

"That's what I want him to do," said Ransome. "We'll just sit down here and look things over and let the king settle into his kingdom. You know, Larribee, the worst thing for a horse or a man is to despise danger just because he's been beaten to it once."

"You mean that for me, Ransome, I suppose?" said Larribee.

"Mean it for you?" said Ransome, sneering. "Why should I mean it for you?"

"Because I beat you once and put a mark on you," said Larribee bluntly. "You're warning me not to despise you. That's all."

"Stuff!" protested Ransome. "I don't mean that at all. Don't play the baby and grow sensitive. Remember that I'm talking about a horse, and not about a man. I say that Sky Blue has learned to despise us. Well, he may have to pay for that with a saddle on his back one of these days."

They settled down in the middle of the valley, with water close by and plenty of food. They built themselves a small shack, which they knocked together in half a day, and they found that they hardly needed to stir from their shelter to shoot all the game they could possibly use.

For two or three days they allowed the horses to rest, and like all wild or half-wild things, they recuperated rapidly. After that they made a gradual exploration of the valley.

Their first day's ride taught them that Sky Blue had increased his herd. First they found the sign of many horses. Next they saw in the distance three- or four-score mustangs, with the noble form of the blue roan at the head of them. Finally, in a broad meadow, they found a great stallion, iron-gray, with four black stockings and a starred forehead, lying dead. His skull had been beaten in by the strokes of Sky Blue's forehoofs. There were few other scars about him, and the ground was not greatly trampled.

"You see how the tiger acted?" said Ransome with his usual sneer. "He went in with a rush. This is his stride, covering the grass. He lunged. There's the sign of his teeth on the throat of the gray. When he missed a good hold, he wheeled here . . . this is the mark of his hind hoofs as he stood up and smashed in the skull of the gray with a stroke or two. I'll wager that there's hardly a mark on him from the fight. Here's where he went off, and no blood dripping over the green."

That seemed to be the story. They looked again at the stallion in the distance, and he seemed as thin, still, as the desert had left him, but prouder than ever.

Where had the strange stallion come from? Over the mountains? They followed the back trail of the herd and they found that it led into a little box of a valley about two miles long and a quarter as wide. Into it there were a pair of entrances that communicated with the larger valley, a little creek winding in at the upper one and coming out at the lower through these narrow gaps. It was a small freak of landscape architecture.

"What does it look like to you?" asked Ransome.

"Like a grand place to build a home," said Larribee.

"Shall I tell you what it looks like to me?" said the other.

"Go on, Ransome. Your bright little eye is telling me that you've found an idea. What is it?"

"I'll tell you, then. It looks to me as though we've found the trap for the big boy. This is the open pair of doors. All we need to do is to slam them both and lock them in his face and there he is, Larribee, ready for the hand of the master trainer."

And he bowed to Larribee and sneered in his very face.

CHAPTER THIRTY-SIX

It was Ransome's theory that the horses would use the entrance and exit to the smaller adjacent valley as a regular means of escape from pursuit. So he and Larribee ran the herd three days in succession to try out the theory with fact. Ransome was right. If Sky Blue led the herd through the lower gate, he would come swinging out again through the upper one and back once more to the lower, making it like children's chase around the table, endless and never to be won.

When this habit was established, the two began to work out Ransome's scheme. He was the director of everything. Larribee was merely the slave who labored and rarely spoke. There was no pretense of good feeling between them. Ransome openly and thoroughly hated the larger man, and Larribee felt envy and deep distrust for Ransome. He envied the keen wits of his companion; he feared them just as much.

Now for many days they worked after sunset and slept in the hours of sunshine. This was at Ransome's direction. In the nights, in the beginning, they went to the upper pass. Across it they dug a series of eight holes. Between the steep walls of the gap was a space of some thirty yards, and the idea of Ransome was to prepare so that a fence could be thrown up quickly at a moment's notice. To that end they felled eight saplings and cut them twelve feet long. Four feet of the base would fit into the holes. Eight feet would project above the ground.

They prepared other lighter poles that could be lashed across the uprights to make the fence. The better to secure it in the closely wooded slopes on either side, they felled a quantity of thorny brush fit to make a formidable *cheval-de-frise* or abatis. The holes, as they dug them, they blocked securely at the top with pieces of wood fitted for the purpose, and laid over all a few chunks of earth. The horses might very well notice the scent of man, but the ground was firm beneath their hoofs, and the trap was too thoroughly concealed and incomplete to alarm them greatly.

Moreover, the length of time during which the work progressed gave the herd a chance to become accustomed to it when it chanced to come that way. For ten nights, working constantly and with fervor, the two men toiled. The felling of the trees and the brush was the least part of the work. The excavations were what required the greatest time.

Now that the upper gap was ready to be closed, they turned their attention to the lower. This was of a slightly greater width, and the trees did not grow so conveniently near. On the other hand, there was a great quantity of brush available, and Ransome suggested that the fence should be composed of this alone, a young mountain of thorny branches to spread across a hundred feet of grassy floor, from rocks to rocks. The brush they cut night after night and piled up in enormous masses.

At last Ransome declared that the time had come.

They waited half a week, until a day when Sky Blue and his followers were grazing on the opposite side of the valley. When this was discovered, in the dawn of the day, they went immediately to the lower gap, and there started furiously to work dragging the brush onto the level. It had been prepared in vast bundles, tied about in the center with long arms of runner vines. A bundle at a time, each man hitched himself to a burden and dragged it across to its place. They made the wall two bundles deep; that is to say, about fifteen feet, and they piled it two and three high, which gave a wall of twelve to fourteen feet. It seemed to Larribee that the dimensions were twice as great as need be, but Ransome assured him that wild horses, driven frantic, might stampede into a much more solid wall than this and knock it flying.

By noon they had completed barely half their wall. By sunset, trembling with fatigue, they threw the last bundle of thorns on top of the structure.

"And now," said Ransome, "we'll start the drive."

It was not so easily done as said. In driving the horses forward, they had to make sure that they were confined to the upper end of the valley, so as to make it more probable that they would use the upper gate. Ransome, riding one of his pintos, got behind the herd and started it drifting from the eastern side of the big valley. Larribee, keeping to the north and as much out of sight as possible, rode the black at a distance, ready to turn, if he could, a rush of the horses in his direction.

It went very smoothly until almost the end. Ransome got the herd across the creeks, one after another, without driving them too hard. In fact, the wild brood paused to graze here and there. They were thoroughly used to man by this time, and thoroughly trusted their powers to defeat all his purposes.

But when they got across the last creek and were heading through toward the upper pass, some freak of fancy caused Sky Blue to turn to the north. With one ringing neigh, which Larribee heard like the call of a trumpet to battle, Sky Blue gathered his followers and led them at a rapid gallop toward the broader end of the valley that lay northward.

Larribee, dismayed, looked at the broad front of that charge. He had not a chance in ten thousand of turning them. They would simply split in two parts and flow around him as easily as water flows around a rock in the bed of a course. No shouts or

219

brandished hands would stop them. They were too accustomed to these things.

He watched that rush of fine horses through the twilight and told himself that their labor was lost, for, as the horses ran north, they could not help passing the southern gate to the inner valley, and so discover that one of their two entrances was blocked. So wise a brain as the blue roan's would shun the sanctuary from that moment forward.

It was no process of careful thought, but mere despair that taught Larribee what to do then. He simply called on the black, and, driving it forward at furious speed, he let the reins hang loose, took a revolver in each hand, and began to fire. The noise wakened the echoes on the hillsides, and they came tumbling back with a confused roar. The guns spat fire on either side of the head of Larribee, until he must have looked to the oncoming mass of animals like some frightful beast with horns of electric flame.

They wavered. He saw the host shake. They rolled to either side, and, with a groan, he saw that the mob was splitting in sunder just as he had foreseen.

He felt he had one chance left. With a wild screech, he drove the black stallion at a racing gallop straight at Sky Blue. He saw the great roan dodge to one side, then swerve to the other. But the exploding, flashing guns of Larribee were too much for Sky Blue. He wheeled about, turned tail, and, with a frantic neigh that called his followers after him, he fled south toward the head of the valley.

Larribee pulled the black horse down to an easier stride. Through the dimness of the twilight, toward his left, he could see Ransome on his pinto coming in. Ransome also galloped his horse easily. Speed was not necessary now. They held back and watched the mass of horses pass, boiling through the gap.

Crowding close together, the colts and the old mares went

last of all. The thunder of their hoofs roared upon the ground, reëchoed from the rock walls on either hand.

Then Ransome and Larribee threw themselves to the ground and began to work with a frantic energy. They did not strive to thrust the posts into the ground. That was a slow and wretched labor. Instead, they dragged out quantities of the brush they had heaped up, and scattered it in bunches here and there.

They worked with a frantic speed, for in the distance they could hear the long, withdrawing thunder of the herd as it swept down to the lower pass, and then their hearts stopped. The roar of hoofs had ended. It began again. It swept furiously back toward the upper pass.

"Now fire!" shouted Ransome, his calm gone, his voice a choked scream. "Light the brush, Larribee! Light the brush! Quick!"

They kindled small piles of tinder. They ran from one pile to another. It seemed that the obdurate flames would take no hold. They licked at even the driest brush and would not set fire to it for seconds of frightful length and import. But slowly smoke rose, then flames crackled, and the men could leap on to the next pile of brush. They had hoped to have time to make a solid sheet of fire across the pass, but there was no time for that. Into the throat of the pass came the roar of the returning herd.

And the two sprang out before their own rising line of fire. Each with a pair of revolvers fired rapidly into the air. Behind them the smoke rose, the flames darted up, and the head of the herd, rushing down on them like a great leaping river, swerved to the side.

Larribee was struck in the face by heavy lumps of turf gouged up by the hoofs of the swaying horses. He heard them snorting with fear of the trap and fear of the men and the fire before them. He saw their sleek, shining bodies and the wild light of their eyes. And he began to shout wildly, drunkenly. He hardly cared what the outcome might be. He was drunk with the joy of the picture that raced before him.

They had sheered off, and in the rear was revealed the force that had driven them on—the great blue roan himself. He came on almost alone now. He had thrust the herd before him at the danger like a good general. Now he came to lead the last charge in person. He came hard and fast, aimed straight at the widest gap between two of the flaming brush heaps.

Larribee leaped back to the nearest pile. He caught from it a mass of flaming brush, and, running forward to meet Sky Blue, he swung it in the air and dashed it upon the ground. Showers of sparks spurted along the ground under the very hoofs of the stallion. Fresh volleys of them were flung into the face of the great horse. He planted all four hoofs. He slid to a stop, his face not a foot from the face of the man. Then, flinging himself backward and around, he darted back into the darkness behind the herd.

CHAPTER THIRTY-SEVEN

Larribee found Ransome at his side; far before them the herd was vanishing with a roar of hoofs.

"That's the special value of the hero," Ransome was saying. "Not brains. Not the sense to plan things. But a way of doing 'em when the pinch comes. Take me, for instance . . . I wouldn't have ridden my horse right at that herd, in the first place. In the second, I wouldn't have run out there with a firebrand to stand against seventeen hands of fury charging at full speed. Larribee, you're a man, and a rare one. Now we've got to work all night at this fence."

They did work all night. They worked all the next day, also, making it impregnable. First, there was the unplugging of the holes, then the planting of the ponderous uprights, tamping the ground firmly about them, and the tying of the cross poles to the posts with green withes. After that, they reinforced the fence with brush until it offered an eight-foot barrier from end to end. That, surely, would be enough to withstand the mightiest of jumpers. Even the critical Ransome was satisfied!

After that, they rode around to the lower gate, and there they found the heaped thorn bushes intact, although the ground in front of it was heavily beaten, as though several times the herd had been led in a charge against it, swerving away from before its impregnable face time and again.

They cleared a narrow gap at one end of the barrier, went through with their horses, and rebuilt the cruel fence behind them. For their work was now all on the inside of the smaller valley.

They rested a full day and night after their labors. Then they set about the work still to be done. It was not difficult, in the first place. Compared with the expanse of the outer valley, this was a mere corral, and they only had to constrict the herd to a smaller and narrower end of it. They did it without trouble.

The stallion seemed to know that serious danger was before him. He could be seen galloping restlessly about the narrowed enclosure and scanning the walls, as though he sought for escape over them. But he permitted the two men to drift him with all his herd down the valley to the narrows at one end. No doubt, he would not have allowed it, had it not been that all of the ground here was overgrown with trees. Under the shelter of these, screened from the eyes of the men, he sought refuge with his companions, and the two men built across the neck of the gap their third and last fence.

It took them two days of steady labor, but there was never a danger of a charge on the part of the herd, striving to break through. They built the fence with leisure, the more so as both of them knew that the crisis was on them, and that the final question was soon to be answered. Could Larribee succeed in riding the stallion, fairly and squarely, as he once had succeeded that other day at Fort Ransome?

He himself had a heart-sickening doubt, when he looked at the great horse, lithe as a serpent, strong and swift as many tigers. But there was no question about their ability to rope the stallion. For Sky Blue, after escaping from men repeatedly, after crossing half a continent, after winning a herd, losing it, and winning another, had now been tricked into a compass no larger than a corral. The very trees that gave him shelter, they would give a priceless shield to the men, also, in the fight that was coming.

They left their horses outside on that third day. What they had to do would be better accomplished with their hands and their ropes. They had for the purpose two fifty-foot rawhide lines, tough as steel cable. They were of Indian workmanship, well tested, supple, and sure to hold. Yet it seemed to Larribee, as he and Ransome walked in from their third fence toward the trees, that they were carrying ridiculous tools in their hands.

The herd was everywhere in sight, dappled under the shadows. The wild horses scattered back on both sides, and the men walked at short distances from one another down the center of the natural corral. Before them, sweeping from side to side, beautiful as panthers, the wild mares and their foals dashed. They bounded high. They struck the lower branches, and the trees were stirred as if by the blowing of a strong wind.

Then Larribee saw the blue roan in the distance, at the very end of the enclosure. The big fellow stood alone. The rest of the herd fled from him like quicksilver, flashing through the patches of sun and shadow, and there was Sky Blue with his head high, surveying the approaching danger.

One certain realization came home to Larribee, then, that soft words and a gentle touch would never have any effect upon the big horse now. One knows the ferocity of the leopard, not by its ceaseless pacing in front of the bars, but by the grim light of its eyes as it lies in the shadow and looks out at the world it hates. So Larribee knew the heart of the stallion as he stood nearby, not attempting to bolt, but measuring his adversaries with a steady glance.

It had the look of a thing for which men go hunting, not with ropes but with guns. Larribee could not help touching the handle of a revolver as he paused and surveyed the quiet monster. In that pause, Sky Blue came forward. He walked with a light, quick step, as though he were treading upon marshy ground, and then, his mind made up, he dashed forward, straight at Ransome. Larribee heard the harsh, alarmed shout of his companion, and turned in time to make his cast.

He was not a bad hand with a rope by this time. Every day of the march he had had some practice to while away the hours. Now he dropped the circle well before the bound of the stallion, then jerked hard against the noose and felt rather than saw, its shadowy finger catch around both the forelegs of the roan. The mere weight of his body thrown back was enough to trip the horse. Sky Blue tumbled head over heels, and then strove to lurch to his feet. But, by that time, the lariat of Ransome was over his head and passed in a slipknot around the body of a sapling.

"Let him up! Let him up!" yelled Ransome. "I've got him tight enough. I've got him, Larribee!"

He had him well enough. For when Larribee dubiously, but obediently slackened enough to allow Sky Blue to get to his feet, and the stallion went forward at a hobbled gallop, the pull of Ransome at the other end of the line brought the roan's head to within three feet of the sapling.

Only once the big horse flung back. The burn of the rope against his neck seemed to teach him in an instant that further struggle was useless, and he stood perfectly still. It was odd to see that his ears were pricked and his head was up as high as the rope would permit.

"He's thinking things over," said Larribee, coming up. "He's thinking things over, trying to make up his mind, Ransome." He wondered at the tremor in his voice. And he saw Ransome leaning against a tree, embracing it with one arm, like a man who would fall except for the support he was receiving. That white, drawn face of Ransome meant a great deal to Larribee. For he knew that his own color and expression were the same— that of a miser looking on at a revelation of untold riches.

For Sky Blue was no longer what he had been in the corral at

Fort Ransome. Between his old and his new self there was the difference that exists between the half-grown boy and the mature athlete, between the clumsy bird that has just begun to find its wings and the grown adept, able to skim and soar. He was one entire piece of silk velvet drawn over the sculptured strength of muscle and mighty bones. He did not win the eye as did the graceful beauty of the black stallion. But he commanded the mind, he overawed the judgment.

Standing quietly there with the rope binding his neck, he looked wilder and more terrible than in the midst of his bucking in Fort Ransome.

The heart of Larribee suddenly trembled and grew cold within him. "There he is, at last," he said huskily. "There's all of him, Ransome."

Ransome nodded and moistened his white lips before he could manage to speak. "There's only the picture of him," he said. "The man that can ride him, he'll know the truth. And that's you, Larribee. You can know him . . . nobody but you could ever ride that beast."

Larribee drew in a great breath. He closed his eyes. "I'm going to try," he said. "But first we've got to get him out from the trees."

"We'll warp him out like a ship," said Ransome. "It won't be hard. He knows the touch of a rope."

It was true. Sky Blue was not a blind fool, to fight where there was no chance of winning. Larribee loosened his rope from about the legs of the horse, coiled it in his hand, and then walked up to the head of the stallion. There was no danger, for that head was now hauled close against the tree. As Larribee came near, he saw a single tremor run through the body of the horse. Then, stone still, with ears that ever pricked, Sky Blue faced the man.

"By heaven," muttered Ransome, "he remembers you. He'll

be yours for a touch, man."

But Larribee shook his head, for he saw that the eyes of the horse were fastened far beyond him, unseeing. And he said: "The thing that you did, Ransome, it's not undone as easily as that. Now that I'm here at the head of him, I see the truth of it. It means pretty near death for one of us." He dropped the noose of his lariat over the head of the horse and Sky Blue did not flinch. Only a shadow flicked across his eyes, Larribee thought.

As Ransome had suggested, they warped the horse out of the wood like a boat, always having one rope passed around a tree trunk, while the other rope was taken ahead and fastened to another trunk with a slipknot. Like a heavy boat, slowly, but with never a backward leap, the stallion let himself be drawn through the trees, and through the gap in the fence.

And now he stood outside it, ready for the saddling.

CHAPTER THIRTY-EIGHT

It was not hard to saddle Sky Blue. They held him with one rope close to a post of the fence, and, standing on a rail of the fence on the opposite side, they worked blanket and saddle upon his back. And always he was quiet, with that still, expectant eye of his fixed upon the future, as it seemed. He accepted the bit of the bridle, also, meekly parting his teeth.

As Larribee passed the hard iron of that bridle that he had carried so far into the velvet mouth, something stung his brain with a savage exultation.

"Well," he heard Ransome saying, "I suppose that he's ready for you, Larribee. Are you ready for him?"

"Put it another way," said Larribee. "Ask me if I'm ready to die. And I'll answer you this way . . . I'd rather die than not to take the chance at him." But he hesitated. He was not gathering his courage, but he was thinking over all the incidents that bound him to the stallion from the first—the glimpse of him in the corral at Fort Ransome, Gurry's talk, the wager with Arabelle Ransome—and then the trail itself—the fight with Shouting Thunder, the life among the Indians, the end of poor Gurry, the disappearance of the colonel, the river that ran like a thousand flashing swords to shut him away from the Cheyenne, the finding of Ransome, and now this final day when they were to close with one another for the second time. Of all these, only two things seemed important—the dark, lovely face of Arabelle Ransome, and this moment when he stood beside the stallion about to take up the fight, hand to hand again.

He could not say that the long hunt had been worthless. The horse was a new horse—keen, cruel, indomitable, wary. His soul was newborn in pride and evil, it seemed to Larribee. His own soul was new, also. What it was now he could not say, but the man who had lounged and gambled and fought in Fort Ransome seemed a different creature to be looked at outside his own life and experience, as a stranger.

He laid his hand on the top of the post. "You know that ring, Ransome?" he said. He was astonished at the answer.

For Ransome replied with his usual sneer: "You shouldn't do it, Larribee. You shouldn't show your teeth like a cur. Not at a moment like this, when you're about to take the center of the stage and play the hero. Heroes don't show their teeth, Larribee. They're always noble."

Larribee did not turn his head. He continued to look at the blue roan, but he answered: "I wish you'd tell me what you're driving at, Ransome."

"No, you don't know, of course," said Ransome.

"I don't," said Larribee.

Ransome spoke in a tone of such genuine agony that Larribee suddenly twisted all the way around. "Man, man!" he cried. "Do you want me to do murder? Do you want me to shoot you through the back?"

"Old son," said Larribee, "you're wrong to talk like this. I can tell you all I know about it in ten seconds. She wanted to make cheap of me before I tried my hand with Sky Blue. So I made a wager with her offhand . . . a thousand dollars against the ring."

"You lie," said Ransome. He shook with rage.

"All right," said Larribee. "Let it drop. Let it rest there. Only I want to give you my word . . . when I asked you, just now, I didn't know that the ring meant anything to you."

"You lie again," said Ransome. "Damn you, you lie again. You haven't been flashing the thing under my eyes, day after day, on purpose? You've had no meaning in that? Do you suppose that I'm a complete fool and that I don't know you're the coldest-hearted devil that ever walked the face of the earth?"

Larribee gazed at him with the calm of one who realizes that an explanation is hopeless. Then he turned his back, still quietly wondering. He had thought that there was simply a natural well of bitterness in the heart of the man, a natural viciousness that poisoned his mind, but now he knew. In some mysterious manner, he had been tormenting poor Ransome to the point of madness with that daily showing of the ring. He put the matter out of his mind or, rather, he thrust it far back. But he felt that the circle was now complete. He and the stallion and Ransome and Arabelle Ransome were all linked together by that green stone, with the pattern cut into it. If he lived, he might learn the solution. But as he faced toward the roan again, he doubted his future with the utmost gravity.

Once, when he was a boy, he had felt a peculiar stroke of fear and wonder when he saw the circus trainer step into the ring among six snarling tigers. That memory and that same fear came back on him now. But he forced himself ahead, mechanically, as pride always forces a man in the face of a great terror.

He climbed the fence, swung his left leg over to an inside bar, and then slipped easily into the saddle. Sky Blue sank a whole foot beneath him, then slowly righted himself as Larribee fitted his feet into both stirrups. He made a small movement with his head, seemed to feel the pressure of the rope, and did not stir a foot.

"Are you ready?" said Ransome, who was leaning on the fence. His face was as white as ever, and his eyes blazed like the eyes of a madman.

"Wait a moment," said Larribee. He pressed his knees against the barrel of the horse. There was small give to it. It was as hard as India rubber with muscular strength. And his knees swayed a little out and in with the deep breathing of the horse.

He looked down the line of the neck. It was much thinner than his memory of it, and the head was a trifle higher. The shoulders were more sharply defined. The overlying gloss of fat removed, one could read more accurately the slope of the bone and the muscle. And under him, although the horse stood perfectly still, he had the sense of sitting upon immense coiled springs that were likely at any instant to be released.

Then he looked away across the fields, richly green, and at the russet of the hillsides, with one great white cliff of limestone or chalk, faintly streaked across with the blue of distance. And he looked up to the sky, where a hawk tipped on an uneasy wing, steadying itself against the force of the breeze.

It seemed to Larribee a beautiful and a kindly world, a world of opportunity, in which a man easily could find his proper place. This was his place. As he looked hungrily over the valley, he told himself that the country fitted him, and he fitted the country. If he had hunted Sky Blue half across a continent, the horse had led him, at last, to the very post of the wishing gate itself.

The old pleasures were far behind him; the old life was dead. It was blown out of his bones. As the horse was new, so was he, Larribee, new. He had shunned labor. Now he felt his great muscles ache to take in hand the building of a home in this glorious, open-faced valley. He saw the very hill that he would crown with a house. He saw the flash of the small creek that skimmed around it in an easy curve, and the shadows beneath the trees where his children, perhaps, might play.

Then Larribee turned to Ransome. "Cut the rope," he said. "It's time to begin."

The knife instantly flashed in the hand of Ransome. It was

like the cutting of a line that supports a great stone on the verge of a cliff and lets it fall with a shattering momentum toward destruction at the base. So the stallion, the one instant standing stone still, shot away from Larribee, except that his flight was forward, not back.

The thrust of the first leap, braced though he was, knocked Larribee far back, and he needed the bracing that the cantle of the saddle gave him.

They shot across the narrow of the valley like a bullet straight for the lower pass, and it was not until the stallion was under the brow of it that he seemed to realize that the way had been blocked. Had he been blinded with fear or with rage? He struck into a frenzy of bucking. It was unlike the pitching that Larribee had endured in Fort Ransome. Every shock struck him like the solid smash of a sledge-hammer. He was stunned. The base of his brain ached. A mist shot across his eyes, and the great hills, the solemn mountains beyond, whirled slowly around him, yet he retained his place. He lost a stirrup. He lost them both, and the stirrup leathers danced up before his face and swung down against the sides of the horse. Still he kept his place. He could thank his fortune, now, for the many days of riding the black stallion without artificial support. The grip of his legs was a grip of iron, and never relaxed.

Then came the thing for which he had waited, the most murderous of the tricks of a fighting horse. The blue roan suddenly cast himself on the ground, rolling. He did not rear and topple backward, a maneuver that usually gives a rider time to slip free, but he hurled himself sidelong on the ground like a football player at a ball.

Down he went. No forethought of Larribee saved him. It was the force of the fall that flicked him out of the saddle and threw him clear, rolling him over and over. But he came to his feet only half stunned, and ready as a bulldog to rejoin the fight.

Far away, in a misty glimpse, he saw Ransome coming, whipping up the horse he bestrode. And that horse was the black stallion, not one of the little short-striding pintos.

Up from the ground Sky Blue was starting. His forehoofs now off the ground, his hindquarters were gathering when Larribee hurled himself at the big horse and felt as though he had dived at a moving train.

CHAPTER THIRTY-NINE

Such was the impetus of the stallion, even from that half-prone position, that Larribee was almost wrenched from his grip by the sheer speed. Had Sky Blue bucked then, with the least sidestep, he would have dislodged that heavy burden, but he trusted to speed itself to shake off the human thing that clung to him. And speed alone was not enough.

Larribee freshened his hold, and in a moment he was firmly planted in the saddle. Off to the side, as he gathered the reins, he could see Ransome putting the black stallion to full speed. And here was a fair test, no doubt. For the black was galloping all out, its ears flattened, head to tail stretched in a straight line with the greatness of its effort. Yet Sky Blue, with a far greater burden in the saddle walked steadily away, cast the image of the black behind him, and still strode forward with a greater and a greater momentum.

The valley dissolved at that rush of galloping. The hills swung together, jostling one another. The clouds seemed shooting close overhead to the dazzled eyes of Larribee.

He had thought, that day in Fort Ransome, that nothing living, could have moved as the stallion ran then, but, compared with this race, it was as nothing. He never hoped to see its like again.

Straight up the valley they flew, and, coming to the upper gap, the stallion swerved at right angles and plunged toward it. He could see the fence, and now he shortened his swinging

stride to a sort of buck-jumping like the sky-hopping of a rabbit, as, with his head high, he gazed at the obstacle. His mind
was made up in that moment. His head went out, and he dashed
straight at the fence. He picked the lowest part, but what horse
could carry two hundred pounds over an eight-foot jump like
that?

Larribee, with a wild shout of fear, cast back his weight
against the reins. They were made of the best material in the
world to endure a strain—they were the toughest of tough
rawhide, round as iron rods. But under the pull of Larribee, the
rein on the right hand snapped close to the bit. The jerk of the
released pressure cast him far back over the cantle, and the
other half of the rein flew from his hand and whipped in the air.
All he could do was to regain his position in the saddle just as
the big fellow rose for the jump. Larribee set his teeth and said
to himself, grimly, that he could only hope that death would be
quick.

Up they shot. They hung, as it were, on the wing, in the
middle air. For a dizzy instant, Larribee felt that they might
clear the jump, huge as it was, but then they struck. It seemed
to him that he saw the earth suddenly above him and the sky
beneath. Into that sky he was falling like a flung stone. But it
was the earth that he struck with a stunning shock. The force of
it turned him over, and brought him to his staggering, bending
legs.

He saw the stallion rolling—not one stallion, but half a dozen,
all tangling into knots he thought he saw, and, wiping a warm
flow of blood out of his eyes, he reeled toward Sky Blue.

They had tumbled across the barrier. The thorns of the upper tier of brush had cut and pricked the roan to the blood in a
hundred places, but they were outside the fence, after all, and
there was Sky Blue slowly pulling himself to his feet.

When Larribee reached him, the weight of the man almost

cast down the stunned horse, but he rallied again. He gained his four legs, and, when Larribee reached down along his neck to catch at the flying rein, the horse suddenly thrust out his head to keep the rein from reach, and began to run again.

It was a beaten, a wearily drunken stride, at first, but as though the wind of his own gallop revived him, so the great horse lengthened and strengthened his stride, and presently he was rushing at full speed again.

Where? That made no difference to Larribee. As he looked down at the blood that flowed over the shining coat of the horse, he told himself that Sky Blue was running for the last time, and the end of the race was death. No other man ever would be hurled forward through the air by living flesh and blood as Larribee was now borne, he thought. And let it end soon or late, Sky Blue would die free. He would be no man's slave.

A sort of glory in the stallion filled the heart of Larribee. Although this might of pride was fighting against him, yet he gloried in it. So the bravest men would die, marching silently in the charge for a lost cause. They were in that great outer valley that Sky Blue had adopted as his home and refused to leave. And he had been right, Larribee felt, for here he would die.

They were running down one of the many little gorges that the streams had cut through this outer valley. The water flashed beside their feet, the rocks went by them like bright bits of flame. And still the strength of the horse did not falter.

A little tributary creek ran into the larger one through its own small cañon. Sky Blue leaped it far and wide and flung onward. He was not weakening, for all the wounds he had received, and Larribee, bending from the saddle to scan this horse—now crimson almost from head to foot—was amazed to see that nowhere did the blood run fast. At last he understood. There was no deadly gash whatever. Sky Blue was simply cut in a thousand places by the cat-like claws of the thorns. But his speed was not diminished. His heart was not harmed. He galloped now as ever before, with a most dauntless and an unfailing heart. Well, let him run. Let him run to a stagger, and then Larribee would dismount and tether him, with the battle won.

Now it seemed to Larribee, as this thought came to him, that he heard a voice shouting in the distance, or was it singing? His memory flashed back to the strange chants of the Cheyennes, and yet those chants were not like this strange song that came wavering out of the distance, without words.

It ceased. He told himself that he had simply heard a ringing in his ears. He had been struck hard enough upon the head to cause that delusion. Now, as the wound in his scalp grew cold, it began to ache and sting him to the quick. But it was like the hurts of the great stallion—a small price to pay for a most glorious gain.

The odd chanting sound that he had heard in the distance now swelled louder, and, as he turned an elbow of the ravine, it broke in a roar upon his ears. He could see the cause in the same instant—the white rim of the waterfall that here leaped over a small cliff and dropped thirty feet to the pool that the stream of water had hollowed in the rock below.

It was a furlong away, and Larribee raised himself a little, anxiously. There was a way of padding the declivity, he remembered, on either side of the falls, but the way was a mere narrow trail, and now, beneath him, he recognized the quick, increasing pulsations of the horse as it gathered speed for a final effort.

It ran like a racer for the goal, straight and sure, and a horror came over Larribee. He reached again, far down the neck of the stallion, to get his hand on the rein. For if they tried to negotiate the trail on this side of the water at any speed, there was sure to be a ruinous fall to the rocks below. As he reached down, Sky Blue pitched high in the air and bucked thrice. It almost unseated Larribee, the wild pitch of the stallion. He barely had managed to twist himself straight in the saddle once more, and then, as he straightened, he saw the destruction before him and realized what was happening.

It was freedom that the stallion wanted. Freedom from the controlling hands and the clinging burden of man. For the sake of that freedom he was willing to die, and this was the surest death that he could find.

From the slight upward pitch of the slope above the falls, Larribee could see the full picture. The waters of the creek, running strong and fast, arched well out from the edge of the rock and, smashing into the pool below, sent spray and spume dashing as high as their starting point, so that the wind picked up a continual cloud of water vapor and blew it in slanting smoke aside. That was not all. He who escaped from the falls would be carried straight down into the cataract below the pool, where the water shot down a steep descent for a quarter of a mile breaking itself to white foam among ten thousand jagged rocks. Those were teeth that could tear to pieces a far larger morsel than a mere horse and rider. Unquestionably, toward the falls, with no thought of the safe trail down either side of it, the roan was traveling.

Larribee looked aside. They were running over smooth, green turf. If he threw himself from the saddle, the fall would be frightfully hard, but, by swinging low from the horse before he dropped and by relaxing every muscle, he might survive the drop without even so much as a broken limb. He swung himself quickly to the side, ready to drop. And then he found that he could not. It was like giving up a part, not of his body, but of his soul. So well had Sky Blue galloped into the depths of his heart that he could not leave the stallion. All that was rational and reasonable in him told him to leap. But a blind impulse rose up in him, choked him, blinded his eyes.

Vainly struggling against it, he suddenly found himself sitting bolt upright in the saddle once more, waving his hand, striking his heels into the sides of the great horse, and shouting some madness that had not even words. He was like one gone berserk, rejoicing in the naked face of death.

So they reached the lip of the cliff, and the stallion leaped straight out above the spray-ridden waters beneath.

CHAPTER FORTY

Then Larribee saw the raging mist and the spume below him, he knew that this was death. And again he cared nothing. He felt the big horse spin over. His grip on the barrel of the stallion loosened. He was flung far from the saddle, and, landing on the back of his shoulders and his neck, he felt that he had fallen on the flat surface of a rock and that every bone in his spine had been broken. Then ice-cold water closed upon his face and choked him. He struck out with arms and legs, and, his head coming above the water, he found himself able to stand in the shallows. He had been flung to the verge of the pool, where the mist of the beating waters was like a driving, showering fog about him. And the outer swirl of the current washed up his leg in a steep ripple.

And the stallion? He saw nothing of Sky Blue. Looking down the cataract, he expected in an agony to see the brave head of the stallion appear for one moment, at least, among the rocks. There was no sign of him. Perhaps already those teeth had ripped the great body to small pieces and carried it away in a crimson lather that in turn would dissolve, leaving no trace of that glorious machine that had been Sky Blue.

Larribee was dazed. He thought of the herd, still penned in the smaller valley, masterless and leaderless. In itself that herd was a treasure. It was no chance assemblage, but seemed derived from some common ancestry. Almost all of them were grays, the color of the leader deposed by the roan. Almost all of them were bigger than the average mustang. Whoever collected those horses would have a small fortune in his hands. What would not fighting plains Indians, like the Cheyennes or the Pawnees, give for a collection of horses like that? But all of them, gathered together and multiplied by ten, made not a tenth part of the value of Sky Blue himself. So Larribee thought, and so he knew. Breeding and care could make such animals again as that fine, fleet-footed herd. But Sky Blue was the product of chance.

And he was gone, and the deafening uproar of the waterfall seemed a chant of triumph in which blind, brutal Nature gloried over the death of her princely son.

Still half stupefied, Larribee was about to turn and climb from the edge of the water when he saw a shadow, a hint through the white falling of the water mist. Then he made out the snaky head and neck of a horse coming out from behind the plunging water.

Dead? Aye, every bone shattered, no doubt, and now the carcass was being swept around by the circular current that churned about the pool. Then he saw the gleam of the eyes, and knew that Sky Blue lived. What happiness was Larribee's, then?

It was no longer his wish that the great horse should be saved from the water and come into his hands. He wanted the stallion's life, but for the stallion's own using. The thing seemed blindingly clear to him now. He had been a child wandering in the dark, but now a door opened and transcendent light shone upon him. The proper place for Sky Blue was exactly here in this great valley, not laboring at the bidding of man, with the iron bit of man's making between his teeth, but leading his herd, making it greater, transfusing into it some of his own matchless blood, so that his sons and daughters might grow up here, a new race, flourishing as if in an earthly paradise. And Larribee? His inward richness of mind would be the knowledge that the horse was free and happy, the glorious king of all around him. So thought Larribee, standing there on the verge of life and death. All his heart rushed out to the horse as he fought for existence.

He came nearer, and Larribee saw the laboring shoulders. Twice and again, the stallion disappeared beneath the surface and once more came up, nearer and nearer.

Larribee waded in until the sidelong force of the current staggered him. He shouted. He screamed against the roar of the water, but he knew that his voice was beaten down and overwhelmed in the greater tumult. He stretched out his arms toward the horse and then groaned inwardly, for had not Sky Blue chosen death by this terrible means, even, rather than the dominion of man?

But the stallion labored on. The flare of his red-rimmed nostrils told of his exhaustion. The flattened ears were proof, and the bulging eyes, that there was little strength left in him. Still the blind instinct, the will to live worked in him and drove him on.

Then Larribee saw the ears prick, and it seemed to him that the head of the horse lifted a little in the water. The direction of it altered, also. It pointed straight toward Larribee, and the man cried out in utter amazement, a hoarse cry, for all the fibers of his throat were torn from his previous shouting.

To him, it was the greatest of miracles. It was as though Sky Blue knew the changed mind of this old enemy and now came to him for succor, seeing that help and not captivity was what he could this day expect. Or was it only the sympathy of one living thing for another? The deer that the tiger has frightened may run headlong into the wolf pack.

Gallantly the horse labored on. The side-swing of the current was driving against it. A high furrow of water curled upward from the swinging shoulders, but there was some progress, inch by inch, and at last there was not a yard's length between the tip of Larribee's outstretched hand and the muzzle of the horse. There the progress ended. A crooked, swirling whirlpool came down and struck Sky Blue like a club, driving him a little away.

Larribee groaned, and then he moved a little forward. He was reeling on tiptoes, and each moment the current threatened to carry him away with the horse, and then both of them would be sent shooting into the horrible maw of the cataract. Still he went forward inch by inch into the deeper peril. For the eyes of the stallion, he could vow, were big and bright with trust in him, and the whole soul of the horse was fighting forward to gain to the man as to a rock of complete safety.

It was no use; it was no good. Back went Sky Blue in spite of all his mighty effort—he who could bound across a gulf on dry land, now enfeebled in the wrong element and blown like a leaf downwind. That same whirl of water that was beating on him now plucked out the rein that floated near his head and sud-denly—it seemed to Larribee forever the greatest of all miracles—a thing like a black snake wavered under his hand. He saw it and did not understand. Then, realizing, he grasped it and gathered in the rein. He felt the pull on the bit. He leaned back in the water. He dug in his heels and moved inches back. And then they came to a dead halt. The force that he could exert was not much. A strong pull would simply topple him forward and send him floating helplessly down the current to death. All he could do was to somewhat counterbalance the pull of the current against the horse.

But, as he laid back on the rein and pulled on it, he saw Sky Blue put forth his last effort, as a good racer does, when the rider calls to it in the homestretch, lowering its head, stretching out its neck, and giving its noble heart and soul in a final burst of speed. So to the stallion down the rein flowed the electric message from the man, and a warm sense of comfort and a deep promise of life came to it. He could forget, now, the red-hot torment of the thorn beneath the saddle blanket. All that was clear in his mind was the message that flowed down the rein: *I am safety. I am salvation for you. Come to me and work my will, and you shall live.*

And the blue roan, with eyes red-stained with effort, thrust back at the water with all the furious might of his legs and his driving hoofs.

It seemed to Larribee, then, that the hand of some higher power was surely controlling him and holding him in a balance, exacting from him whatever was best in his heart. That power he answered from the depths of his own grateful soul: *Not for myself, but for Sky Blue. Not for myself, but for him.*

Was it only coincidence? Was it sheer chance that, fumbling back, his heel caught on a jutting rock that thrust up several feet from the bottom of the pool? He got behind it. His knee bore against it. He could pull now with almost his whole power, and he brought Sky Blue in toward the shore, hand over hand, brought him out of the fiercest pull of the current, got him to the shallows, where the strong legs of the horse could support him.

On the shelving, slippery bank, there was another struggle. He climbed out and laid his weight back on the rein, and, between them both—the stallion pawing at the bank and thrusting upward from his mighty quarters, the man heaving back on the tough rawhide rein—Sky Blue at last lurched over the brink of the bank and stood safe.

He stood safe, at last, with the wind blowing the water vapor in driving clouds over him, and the uproar of the waterfall now, to the ear of Larribee, like a great organ breath of solemn and triumphant music, honoring the feat that had been performed, giving glory where glory was due.

He laid his folded arms on the back of Sky Blue. He bowed his head against his arms. And he murmured with joy and with relief. Then, because the stallion was trembling at the knees with weakness and with cold, Larribee led him out of the driving mist. Sky Blue, stumbling with feebleness, answered the pressure of the rein upon the bit willingly. He stood in the shelter of outcropping rocks, free from the wind, with the strong sun beating down on him. Larribee fell to work to whip the water away from the coat with the edge of his palm, and massage warmth again into the limp muscles.

Chapter Forty-One

When Ransome came out of the valley, he had two expectations in his mind—one, of finding Larribee dead beyond the barrier, and the other, of seeing him get staggering to his feet. In either case, Ransome was ready to curse the hands to which he had trusted the stallion.

Once they had trapped Sky Blue, but they never would entrap him again. From that day forth, the mere scent of man in the distance would be as poison in the air and drive him wild with fear. He would not despise man and man's handicraft from that point forward. But he would be as the wolves are, who have learned that man reaches even across a distance and kills with a bodiless touch. So, gloomily, Ransome rode down the valley.

When he had pulled aside the thorns, and broken down an end section of the fence at the upper gap, he rode through and was amazed to find that neither horse nor man had broken a neck at this jump. He measured the distance with his eye. He looked at some of the down-tumbled thorns and smiled faintly as he saw the blood upon them.

Then, as he cast his eye before him, a sort of half hope came boiling up in the mind of Ransome. It was true that he had seen the tough rein break under the terrible pull of Larribee. He had seen it flying in the air, loosely. And it seemed impossible that any man could sit the back of the blue roan without the reins to control the monster in some measure and give the rider balance and some hold. Yet there was no sign of man or horse ahead

247

down the valley.

Ransome picked up the two pintos, and, still riding the blanketed black stallion, he rode forward along the trail. It was easily followed. For one thing, the mark of the roan's hoofs, as he strode at full gallop, could not be mistaken. It seemed to Ransome that the cantering black needed two strides to measure one of the great horse.

Then they entered the smaller valley, and, like Larribee, he heard the distant voices, heard them suddenly increase to the roar of the waterfall. Like Larribee, he remembered, then, all the natural characteristics of the place.

From the undeviating length of the stride, he saw how the horse had rushed at full speed straight to the brink of the precipice. Horse and man were gone, then. Ransome took a quick, deep breath. Well, it was worthwhile, to him—that exchange, if exchange it could be called.

Then, looking to the side, behind a nest of rocks in the gully he saw the strangest sight—Sky Blue standing still, stripped of saddle and bridle, and submitting quietly to the hands of the man that rubbed him dry. Already he was lifting his fine crest. Already the tremor had gone from his limbs. He breathed freely and deeply. The magnificent power of his well-trained body reasserted itself. He was himself once more, like a chained thunderbolt, but the bolt was not striking.

Ransome, his brain spinning, rode down the side of the falls, along the narrow trail, and, as he came around the corner of the rocks, he saw a stranger sight still. He saw Larribee wave his hand toward the distance, and heard him say: "All that is yours, old fellow. Go and take it. You're free, for all of me. Go and take what is given you, because you're too big for me to put in my pocket." And he slapped Sky Blue lightly on the hip.

Yet the stallion did not stir, but only turned his head idly toward the man. Then, as he saw Ransome nearby, he leaped away. With his head half turned and flattened ears, he bounded up the slope. Over the edge of it he disappeared, as a bird disappears, soaring into the sky.

Ransome came down on Larribee, and saw the other laughing, a bitter laughter.

He faced Ransome. "For half a moment," said Larribee, "I thought that he'd stay of his own free will."

Ransome could not speak. Glowering down on Larribee from the height of the horse beneath him, he finally could say: "Larribee, you've turned him loose. You've set him free, and we'll never have the sight of him again. You've set him free, you fool!"

Larribee looked at him without anger and merely shook his head, answering: "It's a thing that you wouldn't understand, Ransome. It's a promise I made."

"A promise you made, eh?" cried Ransome. "And what about the promise you made to me? What about the partnership between us? Except for me, d'you think that you ever would have got a saddle on Sky Blue again?"

"No," admitted Larribee. "You've had the brains, and you've used them for both of us. I admit that, Ransome. I'll tell you something more. I'm sorry for it. I'm sorry for what I've had to do."

"What you *had* to do?" shouted Ransome.

The hoarse, dull voice of Larribee answered: "I said before that I can't explain. Only I'll add this . . . I'm not ashamed of it. I had to let him go and so he's gone."

"You'll never see hide nor hair of him again," said Ransome. "What right had you?"

"Well, I had a right," said Larribee.

"You had? You had the right of a thief. Half of him belonged to me. Is that a lie?"

Larribee shook his head. "Neither of us had a right to a half of him," he replied. "I saw the truth of that today, Ransome, when I was standing in the water, yonder, trying to pull Sky Blue out of the current. You didn't do that, you know, and so you can't tell exactly what thoughts came to me."

"The thoughts that come to a fool?" said Ransome. "By heaven, Larribee, I think you've gone mad . . . or sentimental . . . and that's the same thing. Do you think that you'll be able to catch him again? I'll answer that for you. Neither you nor any other man will catch him with anything short of a rifle bullet. That's all he's worth to men, from this day onward. Nothing but so many pounds of dead meat. A steer is worth more. And it's because of you."

"Old fellow," said Larribee, "it's best the way it is. I don't ask for him. He's gone back to the world where he belongs. I've no right in him. Neither have you."

"You're out of your head," said Ransome. "Larribee, if you're not completely daft, try to tell me what less right we have in him now than when we left Fort Ransome?"

"I'll try to tell you, but it's not easy," said Larribee. "When we left Fort Ransome, we were trailing a runaway horse. I mean that we were trailing a horse that had a master, a man that had bred and raised it. He owned that horse. He had a right to him. He'd spent money and time and affection on him, d'you see?"

"I see that," said Ransome sternly. "Go on, then."

"That man is dead, Ransome," said Larribee.

"He transferred his rights to the man who could catch the horse. You've told me that. You know he did that!" exclaimed the other.

"Look here, Ransome," replied Larribee. "He could speak the words, but he really couldn't transfer his rights. He couldn't transfer the affection and the time he'd spent on the horse. He couldn't transfer any of that. When he died, no man on earth had any actual right to Sky Blue."

"Do you think that would stand in a court of law?" demanded Ransome.

"There's one court I'm thinking of where that would stand," said Larribee.

"By heaven," said Ransome, "you've gone weak-witted, all at once, if you ever were quite right in the head. There's no good talking to you."

"No," answered Larribee. "There is no good talking to me about Sky Blue. He's gone. I tell you this . . . I'm glad of it. You think you're pretty heart sore because he's gone. I tell you, Ransome, my heart's broken because he's gone. I've had him under my hand, quite as a pet colt. But he's gone. And broken heart or not, I'm glad that he's gone. What could we give him, compared with this?" And he waved his hand toward the great reach of the sky and toward the distant heads of the mountains.

Ransome said not a word.

"Now, then," went on Larribee calmly, "I'm going back. Are you?"

"I'm going back," said Ransome slowly, and his eyes never left the face of the other.

"You're not fond of me, Ransome," said Larribee. "I can't say that you're my best friend in the world, either. But I think that traveling might be easier, if we went together. Safer, at any rate."

The face of Ransome twisted to one side in the greatness of his repulsion. "I'd rather travel with a Gila monster," he said.

"Very well," said Larribee.

"But," went on Ransome, "I suppose that I'd be a fool to go it alone. We'll start back together, then."

"All right," said Larribee.

"You've thrown away my half of the roan," went on Ransome. "I'll take the black, here, as a partial exchange."

A flash came into the eye of Larribee, but only for a moment.

"Take him, then," he said. "And give him the right care, Ransome. Mind you, he reins well. You don't have to wrench at his mouth. It's lined with tissue paper. Keep your spurs off him, too. And you won't need a whip, either. Just talk to him. Learn to talk to him, Ransome."

"He's mine," snapped Ransome, "and I'll handle him in my own way."

Larribee looked at him with an odd smile and with an eye as still as the eye of Sky Blue, when he stared at the distant horizon. "The moment," he said, "that I see a whip welt or a spur mark on the side of the black, I'll break your neck, Ransome. Now let's go on together and be as friendly as we may."

CHAPTER FORTY-TWO

No less likely pair ever traveled together as friends, helping one another as though out of the depths of the most ardent and brotherly affection, and assisting one another in every way through the troubles of the march. Yet all of these services were performed in silence. Each seemed eager to cut the wood, build the fire, do all the camp work. Each was ready to take care of the horses, hobble them out at night, catch them up in the morning. And so the labors of the camp were a mutual contention between one another.

Had a stranger watched them during a day, he would have called them the truest pair of friends that he had ever seen. Had he listened to them, he would have written them down for maniacs. Rather than ask the other to toss so much as an awl across the fire, one would rise and make the semicircle back and forth to get what he wanted. Their salutations in the morning were grave nods and waves of the hand for greetings. If something noteworthy appeared in the course of the march, it was pointed out, but never discussed.

So they went for ten days on the back trail.

They naturally chose exactly the course along which the stallion had come with his attendant mares, for they knew the route fairly well and the position of the water holes in the desert. There could have been several far more direct routes to use in their return, but they chose to accept the safe one in that uncharted wilderness.

Above all that was noteworthy on the back trail was the number of horses that they saw every day. When they moved over this region on the way west, there had been never an animal to be seen, from day to day, except the object of their quest. But now they saw horses right and left or straight before them, or a cloud of dust would dissolve behind them and show, as it cleared, coming nearer, the forms of horses again.

It was no wonder that the mares of Sky Blue's herd had chosen this trail to move over, since for some reason it was so popular a tract with other wild horses.

It was the hardest march that Larribee ever had made. The very first day out, something in the manner of Ransome seemed to convince the larger man that murder was in Josiah's mind. That evening he did not wait to carry out his test.

He lay down immediately after they had eaten and, closing his eyes, simulated the deep breathing of one sound asleep. Through his eyelashes he watched Ransome slowly and deliberately sewing a sole onto a worn-out moccasin. After a few moments, Ransome calmly put the sewing aside, although it was unfinished. Then, drawing a revolver, he rose, and made one step toward Larribee.

Larribee sat up, gun in hand, and for a moment, by the dim flicker of the campfire, they stared at one another.

Then Ransome turned back, sat down, and resumed his sewing without speech.

Larribee got up in his turn. He leaned beside his companion and, unprotected, picked up the revolver that had been laid on the ground by Ransome. He took the other's rifle out of its holster, and, leaning over, he even drew the knife from his belt.

It was as though he were an invisible spirit. Ransome gave him no heed. He took all the weapons back and heaped them under his pillow. It made bad sleeping, but a bad sleep was better than an eternal one.

Thereafter, he kept Ransome constantly in his mind. Night and day, he strove to have the other before him, a position that, during the day, he naturally assumed on the black stallion. Usually he rode some hundred yards ahead of Larribee, the latter bringing up the rear with the two pintos. When they were near, the lack of speech was an irritant, but when they were separated the silence was, of course, natural.

Strange as it seemed, Larribee was glad to have this companion. There might be dangers from worse than animals, wandering Indians, for instance, and, in such a pinch, two riflemen, able to guard one another's backs, were a hundred times safer than one.

So for the ten days that strangest of marches continued. It was on the tenth day, a little after high noon, that Larribee, almost a quarter of a mile to the rear, saw his companion suddenly halt and raise a hand.

He came up at a canter, and, looking earnestly in the direction in which the other pointed, he made out, clearly, two horsemen, a little to the north and east of them, coming straight down toward them.

Larribee, without a word, drew out one of the two rifles and handed it to Ransome. The latter looked silently to the loading, and then balanced the weapon across the pommel of his saddle.

It was the first time, since the first night of their journey, that Larribee had confided a weapon to the hands of Ransome. Up to that time, he had done the hunting for both. And they had fared poorly, because Ransome was far and away the better rifle shot of the two.

Now they awaited the coming of the two strangers, who had the look of Indians in the distance, for they rode on small mustangs, and, as they drew nearer, Larribee could see the length of the hair upon their shoulders. Then it was clear that one was a very small man and the other a very large one. Some brave, perhaps, and a young boy who was passing through his initiation on the war path?

A moment later, Larribee cried out, and, putting the black stallion and the rifle of Ransome fearlessly behind him, he galloped the pinto furiously forward, still yelling as he went and brandishing the rifle above his head.

The smaller of the two riders at once halted his horse. But the larger in exactly the same fashion kicked his horse in the ribs and sent it into a headlong gallop, whooping with a true Indian war cry that would have curdled the blood of better men than Ransome, as he looked at this odd spectacle. The big stranger was waving a feather above his head.

So Ransome saw them come together, halt their horses with a sudden jerk, leap down to the ground as though to fight it out hand to hand, and suddenly fall into one another's arms. They separated a little. It was to be seen that they wrung one another's hands.

The little man in the distance now came cantering up, and suddenly he, also, was a participator in that strange meeting.

Then came, the three, all together back to Ransome. They were laughing. They were shouting, and Ransome thought that the world had gone mad until, as the three came nearer, he recognized first the great shoulders and the noble presence of Shouting Thunder, and then the thin face of Colonel Pratt.

They shook hands with Ransome with an unaffected gladness at seeing him.

Now the colonel was saying, enthusiastically: "Tell us, Larribee, for all of your patience, you've given up the trail of Sky Blue, at last? Isn't that it?"

Larribee looked askance at Ransome. "Yes," he said, "we've given up the trail of Sky Blue."

The colonel laughed loudly. "By heavens," he said, "then we've come up in time to join the hunt once more. You've followed the trail and lost it, though it was right under your nose. But we, Larribee, blindly drifting west, or almost blindly, hoping to find you, hoping to find the stallion, at least, we, by the eternal, have blundered upon him."

"You?" cried Larribee, staring. "You have found him?"

"Yes," said the colonel. "I can point him out to you."

Larribee gaped at Ransome, and the latter actually turned pale.

Said Ransome: "You've had a dream, Colonel. Sky Blue is ten days' march to the west. We'd fenced him in and caught him. He's been ridden and broken, and then turned loose." His face puckered as he spoke.

"You're talking mysteriously, Ransome," said the colonel, while Shouting Thunder, looking with a smile of affection upon Larribee, nodded his assent, "but tell me this . . . could a man who has seen Sky Blue close up ever mistake him for another horse?"

"It's not likely," said Ransome, "but, then, people are apt to see what they want to see."

"Two people?" snapped the colonel.

"Well?" said Ransome.

"This morning, when it was full dawn, I saw Sky Blue from our camp, not four hundred yards away, in the clearest air in the world. Now tell me that I'm a fool and a dreamer, and I tell you that I touched Shouting Thunder, only to find that he was already staring at the same ghost, if you want to call it a ghost, and that same ghost we've followed this whole half day right here to you."

Larribee rubbed his knuckles across his forehead.

Ransome, biting his lips, suddenly said: "The horses that we've been seeing every day, and the dust clouds on the edge of the sky, do you know what, Larribee? It was the same herd, always. It was Sky Blue, following us, following you, I ought to say."

The very sound of his voice was odd in the ear of Larribee, it was so long since he had spoken.

"There, yonder! Yonder," the colonel cried. "Take these glasses, Larribee, and you'll see him as clear as day. Right out yonder . . . under the edge of that dust cloud. If you can't make him out, you're mad!"

Larribee, however, paid not the slightest heed to the colonel's proffered glasses. With a low cry, he had flung himself out of the saddle, and he was running straight across the desert in the indicated direction.

"What's the matter?" said the colonel to Ransome. "Has poor Larribee had a touch of sun."

"Hush," said Shouting Thunder. "There is something on his mind, the Larribee. He has a thought."

"He's going to bring in Sky Blue," Ransome said bitterly.

"Bring him in?" exclaimed the colonel. "What do you mean?"

"What do I mean?" said Ransome. "Nothing that anybody can understand. It's Bible talk. It's nonsense. It's complete rot. But Larribee . . . damn him! . . . is the only man who's given up Sky Blue, and, therefore, he'll be the only man who'll get him."

"Hold on," said the colonel. "What do you mean, Ransome? Given up Sky Blue? He'd rather give up his lifeblood."

"Well," muttered Ransome, "he's given some of that, too. Don't talk to me. Don't ask me. I'm tired of talking, and I'm tired of you."

CHAPTER FORTY-THREE

But out there in the desert Larribee was running so blindly that he floundered through greasewood and fell flat on his face, got up, stumbled, and fell flat again when his toe caught in a hummock of sand. So he ran on, with the sweat pouring down his hot, red face, until he was near the dust cloud and saw it gradually merge into a herd of wild horses.

They were off in a flash, scattering as though gunpowder had exploded under their feet, but Larribee ran on, panting and gasping. Then he saw, from the flank of the herd, a great striding horse emerge, that galloped as though wings were hitched to its heels. And the sun, flashing along the sleek sides of the stallion, made it burn one instant like flame; the next instant, it was a queer reddish-blue, the color of the evening horizon.

Larribee halted. He began to laugh and he gasped, brokenly: "Sky Blue! Sky Blue!"

Around him as though making a tour of inspection before running in to dash him to the ground, Sky Blue cantered, raced, came closer, then, flinging his head up, with his tail arched and his mane fluttering in the gale of his running, he came straight at Larribee and plunged to an abrupt halt thirty yards away.

The breeze caught some of the sand that was knocked up and blew it in a thin rattle against the body of Larribee. He laughed as he watched the glorious beauty of the horse. He laughed, but he stepped not one foot forward. He would not raise a hand.

"You're mine, Sky Blue," he said aloud. "You're mine while there's life in you. You're mine forever and, by heaven, I'm yours. There's no ownership. There's only an exchange. Whatever is in me, it's yours. And a rotten poor exchange for you. You could have had the best in the world. You only get me, a rags-and-tatters gambler, a worthless rat, unless you've shown me the trail to a new life. Stand off there as long as you like, but you've got to come to me, because I went to you."

As he spoke, Sky Blue came slowly but steadily in toward him and never paused until he stood with his bright eyes above the head of Larribee, eyes that shone like two worlds of wonder. Then the stallion lowered his great crest and his soft muzzle touched the shoulder of Larribee.

It was some weeks after this that Dennis Larribee sat down with Major Ransome on the verandah of the Ransome house.

"I've come out here," said Dennis Larribee, a tall man, brown as only sea winds can blow the skin, "I've come out here because I've waited long enough to hear from a boy I sent into this part of the world."

"The Larribee, is he your son?" asked the major.

"The Larribee?" echoed the other. "There are several Larribees, Major Ransome."

The major smiled. "You can call him Alfred, then," he said, "but the Larribee is what he's called out here. The Indians gave him the name, I believe, and Indians give names for a reason, though just what a Larribee may be, I'm sure I don't know. But others seem to understand. We might ask that boy, for instance."

A bare-legged lad with a tattered hat on his head was picking weeds out on the lawn that the major was vainly trying to grow. He came at once in response to the call.

"What's a Larribee?" he asked.

"A Larribee," said the boy, "is kind of smooth and sleek.

Mighty good-nachered. Comes when it's called, sometimes. Sometimes goes when it's sent. It's a great hand at fetchin'. It does all kind of tricks, and hosses get on with it remarkably good."

"There you are," said the major. "That seems to be a definition of a Larribee."

The boy went back to his work. But Dennis Larribee was a man with a serious mind. "There seems to be a joke about it," he admitted. "But I must tell you that Alfred Larribee is my only son."

"One such son is enough," said the major.

Mr. Larribee thrust out his jaw. "Just how am I to take that, sir?" he asked.

"In the most favorable sense in the world," said the major, smiling again.

Dennis Larribee stirred in his chair. "In short," he said, "I've been to see the Dents. My unlucky cousin is dead, it appears. The family tells me that I may find my boy here . . . at your house."

"Not exactly in the house at this moment," said the major. "To tell you where he is, I must tell you a story."

Mr. Larribee, plainly irritated, stirred again in his chair. "If there is no shorter way," he muttered almost rudely.

"Well, then," said the major, "there is in our family an old ring, an emerald ring, that had been with us for a long time. It comes down from an ancient French house to which we're dimly related. This ring has always gone to the eldest son of a Ransome on his twenty-first birthday, and he's always given it, in turn, to the woman who has promised to marry him. So, when a pretty cousin of ours came out here to visit us two or three years ago and my boy fell in love with her, he asked her to marry him and offered her the ring.

"She, however, is an odd child. She told my son frankly that she liked the ring better than she did the Ransome who owned it. But, what with one persuasion and another, she promised to take that ring and marry my boy later on, unless she found a man she liked better.

"Later on, not so many months ago, she made a wager, do you see? And the wager was that ring against a thousand dollars. And she lost."

"One of these heartless, cold, flippant, objectionable modern chits," said Dennis Larribee, frowning.

"The man she gave the ring to . . . or lost it to, one might say . . . is your son," said the major. "And just now your son and my son have gone off for a ride, and they've taken Arabelle Ransome between them. When they come back from that ride, she will have made up her mind about a choice between them. I've been waiting here to see which fellow returns with her, for I think that the unlucky fellow is apt to take a gallop across the fields to blow the shadows out of his mind."

"The strangest story," said Dennis Larribee, extremely displeased, "that I have ever heard. The very strangest. The only son of. . . ." He stopped himself short.

"I think I hear horses coming down the side lane," said Major Ransome. "It's getting dusk and my eyes are no infernal good. Do you make out anything?"

Larribee leaned forward, shading his eyes. "I see a horse with a woman in the saddle," he said presently, "and another horse being led alongside by a man."

"*Humph*," said the major. "And what color is the horse that's being led by the man?"

"Dark," said Larribee. "Black, I should say, but this light is bad."

The major leaped from his chair. "Black, did you say?" he exclaimed. "A big, powerful-looking black horse?"

"No, not big. Compared to the horse the girl's riding, it's no more than a pony."

"Compared to the horse that the girl is riding?" echoed the major, baffled, and straining his eyes vainly. "But Arabelle's little mare would never . . . what sort of horse is she riding, then?"

"A high-headed demon," said Larribee, "that dances along like a racer on parade, a light-colored horse, a luminous color. He has the head of a stallion, I'd say. I've never quite seen the like of him."

Major Ransome dropped heavily back into his chair. "I had one moment of hope," he muttered. Then, sighing, he sat up again.

"Well, that's the way with hope. It nudges one at the elbow, and then it's gone again. I should have known, however. I really did know how the thing would turn out," he said.

"And how has it turned out?" asked Larribee.

The major, however, had started again from his chair, and Larribee followed him somewhat unwillingly down the steps and to the gate that opened upon the side lane, with its big double row of trees.

The major had passed through the gate before him, and there in the evening light Larribee recognized the burly outline of his son's shoulders. In the saddle of a great, blue-roan stallion, the palest color he ever had seen, Dennis Larribee saw the loveliest girl in the world, who smiled the most charming smile, save one, that he ever had seen.

"Well. . . ." Major Ransome sighed. "It's ended, then?"

"It's only begun," said Arabelle Ransome. "Look where I am. Sky Blue has carried me all the way home, and never made a wrong step."

"He's left his wrong steps behind him," said the major. "So has another strange creature, I think . . . the Larribee, in short."

ABOUT THE AUTHOR

Max Brand is the best-known pen name of Frederick Faust, creator of Dr. Kildare, Destry, and many other fictional characters popular with readers and viewers worldwide. Faust wrote for a variety of audiences in many genres. His enormous output, totaling approximately 30,000,000 words or the equivalent of 530 ordinary books, covered nearly every field: crime, fantasy, historical romance, espionage, Westerns, science fiction, adventure, animal stories, love, war, and fashionable society, big business and big medicine. Eighty motion pictures have been based on his work along with many radio and television programs. For good measure he also published four volumes of poetry. Perhaps no other author has reached more people in more different ways. Born in Seattle in 1892, orphaned early, Faust grew up in the rural San Joaquin Valley of California. At Berkeley he became a student rebel and one-man literary movement, contributing prodigiously to all campus publications. Denied a degree because of unconventional conduct, he embarked on a series of adventures culminating in New York City where, after a period of near starvation, he received simultaneous recognition as a serious poet and successful author of fiction. Later, he traveled widely, making his home in New York, then in Florence, and finally in Los Angeles. Once the United States entered the Second World War, Faust abandoned his lucrative writing career and his work as a screenwriter to serve as a war correspondent with the infantry in Italy, despite his fifty-one years and a bad heart. He was killed during a night attack on a hilltop village held by the German army. New books based on magazine serials or unpublished manuscripts or restored versions continue to appear so that, alive or dead, he has averaged a new book every four months for seventy-five years. Beyond this, some work by him is newly reprinted every week of every year in one or another format somewhere in the world. A great deal more about this author and his work can be found in *The Max Brand Companion* (Greenwood Press, 1997) edited by Jon Tuska and Vicki Piekarski. His Website is www.MaxBrandOnline.com. His next Five Star Western will be *Outcast Breed*.